WEB OF MADNESS

Kseniya Kirillova

Translated from the Russian
By
Michael R. Davidson

Web of Madness

Ksenia Kirillova
1300 Clay St, Ste 600
Oakland, CA
kseniavkirillova@gmail.com

Library of Congress Control Number: 2020915285
ISBN: 978-1-7355844-0-9

Russian-English Translation and editing by Michael R. Davidson

The life of young Soviet psychiatrist Irina Krasilnikova changed radically when upon finishing her studies she was assigned to a special "closed" psychiatric hospital on the outskirts of a small town in the Urals. Instead of the noble work of healing she expected she was to become just another cog in the merciless system of punitive psychiatry the victims of which were dissidents and famous scientists. There was no way she could have anticipated landing in the epicenter of the cruel activities of the world's most powerful secret services.

It was a time when the arms race between the Soviet Union and the United States was gaining momentum. The Soviet side intended to equip its surface to air missiles with nuclear warheads that would threaten not only the enemy, but also the peaceful population of their own country. The development of the new missiles was conducted in secret so as not to interfere with disarmament negotiations between the superpowers. A leading military engineer, Colonel Aleksey Golubov does his best to halt the death race, but to do so means acting against his own country. Will he succeed in contacting American intelligence while imprisoned in the far distant Urals, and can a CIA officer manage to contact him inside the psychiatric gulag?

Where is the line between sanity and insanity, conscience and patriotism, pretense and sincerity? Is it possible for a professional spy to permit himself normal human feelings, and what price must he pay for such weakness? Where is the truth in a country trapped within a hypocritical ideology? The heroes of this book seek the answers to these questions through action and betrayal, valiant deeds and irredeemable mistakes, all the while in the hope that despite all difficulties, some good can be achieved despite the shortcomings of their own lives.

WEB OF MADNESS

This is a book that cuts close to the bone and exposes the excesses and cruelty of an authoritarian system that brooked no dissent. The reader should not doubt the truth of what Kseniya has written. As an author myself, I admire the way Kseniya puts words together and creates completely believable characters. I hope I have done her words justice with the English translation."

Michael R. Davidson
Author of 13 novels
https://michaelrdavidson.com

Dedicated with tremendous gratitude to my friend and associate Leonid Polyakov who provided priceless material for this book.

Table of Contents

Chapter 1

1968 was coming to a close and it had been an incredibly difficult year. Dimitriy Rakhmanov sat behind a massive desk in his office at Lubyanka looking through typewritten pages. The words covering the thin paper (clearly it had been a new typewriter ribbon) were clear. The pages were scattered over his desk, although at first glance they clearly were not meant for his eyes. The "Chronicle of Human Events," or $KhTS^1$, was yet another outlet of the dissidents Dimitriy hated so much.

To be precise, the flood of anti-Soviet writing had gathered steam the previous year following the stir raised by the "Sinyavskiy and Daniel" trial – writers who had published their novels abroad. Letters in their defense included denunciations of the trend to rehabilitate Stalin and were signed by writers, movie directors, entertainers, artists and academics. Dimitriy was constantly amazed at the astonishing short-sightedness of certain representatives of the Soviet intelligentsia. They might be experts in the most abstruse field of science or possess rare talent, but in this case, they were incapable of discerning the laws and processes of real life, let alone international relations. In his view theory divorced from practice drove these people to dubious and even harmful acts – and this was the best case if one did not suspect malicious intent.

Dimitriy usually tried to approach work responsibly by carefully distinguishing between what was "malicious" and what was "mistaken." He unquestionably believed both merited punishment, but the level of punishment should be measured. The "mistaken" should be admonished while trying

---

1 Хроника текущих событий – Chronicle of Human Events

to convince the "malicious" of anything was useless. Thus, it was necessary to isolate such people by any means.

Some of the criteria for distinguishing one group from another were the creation of underground circles and groups and contact with foreigners. Indications of such contacts might first appear outside the courthouse where on a frosty winter's day a case was being judged. Dimitriy himself had observed how foreign correspondents, casting cautious glances, sought out the ones they knew were approachable in the freezing crowd. None of them dared open recruitment. For the past year Rakhmanov had received reports of the emergence of a relatively well-established channel of cooperation between dissidents and imperialist governments.

One of the most active agents providing anti-Soviet materials to foreign spies was Andrey Amalrik. Convicted recently of parasitism, he had begun work as a freelancer for the "Novosti" press agency, which he used to contact the "Yankees." Dimitriy personally saw to it that "Novosti" fired Amalrik, something that had occurred only a few days ago. The last straw had been in October when he had passed to foreigners his thoughts on the so-called "Trial of Four."

The difficult year began immediately following this trial. In January there was a trial directly connected with the matter of Sinyavskiy and Daniel: night school students Aleksandr Ginsburg and Yuriy Galanskov had not simply compiled a collection of forbidden documents relating to the trial of the writers (the so-called "White Book"), but had been unwise enough to pass it to the West. And now it seemed that Amalrik had done the same thing – this time concerning the trial of the two students.

This shameful denunciation of events in the USSR, a distorted denunciation in his view, gave birth to Dimitriy's habitual indignation. He had long ago learned to live with this feeling which made him a cold-blooded professional with an even temper as befitted his station – an even temper based on a firm conviction of the importance of his work for the Party and government and on a fierce pride in the exceptionalism and advantage bestowed by his status as an "employee" of the organs of State Security so feared by the citizens of the USSR. And yet his indignation was not feigned – he had a nearly nauseating aversion to the vile betrayal of one's own country which in his opinion could be defined in only one way – treason against the Motherland.

Dimitriy Rakhmanov could not understand such behavior, and to tell the truth never tried. In his eyes those capable of this ceased to be people, and he could conduct a borderline polite conversation with them thanks only to professional habit and the demands of the law. Since the time he was studying in the KGB Academy he had been well aware of the American "Totality" Plan that had been devised in 1945. This was the plan for atomic war against the USSR leading to the total destruction of the Union. The Americans planned to carry out nuclear attacks on seventeen Soviet cities, including Moscow, Leningrad, Gorkiy, Sverdlovsk, Novosibirsk, and many others.

The epitome of American military fantasies, as the instructors assured them, was the "Dropshot" plan: after the massive destruction of the population with nuclear bombers the intent was to occupy all the territory of the Union. Dimitriy shuddered to think that these feverish plans might have become reality had not Soviet intelligence and science uncovered the secrets of the atomic bomb. To even think that they planned to unleash three hundred atom bombs on twenty Soviet cities in order to destroy not less than eighty-five percent of the Union's economic potential. Apparently, no one in the Pentagon ever thought about human losses.

They might no longer be alive: him, his wife and daughters, hundreds of thousands of other children who would never have been born. The purple mushroom cloud that had risen over Japan would have darkened the country he loved more than life itself. What sort of human rights did today's dissidents have in mind when they fraternized with people that at one time would not have left them with a single right – the right to life?

"Do you think they're any different today? Do you think they wish us the best? Who in Washington cares anything about you, really cares? They use every possibility to destroy our country, but you are happy to deliver to them anything that would compromise your own country?" This was his usual rebuke during interrogations. "They would have dropped bomb on your home without a thought that you are a human being. They wouldn't have given a fig about your existence, let alone your rights. You don't believe it? So you prefer to believe them? Have you forgotten in which country you live?"

And his interlocutor more often than not would sit opposite him and stare boldly and defiantly in the eye, and there was something steely and compelling about that stare that under different circumstances Dima might have called noble, but not in these circumstances. They would say something about the elementary rule of law, about human dignity, and about how regardless whether America even existed no one had the right to mock and slander people, to destroy a person because of the books he reads or how he things. They talked of starvation rations, repressions and debilitating work in the camps, about freedom of expression or persecution for an attempt at thought.

For Dimitriy such talk smacked of the contrived ravings of egotists who seemed to have discovered for themselves special rights beyond the requirements of normal people, those who step right up to the edge of the law and make appeals to society that provoke a response and then scream that their rights have been violated. It angered him that for the possibility of behaving scandalously and extravagantly, forsaking all the possibilities for happiness offered by the Soviet Union, these people were prepared to betray the Motherland and millions of their fellow countrymen.

"I don't understand the logic," he would answer with malicious irony. "You and your comrades behave in an openly unlawful manner and then complain that you have unhappy lives? Maybe all that's necessary is to stop doing harm for life to be easier. Have you tried it? If you did, you wouldn't need America, at all.'

He was sick of these never-ending conversations. He already knew that the subject of interrogation would begin to convince him that he had done nothing against the law, that in the materials he had distributed there was no anti-Soviet propaganda, that he had gathered only facts and discovered that the law was being broken in these trials, that the defendants were innocent, and generally good Soviet citizens.

And they would say the same about the *KhTS* that now lay on his desk: nothing but facts here, nothing more than a common chronology. In good faith Dimitriy read the entire "Chronology" and concluded that this was a lie. Protest letters were cited with too much detail – with no mention of the arguments of the prosecutor. There was too much detail about the content of protest leaflets, the words "repression," "persecution," "stool pigeons" appeared with excessive frequency, inevitably followed by imprecations of illegality and the cruelty of the measures taken by the organs.[2]

"These three examples of how the organs of State Security

---

2 Organs – security and police

conduct searches by someone else's hands under the pretext of false criminal charges that later are discarded as useless and forgotten," "cruel and illegal instructions grossly violated" – were spread about by the "Chronology."

The texts that had fallen into Dimitriy's hands contained in addition to lists of the repressed and brief recounts of their stories, the leaflets of the "Church" group were cited. They tried to distribute these in Mayakovskiy Square and included commentary claiming they were "not anti-Soviet in nature."

The editions were filled with the statements of dissidents, quotations from their final statements at the trials, letters from the zone[3], and comments on the most important events. There was a retelling of the story of the publication of Solzhenitsyn's novel abroad and a letter from the dissident Anatoliy March-enko, and leaflets protesting the so-called "occupation" of Czechoslovakia.mNews about dissident demonstrations was spread by those participants remaining at liberty, and in the latest edition from October they spoke of political searches carried out on the pretext of fabricated crimes.

In the depths of his heart Dimitriy knew that some formal bending of the law mentioned in *KhTS* had occurred, but he was firmly convinced that in such cases the end justified the means. He had no doubt that the documents on his desk could under no circumstances be called neutral. They represented a fully defined attitude toward the authorities and the heroes of the publication. This attitude was so contrary to what Dimitriy felt that the fate of the authors was predetermined in his eyes. He never relied on emotion, but his feelings about this were instinctual. Through long years of service he had learned to spot the tiniest animosity toward the existing order and grasped it intuitively, and in this case the hostili-

---

3 Prison

ty was undisguised. Take, for example, the words "Appeal of the representatives of the Crimean Tatar people to the world community." Wasn't he correct in believing that the so-called dissidents were creating underground groups with the aim of recruiting others to oppose the Soviet authorities? Now they were supporting nationalists of all stripes!

Winter already was filling with the joy of the approaching New Year, and the "Day of the Chekist" was just around the corner, but Dimitriy couldn't get into the holiday spirit. He knew that the *KhTS* was being sent abroad, and he was writing an analysis of the clearly explosive nature of the document. Rakhmanov understood it was too early to arrest the editors. In the first place he didn't yet have the identities of all of them, and secondly putting an end to it had to wait until he had uncovered the entire information network and its channels of distribution. If in the first edition there had been only information from Moscow and Leningrad, but Novosibirsk, letters from the Gulag, the Crimea, and even Latvia had appeared later. The authors had a definite network of informants who might in turn lead underground circles in their own cities and republics. A major of the KGB simply could not let any of them remain unidentified.

The channels for transmitting the *KhTS* and a lot of "samizdat" abroad also were unclear. The facts indicated that besides Amalrik, others had Western contacts that were still unknown to state security. He did not doubt that foreign spies were doing everything possible to increase the numbers of such people.

In this regard Dimitriy was reminded again and again of Andropov's speech of the year before on the subject of ideological sabotage. "In conducting these operations, the enemy special services made wider use of various foreign policy, military, propaganda, and other institutions... The intelligence services more often act as coordinating links even in those instances when ideological sabotage is 'openly' conducted via official propaganda channels...," Yuriy Vladimirovich had said. Andropov stated that the Americans had created a special coordinating committee for "strategic psychological operations" that was directly under the President, and in March 1966 a senior inter-agency group was created in the Department of State. According to intelligence reports the CIA oversaw the operation.

It had been for this reason, in view of the difficulty of the situation that Dimitriy had agreed to transfer from the Second Chief Directorate, responsible for counterintelligence, to the new Fifth Chief Directorate, created by Andropov the previous autumn to concentrate directly on the battle against ideological sabotage. The experienced counterintelligence officer was not surprised by the Americans' efforts – what impressed him was the willingness of some supposedly Soviet citizens to take the Americans' bait. An example was the appeal of Bogoraz and Litvinov. Was it any wonder that it had been seized upon by the West? Intuition told Dimitriy that the danger was only just beginning, and if it was not suppressed at birth it would only continue to grow. The greatest amount of information must be collected in the shortest amount of time and a pre-emptive strike carried out – just as he had done in a recent interrogation...

"Have you managed to read the filthy writings of Solzhenitsyn?"

"No, I haven't."

"Really? Is this yours?" Rakhmanov tossed a packet of papers onto the table and squinted to watch his interlocutor shiver under the harsh light of the lamp and shrink back into the chair. Dimitriy could read all such reactions with lightning speed, but rather than rush things he gave the girl the time required to become anxious.

She lowered her head to hide her face in shadow, but Dimitriy knew there was fear in her eyes even without seeing them. It was useless to scoff at people in situations where they were dependent on him. Although he wasn't fond of it, he did not refrain from pressing the victim at times, playing on her weaknesses. Dimitriy never overdid it, threatening only as much as necessary to achieve results.

"Where did you get this?" she asked in a frightened voice.

"So, it's I who must answer you?" He added a touch of threat to his voice, sensing that this was the moment to increase pressure. "Rather it's I who should ask where YOU got it."

"I typed…"

"I understand. But as it turns out, you are not Solzhenitsyn. Who gave you the copy to type?"

He knew that her answer would be silence, and by the increased rhythm of her breathing he knew it was difficult for her.

"You're studying journalism," he began slowly. "You work as lab assistant in the department. Sometimes you take work home, and the sound of your typewriter doesn't alarm the neighbors. You've already published a couple of articles in serious newspapers. I read them … your style needs some work, but all in all … it's not so bad. You could have a decent career and a completely happy life. You're very young, after all, yes? You should have finished the uni this year?"

"Why 'should have?'"

"Because you've placed your future in jeopardy: a diploma, the possibility of work in your specialty, the respect of friends and neighbors. In five years or so you'll regret this stupid heroism, but it will be too late, and there will be nothing you can do to make things right. And for what? How much were you paid to type this vile fiction?"

"I wasn't paid…"

"Did some young man ask you to do it? A friend? You like him, yes? You're ready to stand by the man who set you up?"

He took the chair next to her and leaned very close.

"Nastya... My work now includes criminal activity under Statute 70UK – anti-Soviet propaganda and agitation. Several people already have been arrested for this. Their task was very simple: pass to our enemies materials that can be used to blackmail our country for "non-observance of human rights" and demand that our leaders take actions leading to the fall of our state. This is no less serious, for example, than military espionage. Those arrested knew what they were doing and were paid a lot of money by foreign spies. But you weren't paid anything. Our task now isn't about what you did – we know all of that already. We only want to know if you were aware that you were acting against your own country. You, your friend, your whole group. If you were motivated only by curiosity and a desire to read some filth – I'll limit myself to preventive conversations with you all. Right now, you're lying and unwilling to provide answers. This only increases my suspicion that this is more serious than it appears at first glance. You're only implicating your friend more than if you simply tell all. I'll give you just one more chance to tell me everything. Otherwise there is no help for you and your friend."

Her voice shook. "But what will happen to him if I tell you?"

"I'll do my best to help him, if only thanks to your honesty. If he's not a member of the gang living on hand-outs from the West, what does he have to fear? It's possible you could save him by naming the leadership of the organization. Believe me, foot soldiers don't interest me. But if you refuse, you'll go to prison, both of you, and for a long time. I'm waiting, but I don't have much time."

Breaking such girls was easier than anything, and in this

case Dimitriy did not err – surveilling her over the course of two months paid off. And the company her boyfriend kept was interesting; the young rake was not involved with ordinary people...

"Right, so Naumov gave him the manuscripts? Good, and Sergey asked nothing more of you?"

"He asked... I have a separate room in an attic almost in the center of Moscow. None of the others has a more private apartment. He asked if I could take in his friend from Kiev. He's a friend from the *Shestidesyatniki*[4]. They arrested nearly all of them in 1965, and he wants to visit them in the Mordovian camps. And to get to Mordovia you must pass through Moscow. Seryozha asked if he could stay at my place."

"What's the friend's name?"

"I don't know. I really don't." She gave him a pleading glance. Clearly, she wasn't lying.

---

4 **Шестидесятники (Sixtiers)** – The **Sixtiers** (Russian: Шестидесятники) were representatives of a new generation of the Soviet Intelligentsia, most of whom were born between 1925 and 1945, and entered the culture and politics of the USSR during the late 1950s and 1960s — after the Khrushchev Thaw. Their worldviews were formed by years of Stalin's repressions and purges, which affected many of the Sixtiers' immediate families; and World War II, where many of them had volunteered to fight.

Sixtiers were distinguished by their liberal and anti-totalitarian views, and romanticism that found vivid expressions in music and visual arts. Although most of the Sixtiers believed in Communist ideals, they had come to be strongly disappointed with Stalin's regime and its repression of basic civil liberties.

Many of the Sixtiers were intellectuals of roughly two strains: the "physicists" (those involved in the technical sciences) and the "lyricists" (writers, theater and film professionals, and otherwise liberal arts representatives). Bard (singer-songwriter) culture, poetry, disillusionment in politics, and love for camping trips to the farther regions of the Soviet Union were some of the common attributes and pastimes of the Sixtiers.

The Sixtiers had some parallels to the New Left and hippie movements in the West but had more in common with the more intellectual-oriented Beat Generation. (Wikipedia)

"OK. You'll let me know as soon as you find out? Are we agreed?" She seemed hesitant, so he added, "Who is dearer to you, your Seryozha or this unknown Ukrainian?"

"I'll tell you as soon as I find out," she agreed reluctantly and then shyly asked, "Dimitriy Yevgenyevich, what will happen?"

"Nastya, if we cooperate things will be normal for you, even better. Sergey has made a mistake, of course, that's clear, but I'll do all I can, agreed? You should be grateful that I came into the picture now, before you had done something irredeemable."

The name of the man from Kiev! Two months had passed since that conversation, and now Dimitriy was occupied by his reports and the *KhTS*. He couldn't allow the opportunity to pass. This is what happens when you don't take any time off. The year had really turned out to be complicated, and the August entry of the Warsaw Pact forces into Czechoslovakia and the resulting wave of protests across the country only underscored the futility of any thought of rest. Dimitriy knew from official sources that the Soviet forces had been under strict orders not to open fire on protesting citizens, to resort to weapons only in cases of self-defense, and that the only ones who had fired on the crowds had been troops of the GDR[5]. But maybe these damned dissidents could prove something!

There is no difference between the darkness of a winter's evening and the dead of night, and the streetlamps glowed over the emptying streets of Moscow. The report was barely half-finished, but Dimitriy rose from his desk, stretched and wearily reached for the telephone. Before it got too late he should call Nastya to find out the name of the secret visitor from Kiev.

---

5 German Democratic Republic (East Germany)

She did not answer immediately, and it was clear that she recognized his voice.

"Dimitriy Yevgenyevich, has something happened?"

"Where have you been, Nastya?" He injected some accusation into his voice. "I was beginning to think the worst."

"What do you mean?" she faltered. "I just began a session ..."

"Do you want to finish school?"

It seemed she had begun to resent his threats, and this resentment overcame her fear.

"What do you want?" She essayed in a hard voice.

"You promised to give me the name of your Ukrainian guest. Or was his visit postponed?"

"Oh, that," the former bewilderment returned to her voice. "I'm sorry. I forgot. His name is Viktor Butko. But he's as old as you, maybe even older. Seryozha says he's thirty-seven. He'll be here the day after tomorrow and be here for three days. He has to meet with someone."

"Lovely! Nastya, do you know who he's meeting?"

"No, I really don't. Apparently it's some journalist."

With a correspondent! In Chekist usage, this word described foreign correspondents, and Dimitriy was certain – there could be no mistake. Really, what Soviet journalist would want to meet with a Ukrainian dissident? It looked like he had succeeded in finding still another "connected" person.

At such an hour there was sure to be no one but the duty officer in the office, and as best Dmitri could recall, tonight it would be a senior lieutenant from the department he headed. Dimitriy dialed the number, and it was answered immediately.

"Fedotov? Are you on duty? It's Rakhmanov. Listen, gather all the information we have on a certain Viktor Butko, a Ukrainian, and have it ready for me by tomorrow evening. He's supposedly between thirty and forty years old and from

13

Kiev. We have unconfirmed information that he's thirty-seven. He took part in the so-called "Sixtiers" movement and has friends in the camps. He'll arrive in Moscow tomorrow. I'll need to know what train he'll be on, and after his arrival I want his every step followed. You know what needs to be done. That's all – tomorrow at 1600 hours I'll expect you with the documents and a report on Butko. Any questions?"

"No questions. I understand the assignment, Comrade Major."

Dimitriy smiled with contentment. It had been a hard year, but it may well turn out to be productive.

Chapter 2

The floorboards appeared to have been recently painted – the garish, poisonously orange color was the first thing that caught the eye in the small room. The second was the big, irregular spot in the upper right-hand corner. Its uneven edges occupied a portion of the ceiling, lending a bluish hue to the whitewash and faded wallpaper that likely no one had changed since the Thirties. In the corner farthest from the window was a squeaky iron bed with a flat mattress that peeked like an orphan from under the coverlet. There was an old oaken table that looked too heavy to have been moved for many years. It occurred to Irina that the floorboards probably retained their original color, but she had no desire to test the theory.

Worst of all was that the room was cold. After six years in Sverdlovsk, Irina should have been accustomed to the Ural frosts, but the village of Medinskiy was distinguished by its own specific coldness that burned lungs ravaged by the dry, ruthless, winds discharged by the long frosts. There was no wind inside, but the odor of the snowbound village was evident even here – in any event, she did not want to remove her fur coat.

Irina went to the window and could feel the cold seeping through the badly sealed frame. She did her best to see through the patterns of frost on the glass and saw a badly overgrown field surrounded by identical yellow two-story houses like the one she must look forward to occupying. Below were some swing sets, now nearly covered with snow, along with the carcass of a new toy rocket. Following the successful flight of Gagarin such rockets were installed in every courtyard, even in deepest Russia, and it seemed that the general enthusiasm for space travel had reached even this small Ural village that was distinguished only by a copper mining and processing plant. It was as though she had been exiled to the farthest corner of the planet. The thought that she must spend the next three years in this hole was painful and made her feel alone.

With freezing fingers she placed her cosmetics bag on the table and sorrowfully removed the pink lipstick and Leningrad mascara with the thought that in this place she would most likely have no use for them. As though she had read her thoughts, the landlady, a heavy old woman wrapped in a gray down shawl creaked across the floorboards and spoke in a hoarse, chilled voice.

"Irka, forget about this. Your cosmetics. In the first place it'll freeze to your lips and stick them together here. And you're such a pretty young thing. The cold outside will make your cheeks rosier than that stuff, and the boys here are such ..." She struggled to find the right words. "They aren't university graduates. Don't worry, you won't have to say a word. Over there, "she waved vaguely toward the window. "down the street there are private houses. In one of them lives Sevka the Fool. Do you know what he does? He pulls out what's between his legs and chases the girls. And they say we'll soon have Communism." After a pause she added," and what will Sevka do with his balls under Communism? Who will he show them to then?"

Irina was uncertain whether the old woman was being sarcastic or was really worried about the relationship between Sevka's behavior and the Communist future. Regardless, the prospect of having to deal with the village flasher was definitely unpleasant.

The landlady wasn't finished. "So tell me, if you were his psychiatrist would you think there was something wrong in his head?"

"Yes," said Irina with some difficulty. The last thing she wanted right now was to discuss Sevka. "If it's not a tendency to hooligan behavior we do work with this form of sexual deviancy."

The old lady frowned. "So you could cure him?"

"Of course. There are special medications ..."

"There was a boy from our house, and they took him and beat him so hard he couldn't walk for a week," interrupted the landlady. "And for a whole year after this he didn't show anyone anything, didn't even take off his hat in the house. That's a medical achievement! But you ... Drugs ... Socialist Humanism ... Young people don't understand anything," pronounced the old woman as she crossed the room.

"The stove is under the table. It's electric. But don't turn it up at night or you'll burn down the whole house. Turn it down at night so it'll last 'til morning. There are common facilities on the ground floor for everyone. Be happy you don't have to go in the street. Only don't spend too much time in the toilet. Do it all in a hurry so you don't catch a cold. You're so sweet." The landlady gave her a glance that suggested condescending pity. "There's no refrigerator – a former boarder brought his own, and we all used it, but he took it away when he left. But with this cold there's no problem. Hang your stores out the window like we've done our entire lives. The hotplate is in the hallway, but you were used to this in the dormitory, of course. Conditions are simply splendid – one hotplate for two families, but your neighbors have gone north for a year, so you'll be the only one using it. They're really smart, don't you agree? It's as cold there as here, but the pay is better in the north."

Irina shrugged.

The landlady unexpectedly added, "My name is Marya Innokentevna. This is a nice room. You'll like it. And it's cheap. More than that, it's near the center of town. The bus stop is two houses away. You'll be riding for two blocks on the bus until you come to the bus station. You can't miss it. Some construction is going on there. They're erecting prefabricated houses. Well, what am I saying? That's how you got here. There's a movie theater there, and a club where the young people dance. You know that from the bus station you can go all the way to Sverdlovsk. But if you go into the city for a weekend remember that there is nothing moving in this direction after nine, so don't be late for the bus. But if you go in the opposite direction on the 13 bus that goes out of town it'll take you right to your *psikhushka*[6]. But it doesn't always stop there. It's best to leave early for the station and get a seat so you'll be sure to get there. Yes, it's a little less convenient, but it's better than standing at the station and freezing your ass."

Marya Innokenevna's voice softened a bit as though she pitied the young city girl. Finally, she asked the question that obviously had been on her mind.

"How did you come to be here, my beauty? After Sverdlovsk why did they send you to this hole to rot - to work in the *psikhushka?* To tell the truth, it's not a psychiatric hospital – it's a prison. Everyone says so, and it doesn't have a good reputation. They say only criminals and spies are sent there – and who decides that? You should be with normal boys, not crazy people. You're as pretty as that Caucasian captive." She spoke with a kind of crude tenderness.

Irina looked numbly at her reflection in the mirror over the bedside table. To be honest, she had purposely emulated the heroine of last year's cult film. Following the release of the sparkling comedy, "The Caucasian Princess," many girls in the big cities started fashioning their hair "*a la* Natalya Varla," and Ira was no exception – she had even dyed her hair darker.

---

6 Psychiatric Hospital

True, her face was thinner and softer that that of the actress which gave her an especially fragile, old-fashion femininity which did not fit with the "sportswoman and Komsomol" look. Irina had joined the Komsomol, but it had had no effect on her assignment.

"By apportionment," she sighed. "But it's only for three years."

"Everyone says that," chortled Marya Innokentevna. "Three years! You'll find a boy, some factory worker, get married – and you'll be here forever. Believe me. I've seen it many times."

Irina decided in favor of tactical silence to avoid a squabble. She promised herself that she would not be in this place for long. True, she had been unlucky in the apportionment following graduation, but what else could a girl from a small southern Ural mining town on the border with the Kazakh SSR expect? Even with a bribe it was a miracle to have gotten into the prestigious medical institute in Sverdlovsk. She'd been incredibly lucky: the very year she finished school the Oblast Central Committee of the Communist Party of the USSR started receiving letters from simple working people whose children couldn't get into medical school even if they passed their exams with the highest marks. The Party bosses reacted by sending a special commission to the institute with the task of insuring that the children of machine makers and miners could become doctors. Irina was caught up in the resulting wave of Party pronouncements, easily winning a place in the dormitory and status as a student of the "elite" psychiatric department.

But that's where her luck ended. Although young Irina was a good student, places in the best hospitals were still assigned on the basis of bribes. The sons and daughters of professors got the assignments to the Sverdlovsk Psychiatric Hospital (the very place Irina spent her residency) while she was assigned to the special psychiatric hospital, a so-called SPB[7], of the MVD[8] on the outskirts of the miserable village of Medinskiy north of Sverdlovsk.

After the bright and busy capital of the Urals with its bubbling whirlpool of theaters, movie houses and libraries, with the student café, amateur festivals at the institute, long hikes through the Ural forests, campfires and guitars, in a word, after the bright and captivating life of a student that filled the best years of her youth, Irina ended up here – torn from civilization, alone, freezing and of use to nobody. As soon as the old lady left the girl quickly pulled the small heater from under the table and plugged it in to a sagging outlet. It gave some small warmth to the frigid room – soon it would be time to sleep only to rise before dawn and begin her first day of work.

Irina finished her interviews by December and, to tell the truth, hoped they would assign her to her first job after the New Year. But the assistant dean who had complained about her missing Komsomol meetings and similar transgressions that he termed "neglect of duties as a Komsomol member and citizen," decided not to stand on ceremony and sent Irina to Medinskiy immediately. He told her that she must appear at the SPB by the 20th. The New Year's holidays were ruined, and Irina, swallowing tears headed into the frozen depths of the country to begin her unhappy duties.

She awoke in darkness, not from the alarm clock, but from the stinging, exhausting cold that enveloped her entire shaking body. At first Irina thought she would rather die than get out of bed, but she gathered her courage. She emerged cau-

---

7 СПБ – Special Psychiatric Hospital

8 МВД – Ministry of Internal Affairs

tiously from under the blanket and, trembling all over, feverishly pulled on her clothes. She had never had to be at work by five A.M., and now going into the street to brave the pre-dawn frost, she all but choked on the thin, dry air. It was as if her lungs had collapsed from the cold as her body was stung by a thousand sharp needles. She arrived at the bus stop almost at a run but there were no buses running at this hour, so, shivering from the icy wind she slogged on foot in the direction opposite the SPB toward the bus station.

The building was dirty but surprisingly warm and others already were there. They tried not to look at one another and sat at different ends of the waiting room looking glumly at the floor. Irina luxuriated in the heat and finally caught the bus. After a dark, snow-covered journey past a pine forest she arrived at last at the SPB.

Irina discovered that Marya Innokentevna had been correct: the exterior of the hospital truly resembled a prison. There was a high wall topped with concertina wire, a forbidden zone inside the wall, towers at the corners like in a prison camp, and thin tripwires along the wall – it looked like it should be inside the Zone.[9] Also it was guarded as if it were a camp: a young man at the checkpoint blocked her way with a rifle and then studied her documents for a long time. He telephoned somewhere and then unceremoniously searched her before finally venturing:

"Are you the new nurse?"

"I'm a doctor!" She replied sharply, deeply insulted.

"We already have a doctor," said the guard laconically. "So you're a nurse. You can go in." He waved a hand and conducted Irina into the hospital's gloomy corridor.

Inside, the place still looked like a prison: a narrow cor-

---

9 Prison or Gulag.

ridor, massive closed cell doors with small peep holes and square openings for the passage of food. Irina was filled with terror and despair. She felt like one of the prisoners as she plunged step by step into the abyss of camp hell: cruel, desperate, an oppressive freshly washed and invariably stinking concrete floor, institutional paint on the walls and thick doors.

Somewhere in the distance someone groaned – inarticulate and hysterical - and the groans were amplified by the echoing corridors and followed her as she passed door after door, only adding to the horror that seized her.

They arrived finally at the door of the Chief Medical Officer – a small, tough-looking woman with carefully curled blond hair who reminded one more of an indifferent machine designed to follow a clearly defined program than a monster-overseer.

"Krasilnikova, Irina Vladimirovna," she read the name slowly as she looked over Irina's documents and then spoke quickly, as though she wished to pack all the instructions into the shortest amount of time.

"I am Chief Medical Officer Volkova, Svetlana Eduardovna. We have three wards: strict, therapeutic, and working. In the strict ward are the most deranged. That's where we normally put newcomers. The work there is the most important. The patients must be acclimated to our schedule, our discipline, and to the medications. The way they handle this will determine whether they can recover or not. In other words, we'll make them sane and safe to re-enter society, or we won't. Everything is decided then and there. Our primary concern is that either they and their illness win, or we win. Is that clear?"

"It's clear," said Irina, still not recovered from the military prison conditions that reigned at this spooky place.

"We have practically no professional nurses," continued Volkova. "At MVD Special Hospitals the orderlies are young

Militia or Internal Service lieutenants. They can give injections but aren't very good at it – they often miss the vein. So we really need you. But, of course, you need them, too. You won't be able to handle the patients without them. Here we call in the orderlies immediately. There are some very dangerous people in the patient population."

Irina interrupted her. "But I'm a doctor. I have a higher education. I planned to speak personally with the patients, check their conditions, perhaps medications will have to be corrected ..."

"I'm the doctor here," stated Volkova. "Everything will be corrected and checked before you even see a patient. In the strict ward twice a day all patients are given 15 milligrams of Thioperazine – remember that. And at night a hundred gram ampule of Aminazine. Should a patient start to make trouble, we add Haloperidolum. Do you understand?"

"But correctives?" Irina tried again. "Corrective drugs are required with large and repeated dosages of antipsychotics."

"We don't have enough correctives," replied the doctor. "So we provide them only in emergencies. We define emergencies thus: if a patient speaks articulately, don't react. You can't imagine what these sly animals are like: lying, aggressive, treacherous. They'll beg you, plead with you, pretend, and yell – you should pay no attention. If they can talk it means everything is normal. No normal person can lie like a psychotic. But when they begin to groan, wail and bleat in an inhuman voice you can check on them. If they have a high pulse rate, you'll give them Corvalolum. If they're having convulsions, then give them a corrective. And be very careful. Call the orderlies."

These words sent chills down Irina's spine, but she once more risked venturing an opinion. "But these are people. You speak as if they are animals."

"Yes, they are animals!" Volkova apparently was beginning to lose patience. "What did they teach you there in Sverdlovsk? Did you have a residency? Didn't you see that they can appear to be normal – two ears, two eyes – but inside they're beasts? They don't listen to us, they don't understand, they don't accept it. They live in their own world, their own terrible fantasies. They are slaves to these fantasies, and they use them to excuse everything. What they consider their own mind and will is really nothing more than their unhealthy instincts, their hallucinations, and their illness. Our job is to suppress this harmful, sick, and inadequate will. Do what is required to prepare them to be healed, make them surrender, don't you understand? For their own good. So they open up to reality. Until they open up, nothing can help them. And all these medications are necessary for this – to suppress the psychosis so they open up, make peace with reality and give themselves a chance to be cured."

She fell silent, probably exasperated by having to explain things to this little fool fresh out of school.

"I know what sickness is," answered Irina in a firm voice. "But I also know that we should not confuse the person with the disease. Despite any disorder a part of the human psyche functions normally, some of a patient's reactions are no different from our own, and so it's important to make a distinction …"

"Make a distinction?" Volkova laughed derisively in her face. "They created their own separation from society. Do you know who we have in here? Murderers, maniacs, rapists, terrorists who tried to destroy our entire country, defamed Soviet order, tried to make sure that America started a war with us, even a nuclear war. What distinction do you wish to make of them? The last ones are the worst of all. Living among us they learned to hide, to camouflage themselves, to conceal their illness. They are accustomed to hiding behind pretty words the fact that they're dissidents. So no matter what they say, don't believe them. No matter how much they plead – don't listen. Constantly remind yourself that this is a carnivorous, deceitful animal, not a human being with whom you can have a conversation, and his sickness is trying to survive, to save itself, writhing as though it were in a frying pan. They will try to arouse pity, make themselves out to be intelligent people, reason with you, beg you, and try to get you to agree with them. Don't fall for it, young lady. This only shows that they don't want to be cured, that they stubbornly dream only of getting out of here, so they start ruining our lives. And they are clever – really intelligent in their own way. It's not for nothing that they say schizophrenia is a sickness of the mind. You can't talk to them as you would to normal people. You simply cannot. You can't take what they say literally. Have you encountered schizophrenia before?"

Irina nodded silently.

"There you are," brightened Volvkova. "Only one thing is required to help them – convince them to take their medications calmly and obey the doctor. If they agree to this, offer no resistance, aren't rowdy or break the rules it means they are truly repenting and want to get well. It means they are on the doctor's side rather than the side of their insanity. Then it's possible to help those who have a chance to be cured. Tell yourself this: you are not torturing them, you are not forcing them, you are trying to ensure that they have this chance, that they themselves and society are more important than their sickness. They must be prepared to reject their illness, do you understand?"

"I understand," said Irina quietly. "And if they're ready for all this, what then?"

"Then in time we can transfer them to the second ward,

the therapeutic ward. They won't need Aminazine there. We give them Trifluoperazine and Tisercin. The dosage may be gradually lowered, and in the working ward we give them no medications. And so, you see, after three or four years we can return a normal person to society – a healthy, able-bodied person ready to live and create. Isn't it glorious? Isn't it worth it? An animal again becomes a person! He was a cowardly liar who at any cost desired to preserve his madness – but instead became an honest, complaisant, adequate citizen. I've personally seen remissions. But to achieve this, their diseased will must be mercilessly broken. They don't think right and so they pass through all the circles of Hell. And this is good for them." Volkova concluded in a metallic voice. It was clear that she did not wish to waste more time explaining banalities. She called out into the corridor, "Yelena!"

A young woman entered the office. She might have been considered pretty were it not for the coarse sharpness of her features - a straight nose, heavy black eyeliner, thin lips, un-tidy chestnut hair, sharp cheek bones. Irina could not decide whether the face attracted or repelled her. The girl was coarse – this was immediately evident. She fixed Irina with a cold look and turned expectantly to the Chief Medical Officer.

"This is Second Lieutenant Yelena Butenkova. She'll show you where to file your documents, where to draw medications, and so forth. Then both of you go to the strict ward and give injections. For the first week she'll be helping you. Yelena, this is Ira, our new nurse. She has a diploma from Sverdlovsk, and she came here," added Volkova in a mocking tone. "You will help familiarize her with things for the first week. But, listen to me: don't get distracted from work and no old lady gossip during your shift or I'll give you extra duty. Understand?"

"Everything is clear. We have no questions," was Butenkova's dry answer. She shook her head and pulled her hair into a tight tail. "So, let's go, Ira with a diploma. Time to go to work. You already know, right? We give them Thioperazine in the morning."

"I know," echoed Irina, and she followed her new partner in despair. A long day of work stretched ahead.

Chapter 3

"Crap!"

The colonel behind the desk quietly cursed and laid aside the report from the department of special projects he had been reading.

He was rather young, barely forty, thin, with thick prematurely gray hair cropped short. Aleskey Golubov was the deputy chief of one of the leading military research institutes, and he was clearly puzzled. He went to the window from which a high concrete fence was visible and above it the tops of trees in the neighboring park on the outskirts of Moscow in *Marinaya Roshcha*. The colonel lit a cigarette and stared into the distance beyond the park as he uttered a few more curses.

The bad habit of cursing under his breath had begun during the war when in 1943 after the end of the seven-year plan he went to work at a recently opened machine tool factory in his home town of Chkalov which had since been renamed Orenburg. His father, Matvey Golubov had been a lathe operator before the war but had gone to the front as an artillery man in forty-one and thus was unable to break away even when his son graduated from school. Every now and then he sent short letters, but in fact it had been easier on young Lesha. He was able to see how friends who had not expected to see their front-line relatives before the end of the war reacted when they returned unexpectedly: emaciated, nearly unrecognizable, wounded or worse, crippled, helplessly trying to embrace wife and children with the stumps of amputated arms. He was content not to see his father in such a state and read his short letters while he imagined him writing the lines somewhere far away on the front, alive and unharmed.

Lesha's mother, a nurse, was sent to work in a new factory, and she insisted that her son remain close. After all, someone had to look after her four-year-old daughter, Dasha, and her nearly grown son was indispensable. Lesha was an obedient boy and a good student. He discovered yet another, perhaps the most important, quality during those hungry war years – he had the strong hands of someone much older. Like his father, he loved to lift weights and enjoyed how the iron stretched his muscles, and his hands became like iron – strong and heavy. By the time he was fifteen his handshake was stronger than that of many adult laborers.

Aleksey very much wanted to work at the lathe just like his father and requested work in a machine shop. For some reason he loved to watch the spinning lathe and listen to the keening of a drill into metal. He could watch for hours as rough materials were given shape and the way the smooth surface of steel acquired grooves or neatly drilled round holes. There weren't enough workers to man the new rear area plant, and thus he was easily hired. However, within a month, before he could get used to the brigade which consisted of girls, women, and other teenagers like him, he found himself transferred to a neighboring shop with no explanation.

To his astonishment, this shop was "secret." One could enter only with a special pass, and several men already worked there, men who appeared rather old to Aleksey. He was immediately placed as a helper to old Semyon Vasilyevich, a former front-line soldier who limped heavily on the wooden prosthesis that had replaced his right leg. The other men in the shop also were invalids or wore glasses. There were no young girls and teenagers here.

The new shop worked on a variety of "products." These included aiming mechanisms for anti-aircraft artillery. The expensive electronic vacuum tubes for them were supplied by the Allies. These glass tubes were installed with their electrodes into porcelain sockets. This was done by hand and demanded both dexterity and strength. The smallest miscalculation could easily damage the contacts or the body of the tube. It was physically difficult for women to install them, and the frayed nerves of the men from the front could not stand such pressure for long. His youth and tranquil nature, his natural sense of responsibility, and those strong hands all proved quite up to the task. He supplied senior machinist Semyon and sometimes stood in for him. The signal for Aleksey to step in was invariably a string of *sotto voce* curses. Eventually Aleksey adopted this not so attractive adult habit and frequently received a smack on the back of the neck from his mother when such words slipped out at home.

More than two grueling years passed with ten to twelve-hour shifts, the heat of the factory shops, and shoulders that ached at night from the heavy work – without leave and with practically no days off. After a few years Aleksey had matured and was appointed senior machinist. A year after beginning work, when the war had moved beyond the borders of the USSR and the pressure for production relented, he entered night school and graduated with honors a year after war's end. The plant management refused his request to be sent to the front insisting he was too valuable for production. When Lesha tried to argue he found himself threatened by the special department of the NKVD that provided security for the plant and investigated sabotage and monitored plan fulfillment. His father still had not been demobilized, but his letters began to arrive with more frequency, and Aleksey also wrote to his father about his work, school, and his dreams.

Of course, he dreamed of being a test pilot like Valeriy Chkalov or the Heroes of the Great Patriotic War – Pokryshkin and Kozhedub. And he wanted to enter the Voroshilov Military Aviation School in his native Chkalovskoye. Even before the war there had been several well-known educational institutions in Orenburg-Chkalov, including two flight schools: one for pilots and the Second Chkalov Military Aviation School for Navigators. There was the Chkalov Anti-Aircraft Artillery School, as well.

His father had nothing against these dreams, and Aleksey enthusiastically filled out the applications. But during the process members of the military commission discovered something in his physiology that would prevent him from becoming a pilot. His dreams crashed and burned, and the thought of becoming a navigator did not fit in with Aleksey's desire to conquer the skies with his own hands on the stick overcoming gravity just as he had prevailed over the heavy weights and vacuum tubes. Angry with the medics, Aleksey put in his application for the anti-aircraft artillery school. He later wrote his father that "if they won't let me fly airplanes, I'll shoot them down."

The anti-aircraft artillery school was pleased to get Aleksey Golubov. His experience with manufacturing in a related sector also played a role. After six months, thanks to diligent study, discipline and a responsible attitude toward duty that were considered early signs of leadership potential, Aleksey was promoted out of the ranks to unit commander. He had to abandon the practice acquired in the factory shop of muttering curses under his breath in order to avoid setting a bad example for his subordinates. Lesha was amazed and proud to have been the only sergeant named from among the "civilians." The others had had military experience.

In the first years after the war there were constant changes in the army. These also touched the anti-aircraft school. A year after his entrance, in 1947, several laboratories were established, one of which was for radio engineering. Since the weapons guidance installations on which Aleksey worked were related to this field, it was only logical that he should begin to work in this lab – and even more so in that there were few instructor-practitioners familiar with such equipment at the school. The head of the laboratory frequently asked his commanders to send Junior Sergeant Golubov to him, both for consultation and practical testing.

When he completed his studies he tried very hard to convince Aleksey to remain at the school as an instructor, but this was not something Golubov wanted. As before, he wanted to fly, still drawn to new, exciting and interesting experiences. Several classmates, especially those already married, wanted assignments in the big cities where they could find relatively comfortable conditions where wives could find work and children could change schools every year. But Lesha found such comforts unattractive: gray, circumscribed city blocks like a prison with no open space, no heights, lacking the intoxicating brightness of new horizons which had governed him when he was a child.

As graduation approached so called "shoppers" paid increasing visits to the school. As a rule they represented branches of the armed forces or solid institutions that were experiencing personnel deficits that required fast but quality replacements. One of these "shoppers" represented a military installation where new types of anti-aircraft artillery were tested. It seemed that Aleksey had found a place that combined the work he loved and the untilled expanse of the steppes – the dream of an unmarried romantic, especially at the beginning of his journey.

As a lieutenant Golubov landed not only in the world of military anti-aircraft weaponry, but also that of civilian engineers and builders, representatives of manufacturers, and military procurement officers. He gained experience, new friends, and the nearly forgotten habit of expressing himself with strong words. The era of jet aviation was beginning. The speed of military aircraft increased, raising their ceiling and bomb-carrying capacity, but most importantly, the destructive atom bomb appeared. This meant that aircraft capable of carrying them had to be developed, as well as the means to shoot them down.

There was corresponding growth in the caliber of anti-aircraft artillery, and what in dry military jargon was called "the means of detection and guidance." Soviet engineers developed one weapon after another, and guidance systems were developed along with new platforms. But the enemy in turn employed the means to disrupt the signals. Operators had to somehow recognize the jamming, which necessitated constant experimentation to reach the required performance parameters, modernize and again test, and then perfect further.

Aleksey worked to remember all those situations when he had to act, almost like a physician – to discover the cause of failure through diagnosis under testing. Sometimes he asked the help of colleagues from other units and took part in meetings along with the representatives of all participating agencies, but it was often the case that he had to figure out the reason for failure by himself, relying solely on his professional intuition.

By the mid-1950's it was clear to Aleksey that the capabilities of anti-aircraft artillery were limited and that given the great speed and altitude of enemy aircraft, they could be shot down only with missiles. The romance of distant military bases turned out to be a boring routine of repairing the production flaws of others, and Golubov was bored. He decided to enter the Govorov Radio-Technical Artillery Academy of the Soviet Army in faraway Kharkov.

It wasn't difficult for him to get into the academy, but it

was no simple matter to get a transfer from the base command considering the constant testing of new artillery types and early missile testing. The command was reluctant to lose the young workaholic captain who was the ideal candidate for away missions or special assignments. But Golubov was fortunate – he'd received a special privilege for winning an All-Army competition with the boring title, "The best conditions for the rationalization of work." The young engineer, tired of constant repair work, created a device for testing radar station waveguides, which made it possible to significantly reduce the time required for troubleshooting.

Things in Kharkov seemed somehow humdrum, but proceeded quickly. Aleksey managed neither to get an apartment nor amass significant belongings. His parents were a bit more concerned at the time with young Dashka who had transformed from the noisy child that Aleksey had picked up from kindergarten into a lovely 17-year-old girl.

At thirty Aleksey was still unmarried. His tough teenage years at the factory and his youth in the strict Chkalov anti-aircraft artillery school did not lend themselves to romance. Passes into town weren't given often or to everybody, and of those girls who sometimes attended dances at the school no one appealed to him.

His first, as he thought, real love was after school when he was sent from the base to short-term courses in Leningrad at the Dzerzhinskiy Military Artillery Academy. On his off days he managed to find time to explore the legendary city on the Neva. Once as he strolled along the banks of the Neva opposite the Petropavlovskiy Fortress his attention was attracted by a young artist who was painting something on her easel. There was something special about her that made the young lieutenant slow his pace: maybe the thick light brown, nearly golden hair that shimmered as it was caught by the slightest breeze or the deft strokes of her brush, or maybe the depths of her gray eyes or the naïve plumpness of her young cheeks an soft lips … His words were clumsy as he asked her some banality about how to get to the Hermitage and essayed a compliment …

In the end they went to the Hermitage together and that night wandered through the Winter Garden and sat on a bench on the Field of Mars. Accustomed to the girls in his native Chkalov who sought out the attentions of young students and lieutenants, Aleksey did not tell her then that he was in the military, having invented the legend of a design engineer at a military plant.

They were good together and exchanged regular correspondence after he left Leningrad. When he got leave, Aleksey, of course, returned to Leningrad. Their feelings grew, and Aleksey finally admitted that he was in the military. Gray-eyed Svetlana forgave him, but the relationship cooled and soon Aleksey received a letter in which she explained that she was an incurable city dweller and could not imagine herself as the wife of a military man wandering among secret installations and military cities in the wilderness. And so his first real romance ended and he again plunged into experiments at the base – he'd not yet entered the academy …

Golubov loved Kharkov. After provincial Chkalov he was unaccustomed to grand spaces like Dzerzhinski Square, or the wide, noisy streets in the city center. One had only to stray from the central streets a few blocks to find oneself on old streets of the forgotten past, such as *Pervaya Konnaya* (First Cavalry) which retained its 19th Century character untouched by war or progress. In such places he almost felt like he was at home.

Aleksey very much enjoyed studying at the academy despite the constant course changes necessitated by the reorientation of anti-aircraft defense in the mid-1950's from anti-aircraft artillery to ground-to-air missile systems. This meant that the traditional disciplines were reduced in the well-known fields of mechanics and electrical engineering. Instead of partially or fully condensed courses, unfamiliar subjects were introduced, such as the theory of random processes, the elements of mathematical statistics, automation, or the theory of the reliability and exploitation of complex systems.

Near the end of his studies Golubov, now a major, was attracted to one of the new innovations – electronic computing. His broad knowledge of mechanics, electrical engineering and radio engineering permitted him to quickly master the basics of programming the first Soviet computers. This proved to be quite useful to Aleskey in the future when upon completion of the academy he agreed to remain there to conduct research and defend his doctoral dissertation.

There were two reasons he remained in scientific work at the academy rather than serve in the military or return to a military base as he had eleven years previously. First, in the academy former anti-aircraft systems experimental engineer Golubov was seriously attracted by the new radar guided warheads of ground-to-air missiles. This was not a basic subject at the academy, but it called to Golubov not only because he had always loved to master hitherto unknown things, but because he was totally confident of his abilities. He understood perfectly the importance of the military application of missiles – from acquiring their targets, support and guidance to target acquisition, to detonation of the warhead. The appearance of new computers for engineers further stimulated his desire to discover new algorithms to assist in the discovery and destruction of enemy targets more rapidly, at greater distances, at greater altitudes, and with higher confidence of destruction.

Secondly, Aleksey married a year after finishing the academy. He had seen his future wife, Oksana, a few times in the reading room of the academy library. She was studying at a local university and had come to help her mother who was a librarian. She was often exhausted from excursions between the shelves to find books requested by students and academy cadets. In time they developed a close relationship that grew into love and finally – a modest wedding.

After their marriage Aleskey and Oksana lived in her mother's apartment until they found separate rooms in a family dwelling near the academy. Shortly after graduation from the academy their daughter, Viktoria, was born. Oksana had never known her father. He went missing in action at the start of the war, and the family could find no trace of him. Oksana also had no grandparents. Her mother, Olga Petrovna, never wanted to talk about this with her daughter or son-in-law and limited herself only to the fact that they all perished during the famine at the beginning of the 1930's in the village of Bolshaya Pisarevka in Kharkov Oblast while she had survived thanks to distant relatives from Kharkhov who somehow managed to get her into an orphanage.

Aleksey listened sympathetically but did not probe for details. He understood that this was only a fraction of the colossal common tragedy experienced by the entire Russian nation before and after the war. For the most part, Major Aleksey Golubov was quite satisfied with developments in his life. He was involved in important and interesting work, and he had a good family …

In the meantime the international situation heated up, and Soviet anti-aircraft defenses played an important role. In 1960 over Sverdlovsk they brought down an American U-2 spy plane flown by Francis Gary Powers, and in 1962 they repeated this when they shot down another U-2 piloted by Rudolph

Anderson over Cuba. This and other events had a constant influence on the work of surface-to-air missile constructors and military service.

Golubov's career prospered. He successfully defended his doctoral dissertation with such distinction that the young scientist was invited to work at the top research institute in Moscow. In short order he was given a spacious apartment near the institute, his wife found work, and his daughter was accepted into kindergarten. At times Aleksey reflected on the irony of his fate. His old girlfriend, Svetlana, rebuffed him so she could remain in a big city while Oksana, who would have followed him to the ends of the earth unexpectedly landed in the capital in circumstances few even could dream of.

Because then First Secretary of the CC CPSU, Nikita Khrushchev was so taken by missiles at the beginning of the 1960's, aviation experienced a considerable reduction in favor of all types of missile systems. Thanks to this, huge resources and specialists of many different types were devoted to the development of surface-to-air missiles. Designers perfected deadlier means of destroying the enemy. Nuclear weapons, it seemed, could be adapted to nearly every type of vehicle: ballistic missiles, bombs, artillery shells, and even underwater torpedoes. The designers were in a frenzy to develop one generation after another of surface-to-air missiles that carried death wrapped in the steel grip of nuclear warheads.

Lt. Colonel Golubov was promoted in short order from section head to department head, and given the rank of full colonel as deputy director of the institute. In this position, rather than solving design problems, he had to manage the collective and handle relations with scientific and design institutes, especially when he stood in for the director who often was away on assignment. Some of these assignments took him to Egypt, Vietnam, and other Soviet allies who were engaged in warfare. Golubov sometimes made such trips, as well.

Periodically he would receive reports on various promising developments. According to one of these, should the enemy employ jamming, a nuclear surface-to-air missile had been developed with a special warhead. The first such warhead had been created in 1964 and adopted for the S-75 SAM, the same system that had so easily shot down the American U-2's. However, unlike ballistic missiles or nuclear torpedoes, the warhead of the SAM could annihilate the very sites and people it was intended to defend ...

Colonel Golubov could almost feel a chill emanating from the ordinary sheets of paper and the printed letters and figures – a sepulchral, deathly cold that struck him with the force of a shock wave from an unseen explosion. With numb fingertips he flipped through the report from the Special Activities Section concerning the possible consequences of a nuclear air burst *above Soviet territory* resulting from the use of the newly modified missile. The calculations collided in his brain and he saw flashes from his life: his wife and little Viki, the shabby facades of the old buildings in Kharkov, the cozy courtyards and shops of Chkalov, the banks of the Neva. The sterile calculations took none of this into account. It seemed to Golubov that some great chasm had opened inside him, and waves of paralyzing horror engulfed his thoughts.

This paralysis lasted only for a second. In the next instant Aleksey recovered his military bearing, gathered his courage, and mashed his cigarette in the ashtray before grabbing the telephone.

Chapter 4

To put it mildly, the day didn't start badly. While it was still early Dimitriy Rakhmanov bumped into Kiryusha from the First Directorate who was generally considered to be a rare sort of rat. How Kirill ever landed in foreign intelligence was an absolute riddle for Major Rakhmanov – as far as he knew Kirill had never been abroad and did only office work, although very specific office work: nosing out information concerning other KGB divisions. Now, spotting Dimitriy in the corridor he scowled and moved to block his passage.

Rakhmanov nodded coldly and stepped back to allow the man to pass, but Kirill ignored the greeting and got straight to the point.

"Dimitriy Yevgenyevich, did I hear correctly that you had an overseas source? And not just anywhere, but in Czechoslovakia?"

"Not a source; just an acquaintance. Where did you hear this?" Kirill's curiosity did not please him.

"The world is full of rumors," Kirill smiled slyly. "But, OK, you may contact whomever you like. I was only surprised that he left a long time ago and you still haven't sent a report to the Directorate."

"Was I supposed to?" Dimitriy raised his brows in mock surprise. "There was nothing substantive to say. Personal observations from his trip, that's all. He had no intelligence collection mission, if that's what you're on about. I have no right to give such assignments."

"Nevertheless, any information from abroad that comes to your directorate must be given to us. Any information! It doesn't matter what you may think of me, this is your sworn duty." Kirill was indignant.

Dimitriy snickered. "So you've decided to tell me what my duties are? Kirill, I appreciate your concern, but it's not worth it. As for materials – send a request through the front office the way you're supposed to do. It's not within my purview to decide whether to pass anything to you or not."

"Well, I think it's a good idea to work through the front office, too. For over a year now you've shared none of the information you receive about other countries. I think the bosses would find this interesting because it's just not normal. Yuriy Vladimirovich took over the *Komitet*[10] only recently, and he's not yet had the time to see everything."

"Where did you get the idea that we even possess such information?" frowned Dimitriy.

"An inspection will sort out whether it's true or not," Kirill shot back.

"You're threatening me?" Rakhmanov didn't bother to hide his disdain. "Go ahead. Let the bosses know who in the *Komitet* really works and not only can discuss the affairs of his own department, but of the neighboring one, as well, and who is faking it. You'll soon learn how we treat informers."

Evidently Dimitriy's confidence deflated Kirill's sails. "I wasn't making a threat. I only said that things are likely to develop, and the bosses will notice."

"I already told you: thanks for the concern, but we manage things with the bosses on our own." Dimitriy ended the conversation and squeezed past to enter his office. He arrived just in time: the phone rang, and it was a call from Vlad, the leader of the surveillance team he'd sent out early that morning.

"Comrade Major, I report," he began formally, "The subject took a taxi directly from the train station to the address you gave to us. He entered the building three hours ago and

---

10 Комитет – Committee (referring to the Committee for State Security – the KGB.

hasn't come out again. Just a moment ago a man entered who matches the photo of a foreign journalist named Joseph Barlow who is accredited in Moscow – you were right."

"He entered the building?" Dima was vexed. Could the Ukrainian guest be planning to pass materials in the apartment of this young girl, Nastya. Such things didn't happen often – exchanges with foreigners usually were conducted on the street or in secluded spots with no witnesses. In this case, Butko was to be taken into custody the moment he handed the materials over to the correspondent. But now it seemed the dissidents were aware of the danger and had decided to exchange documents behind closed doors. This complicated matters.

"Cover the rear of the building so he can't get away. As soon as the foreigner comes out, arrest him and bring him here, but do it politely: so sorry, a mere formality, the man who gave you the documents is a criminal with pending charges against him, and we are obligated to check ... We'll politely confiscate the materials according to protocol, take his testimony and let him go. We don't need an international scandal. Split up into two groups: one to grab the foreigner and the other to get into the apartment and conduct a search the moment he's gone. You can turn everything upside down, but make sure you find every scrap of their libelous writings. Arrest Butko and bring him to me for interrogation. And if the owner of the apartment is there – a young student, Anastasia – don't touch her."

"She should not be arrested under any circumstances?" Vlad wanted to be sure he understood.

"It's unnecessary unless she starts shooting," laughed Dimitriy, "She doesn't interest me."

And now, after the arrangements had been made, he had only to wait.

Snow fell on the windshield in such large clumps that someone might as well have been throwing snowballs. It shattered on the glass into a mixture of white dots and sparkling crystals that refracted colors and objects. The wipers mercilessly displaced them, and the winter scene outside was again visible – unending snow that lent everywhere an air of glistening purity. Even the hectic tempo of the city involuntarily slowed under the weight of the heavy snowflakes that might have fallen from a fairy tale. And Moscow, frozen into snow-locked patterns and buried in drifts, yielded to the charm of its perfect beauty and awaited a miracle.

Vlad waited, too, tense and nervous, cursing the snow from the depths of his soul because it interfered with his vision. He was relatively new to the KGB and this was the first time he'd led a mission. The thought that he might not be up to the simplest task and fail his comrades, terrified him. The major's orders had been transmitted, and both groups were in position, but the targets had not yet appeared. The snow continued unabated, and the windshield wipers swept it from the glass in impassive, regular intervals.

"The foreigner!" The words over the radio broke the silence, dissipating the winter fairy tale in emulation of the wipers on the glass. Bent low against the snow and raising his collar like a Russian, Joseph Barlow walked out of the building carrying a narrow, foreign briefcase in one hand.

"Go," Vlad commanded quietly. He eased himself out of the car and approached the doorway leaving fresh tracks in the snow. Two of his men were speaking politely but firmly with Barlow, one on each side, and two more followed Vlad through the doors and up the stairs to a room at the top, practically a garret. This scum thinks to betray the Motherland without anyone knowing about it? Ridiculous!

At the top of the stairs the wind could be heard howling

in the pipes. The door was opened immediately as if she expected someone by a skinny, dark-haired girl wearing glasses. When she saw Vlad and the two Chekists behind him, she retreated with a look not so much of fright, but like that of a hunted animal, with pain and supplication. Vlad pushed rudely past her as he flashed his identification. Such looks had no effect on him.

"Committee for State Security," he said. "Who else is in this apartment?"

"Me," a calm, male voice sounded from the interior of the apartment followed by the appearance of an athletically built man with a clear and direct gaze. "If you've come for me, comrades, let's leave so we don't shock the young lady."

"We'll leave when it's necessary," replied Vlad with some heat. He had not expected that the hatred lurking within his soul should be so strong. But it burst out, warmed by the sweet sense of power. Vlad was the master of the situation for the moment, and it made him a little dizzy. For the first time he was in charge of a search in the presence of the owner of the apartment, and he did his best to cover his anxiety with aggressiveness.

"We have a warrant from the prosecutor to search your apartment," he continued, injecting contempt into his voice.

The girl gasped. "A search?" Vlad recalled that her name was Anastasia.

"Sit down," he ordered, and with a sign to his men began systematically to search the apartment. Nastya sat down and turned her face to the window to stare blankly at the falling snow.

"Klim pointed at the man. "Arrest this one right away."

The young man asked, "May I see the arrest warrant?"

"You'll see everything," said Vlad. Irritated by the young man's composure, he became angrier. Nastya turned back to them and watched wide-eyed as her guest was handcuffed. Her eyes betrayed such deeply held guilt, soul tearing guilt that the Ukrainian seemed to understand something and nodded encouragingly at her.

"There's nothing here that can be ignored," said Vlad as he pulled open one of the drawers in an old, pre-war writing desk. A heap of printed pages fell to the floor, and the title of one of them drew his immediate attention: "Will the Soviet Union Last until 1984?"

"Who does this belong to?" Almost choking with malice, Vlad grabbed a page and shoved it into Nastya's face. She said nothing, not having expected anyone to question her. Vlad belatedly recalled that the major had ordered that the girl not be touched, but then, Vlad did not intend to arrest her.

"The Soviet Union will live forever, but people like you, all of you, will soon be rotting in the camps," he hissed. "Do you understand that you've broken the law? So who does this belong to?" With these words he snatched up a book that was so new it still smelled of printing ink. Obviously, it had been published in the West."

"Vlad, I found a camera!" One of the men gleefully pulled a new camera from under a pile of old sheets in a nightstand and pointed at Butko, "The books they had published outside the country were put on film, others were typed by hand. They're agents, alright. They gave everything to the Americans."

The Ukrainian laughed. "Well, that's a clever speculation. Do you want to return to the terrible Thirties? I seem to remember that even the Party had something to say about that."

"Correct," snapped Vlad, "The Party decided, and that's enough, so you have no business talking about it. And not to worry: we are not 'speculating.' Everything will be taken into account by the court in full accordance with the law; has it ever been otherwise in our country?" He narrowed his eyes as he stared at the man in handcuffs.

"In our country anything could have happened," was Butko's quiet response.

"Are the witnesses here?" Vlad shot a glance toward the door where a couple of neighbors had been summoned by one of his men. "So, in your presence we confiscate the anti-Soviet literature we discovered here, a typewriter and a camera ..." He carefully dictated the names, brands, identifying marks, the publisher of the books, counted the number of typewritten pages. It was important that protocol be observed in full accordance with established procedure.

Then he turned again to Nastya. "Tell us to whom all this belongs."

"It's mine," she answered in a firm voice. Vlad realized that this conversation was futile, especially since he could not arrest Anastasia. But he did not want to look like an idiot in front of his men and the witnesses, and he had to find a way to end this improvised interrogation.

"Are you giving false testimony?" he frowned. "Do you want to go to Kolyma?"[11]

"I brought all of that with me this morning," said Butko.

---

11 **Kolyma** (Russian: Колыма, IPA: [kəlɨˈma]) is a region located in the Russian Far East. It is bounded by the East Siberian Sea and the Arctic Ocean in the north and the Sea of Okhotsk to the south. ... The area, part of which is within the Arctic Circle, has a subarctic climate with very cold winters lasting up to six months of the year. Permafrost and tundra cover a large part of the region. ... Under Joseph Stalin's rule, Kolyma became the most notorious region for the Gulag labor camps. Tens of thousands or more people may have died en route to the area or in the Kolyma's series of gold mining, road building, lumbering, and construction camps between 1932 and 1954. It was Kolyma's reputation that caused Aleksandr Solzhenitsyn, author of The Gulag Archipelago, to characterize it as the "pole of cold and cruelty" in the Gulag system. The Mask of Sorrow monument in Magadan commemorates all those who died in the Kolyma forced-labour camps and the recently dedicated Church of the Nativity remembers the victims in its icons[3] and Stations of the Camps.[4] - Source: Wikipedia - https://en.wikipedia.org/wiki/Kolyma

"We followed you all the way from the train station, and you had nothing with you but a small suitcase," Vlad interrupted him.

Nastya's voice rang out. "Everything here belongs to me." There was a kind of distinctive, mindless determination in her eyes. Vlad would remember those eyes for a long time afterwards: the eyeglasses framing them, the whites red from sleeplessness, and dark circles that added more emphasis than mascara. Probably they had once been beautiful, those eyes, but now they were dominated by a frightening expression of heroic madness.

"I have no doubt that they are yours. Where did you get them?" Her reaction had only provoked Vlad.

"Let's go," said one of his men. "Our mission was to conduct a search and arrest the Khokhol.[12]"

"You're lucky. You get off for now, but it won't last long," said Vlad in a soft voice. Suddenly a paper stuck between the pages of one of the foreign-published books caught his eye. "'To Sergey Naumov from Ignatiy,'" he read aloud. "Looks like we found the owner."

"Give it back!" Nastya tried to grab the paper. "How can you do this? You promised. You promised." In tears now, she threw herself at him.

"What did we promise?" Vlad sneered as he roughly pushed her away. He knew it was time to put an end to this spectacle. He was jarred by the thought that he had strayed into forbidden territory. It was entirely possible that Rakhmanov's order to leave the girl alone was not because she was "of no interest," but because she was his source – Rakhmanov wasn't obliged to account for his actions to a subordinate officer, and it wasn't Vlad's place to know such things. He comforted him-

---

12 Khokhol – a derisive term for Ukrainians, Literally, a pickle.

self with the thought that he had not literally disobeyed the order; before witnesses he had conducted a search in accordance with established protocol, discovered many items of interest, and arrested the Kievan as he had been instructed. With a final glance at the weeping Nastya, Vlad turned to the door and ordered:

"That's it, boys. We're leaving. Gather up the material evidence, and don't forget this one," he pointed at Butko.

Then he turned to the bewildered "witnesses" with a heartfelt smile. "Thank you, Comrades."

He was on the stairs again, his passage accompanied by the keening of the wind in the pipes. The first search of his career had been a rare success, producing results, and Vlad could see already how he would present his report at Lubyanka. Materials collected, protocol observed, and the detainee ready to admit that it all belonged to him. Maybe the girl had been frightened a little, but he'd not laid a finger on her.

A wind had come up during the search, and the snow no longer settled majestically to the ground but was swept into drifts and scurried along the sidewalk licking at their shoes. Vlad shoved Butko into the car and slammed the door shut. He had just gotten behind the wheel when a noise caused him to turn his head. The car's side windows were nearly enshrouded in white, and through them, as through a fanciful kaleidoscope, he could just make out the courtyard. Another gust of wind tore some snow from the bare branches of a birch, and it settled softly onto a drift to one side. But beyond the snow drift was something bizarre dimly visible through the icy crust on the glass, something very similar to a human body...

Everyone leapt from the car at the same time, but Vlad was the first to reach the still bundle on the sidewalk. Nastya stared up at him with those same eyes he had noticed in the apartment – open wide but now without glasses, and absolutely dead. Her body lay in an unnatural position on her back, her face to the lowering sky with the snow falling on it.

Vlad knelt and lifted her wrist, but there was no pulse. Only then did he notice the fresh red stream of blood on the white snow beneath her hair.

Behind him, one of his men cursed. "Shit. She jumped out the window. We should have taken her, too. Why didn't we?"

Vlad raised his head and saw the open window just under the roof.

"We couldn't take her," he whispered. "The orders were not to touch her. But I didn't touch her! What did I do? Did I slap her? Did I threaten her with something unlawful? Did I swear at her? Not at all! I did everything properly. I discovered forbidden literature in her apartment and told her people are sent to Kolyma for such things. I asked who the materials belonged to. I was obliged to ask! So, I said a few rude things; what am I supposed to do with such enemies, kiss them? That's right, isn't it?" He looked from one to the other of his gloomily silent comrades.

"Go ahead and think you had nothing to do with it." Viktor Butko appeared next to Vlad. "Are you satisfied now, *gebisty*?[13] You've killed the girl."

Vlad shuddered. Nastya's unanticipated suicide had knocked him completely off his feet. The Kievan might have escaped a thousand times, having been left unguarded. But where could he have gone in handcuffs? Still, it was a good thing he had not run.

"No one is asking for your opinion, you piece of shit. It's your fault for using her, do you understand? We were looking for you, not her. If you had passed your spy goods on the street, no one would have gone to her apartment. It's you who

---

13 Гебисты – KGB operatives

killed her, and you'll remember it for the rest of your life. At night in your cell she won't allow you to sleep." He turned to one of his men. "Maksim, call an ambulance and wait for it here. We don't need the police; we'll inform them later if needs be. Let's go!"

He turned and kicked at the bloody snow before grabbing Butko and turning him toward the car, now almost completely covered in white.

Chapter 5

"Kravtsov." The familiar, calm voice of Golubov's former classmate at the Kharkhov Academy, Lt. Colonel Oleg Kravtsov, sounded in the receiver. Kravtsov was the chief of the ballistics department of the same scientific research institute as Aleksey.

"Oleg, are you busy right now?" Regardless of the difference in responsibilities between the Deputy Director of the institute and a department head, Colonel Golubov addressed him by name. He never took advantage of rank, least of all with old friends, and when it came to non-official matters, he preferred to avoid the question altogether. Whether it was with equals or young subordinates he trusted and valued, he referred to them only by patronymic – Petrovich or Sergeevich.

In this instance Golubov struggled to emulate the calm tone of Kravtsov but did not succeed entirely. Kravtsov noted the tension his director's tone and instinctively replied in a nearly official voice.

"Everything is according to plan, Aleksey Matveyevich. The review of the dissertation of the candidate from the Kalinin Institute will be completed by the end of the week. There are two days left. Plus, the calculations for the next test."

"OK. It's not urgent … It's so nice outside. Summer will soon be past, and we'll be sitting in our dull offices sucking dust. You wouldn't have anything against staying for a while after work? We could find a bench in the park. I have a couple of bottles of cold *"Zhigulevsky"*[14] in the cupboard. There are a few things I'd like to toss around with you."

---

14 A pale lager-style beer.

There was nothing especially urgent about Golubov's request. In good weather Institute personnel often took advantage of secluded spots in the half-empty park to enjoy a bottle of beer or something stronger, but this was a practice normally limited to officers at staff level. Department bosses, not to mention Institute directors normally were not to be found resting on park benches. They had air-conditioned private offices with safes and refrigerators, and when they wanted to have a drink with friends or colleagues, they could do so without leaving the workplace or undermining their authority in the eyes of subordinates.

But Golubov did not want to invite Kravtsov to his office, which would have meant displaying to his old comrade the widening gulf between their relative positions. Although they finished the Academy together Golubov's personal experience and high potential led to promotion beyond Kravtsov, and he was the first of his classmates to be given the high responsibility of Department Director at the Institute. After Aleksey was named Deputy Director of the Institute, at the suggestion of the leadership, he started working not only on guidance systems for surface-to-air missiles, but also the entire range of work on future missile design, he received an early promotion to full colonel.

It was typical of this type of research institute to be entirely responsible for a gamut of activities related to the development, storage, and possible use of nuclear munitions one level above conventional weapons. As a result, Golubov became a colonel at a time when several of his Academy "classmates" were still majors. In the depths of his heart Aleksey admitted that most of his former classmates, including Oleg Kravtsov, also were capable of success. Now they served in typical staff officer positions, at test ranges, as military school instructors, and were content with the more modest rank of Lt. Colonel.

Kravtsov accepted his invitation. To sit day after day in an office with the occasional glance out the window at the summer blooms saturated in sunlight and hear the twitter of the birds in the park next door was not particularly satisfying for a man whose vacation time was still far ahead. Besides, he was eager to find out from Golubov the details of the special activities at the "Emba" test range in northern Kazakhstan not far from Orenburg where he had recently conducted an inspection.

They exited through the security controls and walked into the park and soon left the footpaths normally used by Institute staff. Finding a bench, Golubov extracted two bottles of beer from his briefcase.

"How was your trip? Were you able to visit your family? How was everything?" Kravtsov knew that Golubov's parents lived in Orenburg, but he mentioned them only out of propriety. He was more curious to find out the reason for the invitation from this "high-ranking" officer.

"My parents are fine," answered Golubov. "They're nearly 70 now but doing well. My father's hearing hasn't been good since the war, and these days he can barely hear anything. But mom is always there to help if there is a problem. As for the mission ... Oleg, you know how much it weighs on you when people die because of stupidity or carelessness. Of course, it's not our fault, although there may be some indirect responsibility at the top ..."

He took a pull directly from the bottle of the slightly bitter but bracing beer and briefly described the nature of the incident that had prompted his recent trip to investigate the technical causes.

It all began quite normally, and the Orenburg trip seemed no different from dozens of others. Normally, "typical" test flights of various experimental missiles were conducted at the "Emba" test range. This was standard practice before sending the next batch of rockets to the troops. Everything was proceeding normally when there was a terrible explosion in the area reserved for the construction battalion. The tragedy occurred in the middle of a space filled with people, and dozens were killed. Golubov was a member of the commission assigned to investigate the incident because his bosses had good reason to believe that only the military elements of the missile could have caused the explosion under such circumstances. There were simply no other types of explosives in the area.

At the test range Aleksey learned that during the test the missile had lifted smoothly from the gantry but suddenly diverged sharply from its trajectory and after a short, uneven flight crashed down range. As soon as it hit the ground there was a double explosion. First the rocket fuel exploded in a fiery column that scattered metallic pieces of the missile, and then the warhead blew up with pieces flying everywhere. The missile was designed to blow to pieces when it reached the target or to be destroyed in case of an abort.

Golubov and his institute were not responsible for the manufacture of warheads, but questions of design and abort procedures in case of failure were within their purview. And so as the representative of the experimental staff of the Ministry of Defense, along with representatives of the civilian designers and manufacturers were charged with determining why the rocket motor went awry and the warhead, instead of exploding on impact, had landed amidst the construction battalion.

The investigation showed that after failing to meet military standards the manufacturer sent a batch of missiles with unstable motors. Because of this, the missiles would become unstable shortly after launch and within a short time would fall and explode. However, Golubov could find no answer to the second question – why had one of them not exploded?

"You understand, " concluded Aleksey, "I was able to determine the circumstances but not the reason. At some time following the launch of this defective rocket the testing personnel in the command center did not distinctly hear a second explosion and had some momentary doubts, but they were too lazy to go out to where the missile fell. What must have happened was that the missile fell somewhere near a road used by the construction battalion to reach their facilities. When they saw the cylinder containing the warhead, instead of informing base headquarters, they decided to transport it to their unit ..."

Kravtsov was nonplussed. "What? Didn't they see the markings, or weren't they warned to touch nothing on the test range?"

"Who the hell knows? There are no eyewitnesses left to ask. The fact of the matter is that the battalion commander was driving along the road in his *"uazik"*[15] along with several other troops. He ordered in a crane truck to load this 200-kilogram 'barrel' onto a *KRAZ*[16] - and they hauled it right into their area and parked it next to the mess hall where the troops were lined up for chow. A lieutenant climbed onto the truck with a hammer and chisel and tried to open the object ..."

"But that contains a hundred-weight of the trotyl-hexogen mixture!" exclaimed Kravtsov. "Did anything survive?"

"Nothing was left – just the frame of *KRAZ* ... Not a trace was left of the combat battalion and the others who were near the truck."

Kravtsov expelled a long, slow breath. "Holy Christ," and took a long pull from the bottle of beer. "Why in the world did they do that?"

---

15 UAZ – a kind of Soviet jeep or truck.

16 KPA3 – a large, heavy-duty truc,

"They said they wanted explosives to kill fish in the lakes in the Steppe," answered Golubov.

He swallowed some beer and continued.

"It's a good thing they fire only standard warheads at that range. If this had happened somewhere on a nuclear test range in Semipalatinsk and it had been a special warhead? Imagine if it fell into the hands of some sort of unpredictable thrill seeker. You know what happens to people when a special warhead is fired under real war conditions, even in the case of normal operations at a given altitude. It's the TNT equivalent of Hiroshima."

"Of course." Kravtsov was deeply impressed. "No one even wants to think about it. Hopefully, it will never come to that. Something might have happened in Cuba in '62, but they came to an agreement."

"It was still possible then," said Golubov in a hollow voice. "But it did nothing to increase optimism. Look, Oleg, in '64 they mounted a high-altitude nuclear device on the ground-to-air missile that brought down Powers. And now they want to lower the operational ceiling from six kilometers to a hundred, practically at the surface. For use under certain circumstances ... Do you understand?"

"This is the first I've heard of it." Kravtsov grew tense as the unpleasant thought occurred that Golubov was starting to speak of things that Kravtsov had no right to know. An unpleasant chill of fear churned in his stomach. Golubov was discussing secret matters with him – matters that he, Kravtsov, had absolutely no need to know about. But the forbidden knowledge filled him with a feeling of painful responsibility that he did not wish to accept. The entire work experience of Lt. Colonel Kravtsov had taught him that the best way to survive in the system was to avoid thinking about things that did not concern him. The nearly magical formula that "those

above know best" had always helped him to be loyal and ful-
fill his direct responsibilities without entering the realm of
global problems.

Kravtsov deflected the subject. "Listen, they would hardly
use such things near populated places, more likely somewhere
in the north or in the desert. And maybe in the end, nothing
will happen. After all, under Khrushchev long range aviation was reduced in favor of missiles. Maybe they'll switch to
something else soon …"

Golubov finished his bottle. "Who knows? Maybe it will
change, and maybe it won't. But they're conducting tests not
only in the desert."

Kravtsov gave a dissatisfied grunt and closed his eyes,
without replying.

Months passed with no changes in the quotidian routine
of work and domestic chores, creating an illusion of undis-
turbed tranquility. Regardless of human concerns, in Moscow
autumn followed summer sprinkling the city with golden rain
and pampering her inhabitants with the delights of an Indian
summer. Then frosty and snowy winter came to the capital in-
exorably enveloping the city in cold and the darkness of long
nights. The New Year's holiday was celebrated with songs,
the tolling of bells, enthusiastic speeches about new achieve-
ments and hopes – and disappeared, leaving Moscow alone
with the remaining months of the severe Russian winter …

The Chief of the Third Chief Directorate of the KGB,
known as military counterintelligence, General-Lieutenant
Andrey Bykov, loved to play volleyball. As an undoubtedly
busy man he could permit himself this pleasure in the company of men the same as himself, 40 – 50-year-old comrades
never more than once a week and only on Sunday mornings.
They played in the sports hall at the KGB Academy on Mich-
urinskiy Boulevard where the Head of the Academy, who was

a little older, was always pleased to greet them. It goes without saying that no random player was allowed in their game. The volleyball teams consisted either of highly placed officers of the KGB or retirees who were still in shape. Some of them worked in Party organs but did not want to lose contact with their former colleagues. Afterwards in the relaxed atmosphere of the sauna or the pool, it was possible to discuss important or sensitive questions without having to resort to the tediousness of inter-departmental correspondence, approvals and the other bureaucratic procedures that went with high office.

"You really guarded the net today, Andrey." Bykov accepted the cheerful praise of a graying, sturdy man of middle height, who was publicly known as the Deputy Head of the Defense-Technology Department of the Central Committee of the CP USSR, but who the initiated knew was Colonel Yuriy Kryuchkov of the KGB Active Reserves.

"Yes, Yuriy Ivanovich, as they say guarded 'with complete proletarian hatred' … You understand, after a week of constant tension at Lubyanka it's quite pleasant to let off some steam …"

"I understand. I understand," was Kryuchkov's fatherly reply. Although he was lower in rank his duties in the Central Committee were higher in the hierarchy, and the act that he was older made Bykov's deference completely natural.

"Listen," continued Kryuchkov, "I have a small favor to ask. We're considering a state decision on the improvement of special means to guarantee the destruction of large formations of aviation targets. We've already had a series of meetings on this. You understand that we lag behind the Americans, and this must be overcome quickly and at all costs. But among the representatives of your 'patronized' Ministry of Defense, it is puzzling that a rather special opinion is held by a certain Colonel Golubov of the Institute for Anti-Aircraft Defense. Instead of looking for a way to resolve technical issues, he regularly puts up arguments against the suitability of new designs that are supported by practically everyone else. There is some logic in his judgments, but it is rather pessimistic, not to say defeatist ... He speaks of unanticipated consequences, big risks, the threat to life and the environment, and the like."

"The task is clear, Yuriy Ivanovich. I'll try to work up a report on this 'interesting' colonel, and I'll deliver it personally. What did you say is his name?"

"Golubov. Colonel Aleksey Golubov, Deputy Director of the Institute. The Director of the Institute, General Gerasimenko, is in the hospital following an assignment in Egypt – bad nerves. The Israelis captured one of his missiles there ... it embarrassed the old man ... and something is making this Golubov nervous, too, only no one knows what it is ..."

The following day, Monday morning, the first thing Bykov did was to make an encrypted call on his *ZAS* (as his department referred to the encrypted telephone apparatus[17]) to the head of the special department for military counterintelligence of the KGB at armaments headquarters of the Ministry of Defense to which Golubov's institute was subordinated. This department "looked after" the Institute. As it happened his subordinate officer already had placed Colonel Golubov under observation but had as yet made no report as the investigation was still underway.

"We already have some indications," said the officer, "From a co-worker of the Deputy Head of the Institute, Oleg Kraftsov we have information that Golubov talks too much about closed subjects and pays insufficient attention to the protection of classified information. Also, transcripts of conversations in Golubov's home reveal that his wife, a Ukrainian,

---

17 ЗАС - засекречивающую аппаратуру связи

harbors critical views about pre-war events, especially about questions of collectivization, and also the reason for the famine in Ukraine before and after the Great Patriotic War. Golubov has made several critical comments about the leading role of the Party in the structure of the military – he has in mind the radical reductions in aviation at the beginning of the 60's and the possibility of taking similar decisive steps in the future."

"Interesting," replied Bykov. "And how about his work performance?"

"His work is very good. He's knowledgeable, shows initiative, and is responsible. He knows how to manage people for the successful resolution of creative tasks. It's true that some are not so fond of his penchant for familiarity with subordinates. But the leadership has no problem with him."

"Understood." Bykov ended the conversation. "I want everything you've collected on my desk by Monday morning. You personally are to report. Are there any questions? … No questions? Then get to work …"

The following Sunday Bykov and Kryuchkov played volleyball again. After the game and showers, they sat at an empty table in the anteroom of the Academy sauna. Teapots and glasses had already been laid out on the table. After a few pleasantries, the conversation turned to Golubov.

Bykov concisely reported that as yet there was no basis for serious concerns, by which he meant treason or espionage. An insufficient reverence for secrecy or critical comments and even jokes about the Party and state leadership were not at that time so rare among creative people, including military scientists. And so, in Bykov's opinion, if Golubov's problems were limited to this, then it would be enough to have a good prophylactic conversation with him. At most, he could be transferred to other work, for example, as an instructor in one of the academies.

But the wife's influence and Golubov's noted emotionality when it came to questions of assignments of national importance required more careful study because they could be viewed as indications of more serious problems. Bykov's conclusions about Golubov obviously worried Kryuchkov.

"Absolutely!" was Kryuchkov's rueful response. "He might be put in charge of a project and receive a state prize … He has excellent knowledge of missiles and guidance systems. Now I'm not so certain that Golubov should be permitted to continue as he is … At the very least he should not be allowed to attend meetings of the Central Committee... Did you say he is easily upset?"

Bykov nodded.

"Do you know what?" continued Kryuchkov, "Tell the Chief of Staff of the Armaments Headquarters to send Golubov to hospital immediately for a compulsory medical examination. And make sure he is closely examined not only by a neurologist, but also by a psychiatrist … Do you understand what I'm saying?"

"Are you thinking the same as I?" Bykov frowned.

"I think that a psychologically healthy person would hardly wish for the destruction of his own country and think that everyone but him is mistaken while only he is fit to determine the defense doctrine of the Soviet Union. It's entirely possible that such a man is simply unstable, and we have stumbled upon the source of his instability. Although," he paused to give Bykov an imposing stare. "Only the specialists can make such a determination – not you and I."

"Well, of course." General Bykov nodded coldly. "I personally know some doctors who are absolutely trustworthy."

Kryuchkov was satisfied.

Chapter 6

Early January frosts mercilessly gripped the sleeping city in a prickly cold that could shake the lungs, and darkness pressed in from beyond the reach of the lamp that cast patterns on the glass. But Irina had no time to admire the fairy-tale sketches on the windowpane – she had to hurry to get to work.

"A scoundrel can get used to anything!" She recalled the words of Dostoyevskiy. Yes, to anything. Ira recalled her shock on the first day at the squalor of the cells at the SPB. The bunks were so closely spaced that it was nearly impossible to walk between them, and the prisoners or patients – it made no difference what one called them – literally had to clamber over their neighbors to reach the small feeding hole in the heavy door. At first, Irina thought she might faint from the odor of mold and dampness. The dank, rotten, cold and heavy air exuded such a feeling of hopelessness that a single breath might rob one of the will to live. Water dripped from the bowed ceiling that had long ago lost its color to form a puddle in the middle of the room which reflected the forlorn gray of the walls.

The first time Irina entered a ward with Yelena Butenkova, she was struck by the dim, expressionless eyes of the patients. Only a few of them glanced at her, and she thought she detected some mild curiosity in their eyes, but they immediately lowered their heads when strict Yelena looked menacingly in their direction. Their attitude expressed so much hopelessness and suffering that Irina's heart contracted sharply. Thin and haggard with dull eyes, they said nothing but only reflexively shrank from the syringe. The patients wore thin, cotton pajamas, covered with holes, patches, dirt, and dust.

Gray walls and gray rags stained by the moisture from the ceiling, darkness and puddles on the floor, empty hollow eyes that reflected not so much insanity as vacant futility, the clank of the doors and the groaning of the patients – all of this distressed Irina and gave her nightmares after her first day at work. She twisted and turned, unable to sleep, sobbed softly and then calmed down as she tried to expel the terrible memories. She rolled onto her other side making the springs of the old bed squeak, almost forgetting the strange half-sleep – but pictures of the awful day sprang up again, jangling her nerves and driving sleep away.

The following morning normally harsh Yelena suddenly displayed unexpectedly human behavior. Seeing the dark circles under Irina's eyes, she understood immediately and rudely asked, "You couldn't sleep, eh? It all seemed pretty shitty, didn't it? It's always the same on the first day. I saw a lot of stuff when I started working with the Police, but after the first day here – believe me – I couldn't sleep either. Do you know what helps?"

"What?" asked Irina hoping for some consoling advice.

"Loathing," was Yelena's simple response. "You've got to develop a loathing for them. And don't roll your eyes. I don't intend to lecture you on socialism humanism. I'm explaining how to survive in hell. Do you want to survive? Then listen. Just take a look at these miserable fools. They've murdered, stolen, fought against their own country. They deserve this, understand? And now they have everything done for them, they get free food, they don't work, they do nothing of value, they trample the earth like dumb cattle, and they whine, whine, whine. Isn't it disgusting? So just tell yourself they're cattle, sick cattle. We take care of them, but it destroys and tortures us. And they don't even ask for forgiveness. Because of them we normal Soviet people are forced to be with them in the filth and dampness where one can contract tuberculosis if they spit even once. They have to check us frequently for tuberculosis because of that. So, what's more important, these nut cases or your own health? Feel sorry for yourself, not for them. Love us and hate them."

Irina said nothing. After what she had seen she had no wish to engage in empty and naïve conversations about humanity. Yelena was holding out a psychological straw, and although Ira understood, she wasn't ready to grasp it, she realized only too well that the only means to survive such work was to avoid allowing what she saw to affect her.

No, she did not develop loathing for the sick, but she did become accustomed to them. But after a couple of weeks her resolution was tested for the first time. Irina looked into a cell where one of the patients was suffering from tachycardia and was shouting and drumming on the door. Ira recalled Volkova's admonition to ignore such behavior, but she could not resist and opened the square feeding window to ask the patient to stick his arm out so she could check his pulse.

The prisoner obediently stuck out a bony arm and suddenly grabbed Irina's hair and gave it a yank. He pressed himself against the door as though he hoped to squeeze through the tiny opening and breathlessly whispered, pressing his lips to her palm as he did his best to prevent his cellmates from hearing him.

"Let them know what I say! Please! I beg you! I can't go on any longer, I can't take it. I'll tell them everything, I'll give them all the names. Just please – no more medication. Tell them I have important information. They'll understand. Just tell them. I know a lot. Names, addresses, who couriers the information to Moscow from the provinces. I'll name them all, please!"

"Calm down, calm down." Irina tried to calm him as she

freed her hand. "You're hysterical. I'll give you an injection, and you'll get better."

"Sure, give me an injection." The ill man no longer kept his voice down. "You understand everything just the way you're told. You know I'm not sick. I'm ready to cooperate. Tell them. I'm begging you just to tell them. I've come to my senses."

"If you've really come to your senses you must understand that you are ill," said Irina in a dry voice. "If you let go of me now, I won't tell anyone. I'll bring you some Corvalolum, and you'll calm down. If you keep on, I'll have to call the orderlies."

His answer was silence. The patient slowly loosed his grasp and in a despairing voice asked, "You mean you really don't understand?"

"It's you who does not understand." Irina's voice was firm to conceal her irritation. "You must be cured. The only thing we want from you is that you take your medicine and get better. You should have told everything during your investigation and trial. There's no need to tell us anything. You were diagnosed, and our job is to help you. And we know best how to go about it."

Her heart was pounding as hard as the patient's, and in her head Volkova's words throbbed painfully. *"You can't imagine what these sly animals are like: lying, aggressive, treacherous. They'll beg you, plead with you, pretend, and yell – you should pay no attention ... They don't listen to us, they don't understand, they don't accept it. They live in their own world, their own terrible fantasies. They are slaves to these fantasies, and they use them to excuse everything. What they consider their own mind and will is really nothing more than their unhealthy instincts, their hallucinations, and their illness. Our job is to suppress this harmful, sick, and inadequate will. Do what is required to prepare them to be healed, make them surrender, don't you understand? For their own good."*

For his own good ... The grip of his wiry fingers weakened and retreated through the window. The patient grew silent.

"That's better," whispered Irina and went to fetch the Corvalolum.

Every step along the corridor was accompanied by a pain in her temples, and like a mantra she repeated the words of the Chief Medical Officer: *"So no matter what they say, don't believe them. No matter how much they plead – don't listen. Constantly remind yourself that this is a carnivorous, deceitful animal, not a human being with whom you can have a conversation, and his sickness is trying to survive, to save itself, and is writhing as though it were in a frying pan. They will try to arouse pity, make themselves out to be intelligent people, reason with you, beg you, and try to get you to agree with them. Don't fall for it, young lady. This only shows that they don't want to be cured, that they stubbornly dream only of getting out of here, so they start ruining our lives."*

"It wasn't him speaking; it was his illness," Irina reassured herself. "He believes he is well, that he's being held here because of some sort of information. But this is paranoid hysteria. He'll get better only when he realizes this."

She kept her word and said nothing about what had happened to the orderlies or Chief Medical Officer. She knew what would have happened to the unfortunate man had she reported his actions. More than likely it would mean an increased dose of antipsychotics that could cause him more suffering. After all, she had promised him not to raise the alarm, and he had believed her, had retreated and stopped his entreaties. That meant the patient hoped to get better without additional therapy. Despite everything Yelena had said about loathing, Irina still hoped she could treat the patients as humanely as possible under such conditions ...

Work slowly became routine. Irina was astounded that even here she still was able to find reasons for hope, and her once-faded life began to acquire new shades that were not always hopelessly gray. For example, she managed to have a warm New Year in the club near the train station that Marya Innokentyevna had mentioned.

She went with Yelena who apparently knew everyone in Medinskiy without exception. It was surprisingly cozy inside the little wood-framed club. The place was infused with the pleasant aromas of warmed wood from the walls and hot clay from the old country stove. These aromas were almost like a caress after the deep cold outside, and the bright lights reflected from gold and silver tinsel that decorated the walls. It was a noisy evening, but at the same time homelike. Young people played the piano and sang, happily uncorked champagne when the clock struck twelve, and then they danced.

"Look, there's Kostya and Misha," Yelena pointed to a pair of rustic-looking young men who were leaning against the wall eyeing the girls. "They work at the factory."

"Mikhail," said one of the boys as he cheerfully extended a hand to Irina with a broad smile. He was strongly built, red-headed and freckled. "Yelena, where have you kept this one hidden?"

"Irka only recently came to work with us," said Yelena. "She's from Sverdlovsk and has a degree," she added with a hint of jealousy in her voice.

Irina was suddenly embarrassed by her degree and Sverdlovsk, and she rushed to change the subject. As it turned out there was no need for a long conversation. Misha asked her to dance, and they merrily circled the floor among the wreaths and tinsel. The warm aroma of pine combined with the champagne made her happy.

Later they sat in a corner and talked of unimportant things. Irina did not wish to think about work on this day, and she relished the empty conversation. Misha was nice but boring, but it the holiday did not invite deep philosophy. Irina looked at the glowing number 69 on the New Year's tree and thought that life might not be so bad, after all.

It was back to work after the holidays, and it seemed to Irina that she had become accustomed to her unpleasant job. At least she thought so until that January morning when she entered the SPB ...

Accompanied by two orderlies during the standard morning circuit, syringes filled with medication ready in her hand she looked into one of the cells and froze. The patient who had grabbed her through the feeding window a few weeks earlier was standing among the cots in the middle of a puddle as he gashed his wrist with a rusty nail. He turned mechanically toward Irina as though she were watching a slow-motion film before returning to his task. Catching a vein with the nail he stretched it out, thin and blue, hoping to break it. Stubbornly, it would not tear, but only stretched like a bowstring. But the man pulled even harder at the nail, and the blood burst suddenly from the torn flesh turning the water in the puddle bright red.

During her studies at the Institute, Irina had seen a lot. She had attended surgery several times and participated in autopsies in the morgue. She had wondered at the way the pathologists could cold-bloodedly saw a skull and pull away the face of the corpse like a cloth to expose the bone. She remembered black spots on exposed lungs and the monotone voice of the physician as he explained: "No, these are not the lungs of a smoker, but the normal lungs of a city dweller." But now, upon witnessing the calm but simultaneously horrible suicide attempt, she screamed at the top of her voice. Her scream echoed down the narrow corridors and off the metal doors.

As though through a veil she watched as the orderlies

grabbed the patient and dragged him away as he struggled against them, bloodying their white tunics. Yelena came running and saw immediately what had happened. She led Irina to an examining room. On uncertain legs, Irina followed her into the empty room that reeked of medicine and fell onto a chair. Yelena retrieved a bottle of vodka from one of the cabinets and poured the viscous liquid into a glass, then held it out to Irina.

"Drink."

Irina lifted the glass and felt the bitter tartness of the alcohol against her face. She grimaced and could barely place her lips on the rim of the glass before pulling back.

"How can anyone drink this garbage?" Her voice was soft.

"All at once," ordered Yelena. "Don't sniff it. You must drink it, not smell it. It isn't wine. You don't have to roll it around on your tongue, just pour it down your throat."

Irina obeyed and swallowed the burning liquid before finally bursting into tears. "I talked with him at the end of December," she sobbed. "He grabbed my arm and pleaded, swore he would tell everything, name some sort of names, addresses. But I told him to quiet down and gave him some medication ..."

"What?" Yelena leapt from her chair and grabbed her shoulder. "Did you tell Volkova about it?"

"No." Irina raised tear-blurred eyes to her. "Why should I have done that? It was only his sickness speaking. Volkova herself told me under no circumstances to react, believe, or carry on with patients. If they cause trouble, call the orderlies. But he wasn't causing a problem; he just spoke quietly. Why should I have snitched on him? You understand that it would have only made things worse for him."

"Oh, you little fool!" howled Yelena as she sank onto the chair beside Irina. "You complete fool! Where did you get such ideas? What do you mean 'it was his illness talking,' when he was asking to cooperate? That's why all of this happened."

"How am I a fool?" In her anger, Irina forgot about her tears. "What are we here for? The Chief Medical Officer quite clearly explained that it is a sign of recovery if a patient admits he is ill and agrees to take his medications. It's forbidden to react to anything else. These are sick people, already diagnosed, and the only way to help them is to break their resistance and get them to recognize the obvious. And that man did not do so. Quite the opposite, he insisted that he was not sick, begged not to be given more medication, and again ranted that I had to 'understand' what was really going on – typical paranoid schizophrenic behavior. What was there for me to report? That his condition had worsened? I would have done so, of course, but he calmed down on his own. I simply pitied him. Where do you see any improvement in that? 'That's why all of this happened?' Where's the logic in that?"

"So," said Yelena, finally calming down and now regarding Irina as though she were a mentally defective child. "There's only one kind of logic here: if a patient says he wants to cooperate, report it, ask to be connected with the KGB and the like – immediately tell the Chief Medical Officer. The rest is not your concern. I'm at fault, of course, because I didn't immediately warn you, but I thought you would figure it out on your own. I didn't think you were such a slow-witted city girl. It's a good thing for you that I won't breathe a word to Volkova about your lapse. But in the future, don't dare do anything like that again."

"You mean, it's true?" Irina looked at her incredulously. "He was actually healthy? We gave a antipsychotics to a healthy person?"

"He's a criminal," screamed Yelena a bit too loudly. She went to the door to make sure no one had overheard before continuing more quietly. "He attempted to destroy our country. For people like him the way to redeem their mistakes is to be cured."

"Stop," Irinia interrupted. "You understand what I mean. We're not talking about what he did. We're talking about his illness, about medications. So, he didn't need to be cured, he needed to be made to talk, right? He wasn't really sick. He was telling the truth ..."

Realization washed over her in a great wave. Irina leaned against the back of the chair and closed her eyes. The full weight of the horror of being in an SPB came upon her in a rush, and the thought of what all of this could do to a healthy person who had been rendered helpless.

Yelena didn't say a word.

"What will happen to him now?" Irina asked the emptiness.

"Well, now ... If he survives, they'll restrain him and put him in a bed. They'll shoot him full of chloropromazine and sulfazine or haloperidol. After a week, he'll be back. People try to kill themselves all the time here. It's hard to find the means here, so they resort to cruder methods, as you saw. You'll get used to it. It's hard at first, but then ... you'll get used to it," she added somewhat guiltily.

Irina leapt to her feet. "I'll go to Volkova myself. I'll tell her he was ready to cooperate. He promised to tell everything."

"It's too late." Yelena grabbed her wrist. "You'll only hurt yourself, and it won't do him any good. It's over for him. Forget him. This was a learning experience. If it happens again, you know what to do, right?"

Ira did not answer. She stood staring into space for a moment before asking, "Why do you work here if you know ... everything?"

Yelena shrugged. "Where else is there to work around here? How old are you? Twenty-three? I'm thirty. You were born after the war, but I remember it. I remember hunger and terror. We survived only because I lived in an orphanage. I never knew my parents. My whole life has been in this place. Childhood in the orphanage, then Militia school because if you went there they gave you a room and might later give you an apartment. When I was your age, we were catching real bandits. They say that in the forest around here there are still some cutthroats like you never dreamed of in Sverdlovsk. Later they offered a job here. The work is not dirty, the conditions aren't bad, and they pay well. I'll work a few years longer and maybe I'll get a referral for an advanced training course, maybe even go to Sverdlovsk. I want to get out of this hole," she blurted.

"Why is it that some are lucky and are given a papa and a mama, apartments, institutes in Sverdlovsk, and others rot their whole lives without a family in a hole like this where there is nothing but thieves, psychotics, freezing cold, and drunks? And where is the equality of all workers, where is fairness? Do you think it's fair? There is no justice, and there is no truth, so don't look for it, you little fool."

Yelena became even more enflamed. "The people who get ahead know how to step over others, how to lick ass, know to do what they're told. That's real life; not what they taught you at university. Who would ruin their life for the sake of such psycho-failures? If anyone is looking for justice, they're already crazy. You can't find what doesn't exist. And it doesn't exist – fairness, justice."

"And you never learned anything about your parents?" asked Irina. She was shaken by the other woman's candor.

"Sure, I learned about them," snickered Yelena. "I found my mother in '54 when I was fifteen. She said we had lived in Sverdlovsk before the war, had a nice two-room apartment. But then they arrested my father as an enemy of the people.

At the end of '39 I was only six months old. It was winter, like now, as my mother told me, a freezing January. The day after they arrested my father an NKVD officer came and gave my mother 24 hours to move out. Otherwise she would be arrested, too. Mama filled a suitcase, grabbed some diapers, took me in her arms and left. She didn't know where to go. She heard from my father that they'd sent him to work in the village of Medinskiy, so she came here and sat all day at the station holding me. Finally, some aunt or other took pity and invited her to stay in her room at the barracks where they were building a factory. My mother slept on the floor. People were dying from exhaustion all around her. She couldn't feed me and so gave me to the orphanage. She gave up her own daughter. After that they rescinded her rights to see me and told her never to speak to me again so that I would never learn I was the daughter of an enemy of the people. And she didn't."

"But everything is OK now, right?" Irina asked, filled both with horror and pity for this ruthless woman. "You found one another. Your mother is alive."

"I couldn't care less whether she's alive or dead," said Yelena with some heat. "I sent her away with a curse. I told her I did not want to know her or see her. She'd washed her hands of me. They didn't arrest her or send her to prison. She got rid of me on purpose, and I'll never forgive her."

"But you might have died from hunger. Maybe that was the only thing she could do to save you."

"Maybe," said Yelena coldly. "But I was only fifteen when I found her, and I saw everything in black and white. She tossed me away, so she can go to hell. Can you guess how many years I wept, waited, believed that my mother was still alive and would come for me? And all the while she was just next door in an apartment she got from the factory. She lived and worked right here in the same village. And I was in the orphanage. She probably was able to buy oranges for the holidays and invited guests, made nice salads for them, put up a tree ... But she never once tried to get in to see me. She was no mother to me after that. I can't forgive such behavior ... Oh, well." Without warning she lapsed into silence. "Let's get back to work before they miss us. Wipe away the tears and chew on something so you don't smell of vodka."

She turned and left the room without a backwards glance.

Chapter 7

Snow was falling outside the windows of the thick walls plunging the capital into indulgent somnolence. The world consisted of curious combinations of white: gossamer and solid, thick and transparent, soft and frozen. The scene was entrancing as the snow failed to find a purchase and moved in slender streams like a picture of carved of marble. A winter's fairytale covered Moscow and should have put all anxiety to rest, but it had no effect on Dimitriy Rakhmanov. In fact, what he was experiencing bore no resemblance to normal anxiety.

He had first felt such tangible fear of imminent failure and cruel reckoning ten years earlier in the GDR[18] when he was working under the legendary intelligence officer Aleksandr Korotkov. A decisive and demanding man, Korotkov combined accessibility with a certain severity and equated forgetfulness with hypocrisy. Just a few days before, he had sent a transgressor to Moscow, and young Mitya Rakhmanov had reason to fear that he was not far from being sent home, as well.

As a security officer for the Soviet diplomatic mission Dimitriy was carrying out the order of the Senior Counselor of the Embassy from the First Chief Directorate of the KGB. His mission was to penetrate a West Berlin company to acquire information on the methods of cooling the data banks of complex equipment. Any contact with the inhabitants of the Democratic Sector of Berlin was forbidden to employees of the company, but Rakhmanov had discovered a GDR citizen with a relative who worked in the target enterprise. Through him Mitya was able to arrange a meeting with a Soviet specialist. A cover story was created; the specialist from the Urals arrived

18 German Democratic Republic

and successfully entered the target plant. He should have returned after couple of hours but had so far failed to appear.

Dimitriy and a colleague waited close to the border between sectors which had not yet been blocked by the famous Berlin Wall. It had been as overcast as today, but there was no snow. The approaching winter filled the half-destroyed city with a sharp snowless chill, the sky darkened, and the agent did not return. Dimitriy and the other operative went to the nearest police station to ensure that the Ural specialist had not been detained, then returned to the meeting site and waiting some more. There could be only one conclusion – the agent had defected to the West.

It was then that Dimitriy first felt the desperate and all-encompassing fear that there would be not only a reckoning, but also that his days in the Organs were over. It was inevitable according to the iron rule – the case officer answers for the agent's treason. It made no difference that Dimitriy had spent several days with the agent, a reckoning still hovered over his head like a dark cloud. The silence of waiting increased the sense of impending catastrophe; it was senseless to remain at the meeting site. With resigned sighs, he and his comrade drove back to the embassy only to find that the agent had forgotten his instructions and was waiting for them there …

But the alarm that infected Major Rakhmanov now wasn't the same. It was different not only in that he could not hope for a miracle. This time the unpleasant anticipation of making explanations to his bosses faded into the background considering the achingly irrational and unnecessary sense of guilt. As an experienced operative, Dimitriy understood that he was unlikely to be dismissed for the suicide of the dissident girl that was caused by the thoughtless behavior of a young subordinate. There was something else: he felt sorry for Nastya, and this sympathy infused his heart with a mixture of sadness and anger. He told himself a thousand times that he had done everything properly – but all the same he failed to convince himself. Outside the window the snow fell in its unchanging rhythm and offered no answers ...

There was a knock at the door and the detainee was brought in. Dimitriy turned at the sound and returned to his desk. He'd received the report from Kiev on Viktor Butko and already knew that there would be no dealing with this type.

A talented engineer, Butko from early youth had been interested in history and even had written a book on the 30's and the later German occupation of Kiev which he had survived as an infant. The Party leadership had not considered the book to be harmful but insisted that several "sharp" passages be excised. The young writer did not heed this prudent advice and decided to publish his work as "samizdat" which was then gaining momentum. He made the acquaintance of the so-called movement of the "60's Generation" that legally existed in Kiev in the first half of the decade.

Absorbing their ideas, Viktor became an active member of the Kiev Club of Artistic Youth, performed the works of several playwrights of dubious talent, wrote verse and always sympathized with Ukrainian nationalism. He enthusiastically adopted the tradition of going to the Taras Shevchenko memorial on May 22nd where he read poetry and gave speeches against "forced Russification." It was most likely on one of these occasions that Viktor attracted the attention of the notorious sociopolitical writer Ivan Dzyuba. They became close, and Butko became a regular at every dissident event. Following the wave of arrests of "artistic nationalists" in 1965 he was seen in the crowd that surrounded the court buildings, in numerous acts of solidarity with the accused and even in the demonstrations that followed the dispersal of the people gathered at the Shevchenko monument in 1967.

The following year Butko became close with Muscovites involved in the collection of signatures in support of the *"samizdatchiki"*[19] and carried out especially harmful activities, in Dimitriy's opinion. His last meeting with a foreigner and his indirect guilt in Nastya's death completed the picture – before Major Rakhmanov was an enemy who was owed no forbearance.

The face of the detained man betrayed no fear. Rakhmanov didn't expect to get anything out of him, indeed it was unnecessary because Rakhmanov already possessed all the information he needed. Vlad's second group had confiscated all the material from the foreigner only moments after he received it, and these documents now lay on Dimitriy's desk. Ideally, he could suggest that the accused make a frank confession and identify his accomplices, but instinct told him that Butko was a tough nut from whom nothing could be expected. Major Rakhmanov wasn't especially disturbed by this because he knew that everything would be revealed by the Ukrainian's Muscovite friends. Even if he could get nothing from the Kievan, he would put him away for a long time for the edification of others.

"Have you worked for the CIA long?" he asked with studied indifference.

"I don't work for them," replied the detainee with equal calm. "And if you've already seen the materials you should be convinced of it. There are no classified documents, no military secrets, no strategic information. Only true facts about social life."

"I looked them over," replied Dimitriy. "This is a denunciation - an underhanded, false accusation against your country

---

to our damned enemies who pay well for any *kompromat*.[20] Did you decide to visit your friends in the camps and betray your Motherland at the same time?"

"Where do you see any lie?" Butko looked him straight in the eye. "It's the truth, God's own truth that I, a citizen of *my country*, can't find here in the Motherland. You're fixated on the person I passed the papers to, but why don't you say anything about their content? How many people died when an avalanche of mud inundated an entire section of Kiev? Who answered for it? When the wave carried away houses and people in their own apartments choked on the mud, what did the KGB do? They changed flight paths so no one could see anything from the air. They forbade that telegrams be sent, and the people didn't even know what had happened and couldn't come to bury their relatives. How many hundreds of people perished there because of the stupidity of the author- ities, and why does law enforcement act against those who want to tell about it instead of the guilty parties?"

"I see no reason to tell about it," frowned Dimitriy. "Do you think it will resurrect the dead? Where did you get the idea that the guilty parties were not punished? You can be sure they were dealt with severely. Decisions were made. I see no connection between the tragedy and treason. The people you report to don't plan to drop a load of mud from a broken damn onto your city; they plan to drop an atomic bomb. Like vultures you are overjoyed at the slightest mistake of Sovi- et authorities so you can use it to destroy your own country. Why didn't you complain when the Soviet Union raised itself from the ruins after the Victory, when the government with superhuman effort tried to return to you what the war had taken away? What imperialist country cared about your peo-

---

20 Compromising information.

ple? You didn't write denunciations when a roof was put over your head, when you went to school, when you saw a doctor, when you were given a profession and a job. You were born into the poverty of war and now you're an outstanding engineer. Why didn't you broadcast it to the West when you were given all of this? You waited like a jackal around the corner for something to happen, even a natural disaster, to strike against your own country to which you owe an unpaid debt. Who did you save with all of this?"

Dimitriy felt himself growing angry and knew that he would not hold it in. He would give vent to his anger let this dumbass know what he thought about him and his accomplices.

"So, you've failed – besides the dam breaking, nothing more happened for several years, and they don't pay for old information, do they? And then you decided to join up with the nationalists because they couldn't go wrong, correct? Either nationalism will finally get into peoples' heads and destroy their unity and socialist ideals, or sooner or later they'll start arresting you and you can whine about persecution. In that case you wouldn't even have to mention the dam. By the way, who was really responsible for the dam? Wasn't this tragedy just a little too convenient for you?"

Viktor stared at him but remained silent. He understood that to attempt explanations with this convinced Chekist would be futile. How could he convey to his skewed consciousness that the meeting with the American was a desperate measure – the only way to break through the stone wall of silence and lies. He cringed at the mere thought of pouring out his soul at the Lubyanka about how his favorite little niece had died under an avalanche of mud while on her way to school and how he had despairingly searched for those who might be responsible only to be met with silence and threats.

The pain had receded, but he at last realized that a human being in the Soviet Union was nothing more than a tiny, defenseless piece of dust in the mechanism. In the guise of humanity this mechanism entrapped people, tossing them a morsel of bread, health, and knowledge for which unquestioning loyalty was demanded. Fearing for his place in the sun, this human cog fits into the template and proclaims his loyalty, repeating over and over again meaningless memorized phrases. He sits at Party meetings and repeats the slogans learned by rote at school, all the while hoping he was not like all the others. And even if he did everything he was told, in a single instant he could be erased from the face of the earth by a wave of filth, and everyone close to him were nothing more than wanted and annoying witnesses of the mistakes of those in power rather than victims ...

"I don't care which of these half-wits was 'dealt with' in their offices or who decided what. These people were guilty of the deaths of others and should have answered for it to the people, to the relatives of the victims. You ask who might benefit from it all coming out? At a minimum, those who would commit similar crimes would learn to be afraid. Only the truth can frighten them, and now they are secure in their anonymity. They know that the special services will give them cover no matter what they get up to. And this means that such tragedies happen again and again. Silence begets impunity, don't you see? Our bureaucrats deal only with other bureaucrats, and for them the people are non-entities without rights. They don't consider them to be human beings, they murder them and lie to them for the sake of some greater goal. Before, the goal was to win the war, but what is it now? Simple bureaucratic stupidity? For what will normal people die next? You don't understand that there are some absolute values. One cannot live a lie and should not permit such monstrous untruths. You tried to cover up the truth of Babi Yar[21] – and you buried thousands of people. Then you tried to cover up the burst dam – the result of your first lie – and what will be next? How many lives will you sacrifice the next time? You prattle about humanism at the same time you're ready to persecute anyone who allows himself to think and speak as he wishes rather than repeat your lies. You have a proven method – put the strongest ones in labor camps and drive the weaker ones to suicide just as you did with this girl, Nastya. Are you going to stand at her grave and berate her for her education and free vacations at Pioneer Camp? Can any of that help her now?"

"Enough demagoguery! I've heard enough of these tales of vengeance." Dimitriy stood up with the sheaf of documents in his hand. "A few hundred people died at Kurenevka,[22] and if it were made public there could be riots, armed aggressions,

---

21 Babi Yar is a ravine on the outskirts of Kiev where Einsatzgruppen mobile squads killed at least 34,000 Jews over a one-week period in September 1941. Russian estimates put the number of killed at nearly 100,000. Today, Babi Yar has come to symbolize the horrific murder of Jews by the Einsatzgruppen as well as the persistent failure of the world to acknowledge this Jewish tragedy. – jewishvirtuallibrary.org

22 After the war, Babi Yar was used for garbage disposal. The story of the 1961 mudslide had begun a decade earlier when the Kiev government decided to fill the ravine and utilize the space for beautification purposes.

Khrushchev personally authorized the liquidation of the ravine. The project made use of the pulp dumped by the nearby brickworks. The solid part of it was supposed to settle and harden and the water to flow into the Dnieper River. Instead, the insufficient capacity of the water runoff transformed the ravine into a swampy wasteland. The dam holding that mass in place was made of earth instead of concrete which allowed for leaks, particularly in the spring when the snow melted on the pulp. Warnings were ignored. Complainers were discouraged, to put it mildly, from spreading panic. Subsequent investigation found a few engineers and managers responsible for dam's design and maintenance; they were convicted of criminal negligence. Too significant to pretend that it did not take place – socialist countries were immune to natural or manmade calamities – the catastrophe was briefly acknowledged in the local evening newspaper. Different sources estimate the number of casualties from 1,500 to 3,000, while the official number hovered at below 150. - appledoesnotfall.com

and thousands would die. We are living under war conditions – even if it's a Cold War, but it's war all the same. In war, in case you don't understand, sometimes you pay more for the truth than for a lie. Even more so when the truth is revealed to the enemy. If there is anarchy, if the country falls apart, how many thousands, how many hundreds of thousands might die? Did you ever think of that? And how about this girl, Nastya? I didn't plan to make her commit suicide. I wanted to give her a chance for a normal life. I certainly did not want her death …"

He stopped talking, not fully understanding why he felt compelled to justify himself to this obvious enemy of the Soviet state. When he resumed, his voice was harsh. "Nastya died today, and it is you who are at fault. That dam broke seven years ago. Your nationalist meetings and anti-Soviet agitation have no bearing on one or the other. How do you explain this?"

Viktor leaned back in the chair. Nothing could be explained to such a person. How could he make him understand the joy of creativity, music and songs in one's native language, a rowdy atmosphere full of life: bright like Spring, the free flow of ideas, sincerity, the novelty of words, the warmth of friendship?

He suddenly recalled a small, half-filled concert hall where a year ago they had celebrated the birthday of a popular Ukrainian bard. The artist's friends went onto the stage in Ukrainian national costumes and recited some congratulatory limericks. None of these had been shown to the bard beforehand, and his gratitude was bottomless, as was that of all who heard the words. At such gatherings there were no strained official speeches, no marching songs, and no phony songs about brotherhood. Music, both sad and ebullient, interspersed with impromptu jokes and anecdotes escaped from the hall. A group of theatrical students acted scenes from Gogol into which contemporary political satire sometimes seeped evoking hearty applause. Inspired by the general atmosphere two former front-line soldiers climbed onto the stage with an accordion and performed a melancholy song from the trenches that had never been heard on the radio – followed by some more or less polite soldierly couplets.

The bard later played guitar and sang about love with a bitter irony unusual for "official artists," and this lent special depth to his words. Everyday life was woven into his songs along with eternal longings, and the words were so distant from everything the country had lived through that they were evocative, and the combination of abstraction and intimacy was astounding. Afterwards someone in the audience shouted that he wanted to recite some verses, and he was shoved onto the stage. And he began to read something about Bogdan Khemlnitsky and distant villages. His voice was drowned by applause, and someone took advantage of the noise to set up additional chairs for the people who had been standing in the hall.

The political undertones in such gatherings were not entirely innocent. Indirect confirmation of this was that the authorities tolerated the "Sixties Generation" for so long without denying them halls for concerts and exhibitions. Viktor recalled the mountain of flowers at the Taras Shevchenko memorial, the intoxicating fragrance of May, the songs and poetry. By the time they reached the rear of the crowd, they had mingled so as to drown one in an attar so concentrated as to draw all the oxygen from the air and make one's head spin with a sense of freedom.

Freedom and joy swirled above Kiev as Viktor in a jester's costume went singing through the streets with a group of young people. To be sure, they went a bit too far when they ended up in front of the home of an important Party function-ary. Later, Viktor endured a very unpleasant conversation at his place of work …

He recalled an evening in the studio of a painter where too many people had gathered and had to sit very close to one another – too close. They drank vodka, and his friend, Sasha, read stories he had written in Ukrainian in the style of Zoshchenko, only contemporary. The stories were comical and the style perfect and Viktor laughed in the realization that he would trade none of this for an official career. On his shoul-der, trembling from every touch, leaned Natalya, and the fra-grance of her thick hair enveloped and stupefied him. As if he were frightened of temptation, Viktor went out into the street with some friends and they argued 'til dawn about the recently published *samizdat* piece of a Dneprotetrovsk Marxist showing that the CP-USSR was basically distorting the Marx-ist approach to many things. Butko realized that he could not concentrate on Marx, and the reason was either the vodka, or Sasha and his Zoshchenko, or maybe both – or maybe, after all, it was the beautiful Natalya, the summer evening, and the unrelenting Ukrainian stars.

He and Natalya escaped the crowded studio and strolled along in the light of the streetlamps reading the banners draped on buildings as they passed: "Forward to the Victo-ry of Communism!", Natalya laughed and showed him the drawing the artist had done of her in the studio. In a fit of jeal-ousy, Viktor tore it into pieces and tossed it into the Dniepr. He took her to his house where Natalya, as beautiful as Go-gol's witch, flirtatiously refused him, which was even more seductive. It was a boisterous night that demanded madness and achievement. This was his city, the city of his youth in which he had survived Fascist occupation, and Viktor felt that he could permit himself anything he liked …

They arrested Sasha six months later, and the small world to which he had become accustomed began to fall apart. Natalya, who until then could not choose between him and her Sasha, was now wholeheartedly with Sasha. "Sasha, hold on!" shouted Viktor from the crowd in front of the courthouse as he held her cold hand and feared that if he did not support his friend so loudly and clearly, Natalya would have done so, and it would mean trouble for her ...

"It wasn't about nationalism. There were verses and song, a renaissance of culture, don't you understand?" He said hopelessly to Rakhmanov.

"They gave you time. They watched for several years, and you could have developed your, as you call it, culture. But it wasn't enough for you. You began anti-Soviet speeches, agitation, public criticism of the Party, accusations of 'Russification.' What might you have gotten up to if you weren't stopped?" asked the Chekist.

"So, we're to be judged for our thoughts and words?"

"Public words are the same as actions," specified Rakhmanov. "Our task is to insure the peaceful development of society, both in creativity and work. If we are to resist imperialist encirclement, the people must be united. You wanted to destroy our unity, constantly inciting people – falsely inciting them."

Butko interrupted him. "You cannot impose unity by force. You can't forbid people to think and feel."

"We can't allow them to think like you," said Dimitriy. "All you do is alarm and disorient society – and then people could be driven to the limits of pseudo-nationalism, sexual depravity, and other immorality," he stressed the final words.

"You just love to dig into your own dirty laundry," muttered Viktor. "Those are all abstract values, but real people are more important to me."

"You've already picked up bourgeois mannerisms?" snickered Dimitriy. "Maybe you're prepared to defend fascists and their accomplices? So, real people don't make free choices, maybe work as police? Must you not defend them, too?"

"You make things up," said his detainee. "The fascists shot both my parents during the war. As a little kid, I spent the occupation in a cellar, ran around nearly naked, but I never served Fascism. You're ready to accuse anyone of the worst crimes only because they're not like you? I already said that a government built on lies and force will not last, and America has nothing to do with it. This entire GULAG that you call a country will crumble sooner or later under the weight of its own lies, believe me!"

Dimitriy studied him through slitted eyes that suddenly shone with a cruel and satanic light. "You predict the death of your own country? Tell me, do you think you're right in the head? I think not. I should have figured it out long ago. All your blather about victims, lawlessness, lies, and collapse – this is clearly schizophrenic raving. Have you ever been examined by a psychiatrist?"

It seemed to Rakhmanov that Viktor began to tremble as the first shadow of terror appeared on his hitherto unperturbed countenance. There was none of the former bravado in the detainee's eyes now, and Dimitriy found it unspeakably pleasurable. He seemed to have discovered his enemy's soft spot.

"Were you expecting to be sent to the camps?" he continued slowly, savoring each word. "You would have felt at home there. Half of your friends are in the Mordovían camps, and you were looking forward to heading out of Moscow to them, right? But you won't get off so lightly. You're going to end up in a place where none of your friends will ever find you. And maybe then you'll have some second thoughts."

Viktor said nothing, and his silence enraged Rakhmanov even more. He had no choice but to follow through with the threat. He would punish this stubborn traitor for his fearless scribbling and for his lack of respect for this office, and even for Nastya's death. At the same time, he would prove to his bosses that he could efficiently take care of matters despite unforeseen events. He would destroy this scum.

Chapter 8

Six months later ...

The burning sensation seized his body with torturous intensity, filling his entire being with intolerable itching. Victor knew the feeling well, so similar was it to when his leg fell asleep. Afterwards, it was as though it were filled with lead and then pricked with a thousand needles. One wanted to rub the wooden extremity to wake it up more quickly, to be rid of the tiny, biting needles. The main difference was that now the itching covered his entire body and filled every molecule. It was as though his blood was bubbling and boiling with the desire to burst his veins. And his body boiled along with the shaking and itching. Invisible hooks bit into him from inside, driving him to move, to crawl in an effort to escape the exhausting trembling.

On stiff legs Viktor staggered away from his bed along the narrow passage between the cots, his thin rubber flip-flops splashing in the cold water puddled on the floor. It was the itching that drove him forward, jostling others as he passed, others like him – unfortunates suffering from the effects of huge doses of anti-psychotic drugs.

Behind him, old Uncle Vasiliy walked in circles muttering incoherently. Even in the nebulous world of the psychiatric hospital inmates occasionally were able to talk and learn one another's story. Uncle Vasiliy's story was especially shocking. A native of Belarus, he fought the entire war, from the first days all the way to Berlin only to return shell-shocked but still alive. At home he found a scene that might have been written by Mark Bernes[23] - his house burned along with the fields and

---

23 A Soviet actor and singer who enjoyed great popularity in the 1950's and who is still revered for his contribution to Russian music.

the bodies of his wife and little children who had been executed by the Germans.

It was more than he could stand, and it drove him out of his mind. He began to drink, start fights, and openly criticize the authorities and the Party. Drunk, Uncle Vasiliy, draped in his medals wandered around town shouting about how his entire platoon and raped all the girls in the outskirts of Berlin. He like all the rest, distraught from the hardships of war and filled with hatred from the sight of destroyed cities and burned out towns, vented his anger on the young German girls, tearing their thin dresses and reveling at the sound of their screams. Finally running out of words he fell to his knees in front of the long-closed church that now served as the village club and groaned that the death of his family was his punishment for the sins committed in Berlin; he wept and crossed himself where the church's cupola had been chopped down.

The Party leadership could not tolerate such conduct from the war hero. First, they sent Uncle Vasiliy to a nursing home in Minsk although he was not yet an old man. But he gave them no peace there, crying out in the night and reciting as though they were incantations snatches of German that he had heard during the war. After a fight with one of the residents, they sent Uncle Vasiliy here.

He got no better in the SPB, but he did quiet down and shouted now only because of the convulsions the doctors called "extrapyramidal disorders." They were brought about by prolonged use of anti-psychotic drugs, and almost everyone who had been in the hospital for more than six months suffered from them. Suffering from a seizure, Uncle Vasiliy would raise his head and clamp his hand over the writhing muscles in his neck and howl from the pain. He was lucky if this happened during the rounds of the young nurse, Irina.

As a rule, she ran immediately at the sound of a scream and wisely administered a small dose of corrective medication. The other nurses rarely responded to such calls ...

Exhausted from his pointless wandering, Viktor collapsed onto the damp sheets, freeing the path for others suffering the same as he, driven forward by their itching restiveness. His memory, damaged by mediation, began to clear and fragments of increasingly dissociated thoughts appeared. Nurse Irochka ... It seemed that she had lowered the dose a little – in any event, after her injections he felt better than normal and was able to think more clearly. But the other one, Yelena, was a pitiless bitch. It was as if she blamed the patients for her failed life and detested work. This morning it had been Yelena who administered the injections. This was evident ...

Irochka ... Where had he met her? Ah, yes, in Medinskiy. The village of Medinskiy in Sverdlovsk Oblast. He mustn't forget this. He mustn't forget his long, difficult path to this place. Viktor strained to remember every detail beginning with his arrest and the first interrogation at the Lubyanka because it was vitally important for him. The dark KGB prison, the endless interrogations. He'd told them nothing, wasn't that so? He'd not given up Natalya's name? Or had the investigator already known about her? That investigator with the small eyes and narrow jaw, what was his name? Of course, Dimitriy Rakhmanov. Viktor swore to himself never to forget this name to the end of his life.

He recalled the trial: a closed session where against all the rules, no one he knew was permitted. He remembered the encouraging shouts from his friends in the street as they chanted his name: "Vitya, Vitya!" He remembered the early Moscow spring and how he had believed he would be free before all the snow melted. Six of the criminals who worked there as orderlies beat him in the showers the day he arrived. They beat him severely, and the nurses who had been alerted by the noise administered the first doses of Aminazin and haloperidol.

That night Viktor's memory began to fade. He had nearly hallucinogenic nightmares. He recalled how he had found himself in some sort of dark, narrow cave, scraping his elbows along the walls before emerging into a desert where he fell into burning sand that immediately seared his throat and made it nearly impossible to breathe. Viktor returned to reality and felt as though some sort of object filled this throat and obstructed his breathing. He touched it with his hand and discovered that it was his own tongue that had no feeling and was dry from thirst. His throat was painfully dry, and every breath burned like fire. Viktor crawled on all fours toward the spigot but failed to reach it before collapsing again. He vaguely remembered that the prisoners returning from the exercise yard had helped him get some water. And after a long time, he ended up here.

The season had changed, and in the small courtyard they were permitted to visit an hour daily, he inhaled the fragrance of summer. Even in these harsh climes summer was warm and dry, although there were more mosquitos than in Moscow or Kiev. What month was it: July, August? Viktor could not say for sure. It was hard to return inside afterwards – that's when the medications kicked in.

The itching gained new strength, and Viktor Butko again paced back and forth along the narrow passage. He tried to imagine that he was strolling along the wide Kreshchatik[24] or through Goloseyevskiy Park hand in hand with Natalya or going down to Podol where carefree tourists waited for boat rides along the Dniepr. Just one more step toward the sun,

---

24 Main street of Kiev.

summer, his native Kiev, a blue sky, maple leaves, and the aroma of the chestnut trees. Just one step, a single attempt to rid himself of the invisible needles, a faint approximation of relaxation ... The spasms were very painful.

A tangle of convulsions seized the muscles of his neck jerking his head backwards. The pain drew Viktor back to a bunk, someone else's as he later noted. The owner of the bunk also paced back and forth and with an indifferent glance at Viktor continued his mindless path among the bunks. What was his name? Sasha? Lesha? Ah, yes, it was Aleksey. He didn't remember the last name of this patient but did know that they had been in the facility for about the same amount of time. Aleksey had been some sort of important scientist, maybe a military engineer. Viktor had learned enough about such places to be able to predict that people in such professions would never be released. An SPB was the ideal place for this person to disappear without a trace, and after several years here, many finally lost their minds.

As if he read his thoughts, Aleskey sat on the edge of his bunk next to Viktor and spoke quietly:

"I'm losing my mind."

Viktor's spasms subsided a bit, and he only shrugged. Everyone here was losing their mind – it was inevitable. They all understood they should resist it but did not quite comprehend how to do so or for what reason. What could he say to this poor fellow? Madness might be the best thing for him. Viktor moved to someone else's bunk and saw out of the corner of his eye that the other prisoners had gathered in knots. Some tried to converse among themselves, but the continuous mewling of Uncle Vasya made it impossible to understand what they were saying. "We will become nothing," thought Viktor. Clearly, Aleksey wanted to tell him something. He was trying to pull himself together, trying to organize what remained of his reason.

"I heard that you are a dissident?" Aleksey cautiously ventured. "They accused you of espionage or something similar? Contact with foreign correspondents?"

Have they turned him into a stoolpigeon? wondered Viktor with alarm. *Doesn't he understand that nothing can help him? Given his past employment, nothing can help him now.* He remained silent and it seemed Aleksey understood the reason for his caution.

"You'll get out of here, but I won't." He pronounced these words with a kind of strange, hopeless confidence. "You still have a chance, but I ... I understand how it all will end for me."

"No one knows how it will end." Viktor tried to calm the man, but Aleksey interrupted him.

"I heard that you're an engineer?"

"Yes, but I'm a civil engineer, not a military one."

"That's not important. You'll understand."

He regarded Viktor with such desperate resolution, with such fearlessness in his eyes that Viktor was startled. It was as if the miserable world of the psychiatric hospital had opened to permit the power of the human spirit to penetrate even here – the unbroken spirit.

"You know that a race for anti-missile defense is going on?" Golubov lowered his voice to a whisper. Only now the name of his cellmate flashed into Viktor's mind – Aleksey Golubov.

"I'm not a specialist in such things ..." Butko also lowered his voice.

"It doesn't matter. Just remember what I tell you. At present, all Soviet anti-missile missiles are equipped with nuclear warheads. This is dangerous, very dangerous. Not long ago the A-35 missile was brought into service. It carries a 2 -3 megaton nuclear warhead. Do you understand? The point is that there is practically no reason for them. They provide no guarantee against sea-launched ballistic missiles or an armada of bombers. Should there be a break-through anti-missile defense is useless. Understand? This race must be stopped, or it will destroy everybody.

"But how can we stop it?" Viktor was shocked by these revelations. He kept his voice low even though Uncle Vasya's ranting had risen to a scream, and no one could overhear them.

"If you get out of here and are able to make it to the West or simply get to the American Embassy ... I've made some drawings of the A-35. This is important. I have no chance, but you do ..." With these words Aleksey reached his wizened arm somewhere under his pajamas.

Viktor silently watched him and knew already that he would not refuse the request. It seemed that this was something which could justify continuing to fight and trying to preserve his mind.

When the doorbell of her small service apartment rang, Yelena Butenkova already knew it must be Irina. And there she was – at the threshold stood Irka Krasilnikova in a summer dress, cheerful and looking like she wore no make-up. Her hair had grown out and no longer resembled that of Natalya Varley. The chestnut locks lay on her shoulders. When she was inside, Irina began to sing a silly children's song from the recently released movie "Father Frost and the Summer."

"That's what it's like, our summer," she sang, and embraced Yelena who snickered a bit condescendingly as she regarded Ira as though she were a child.

"What are you on about?" Yelena asked with feigned severity unable to hide the mischievous sparkle in her eyes.

"Well, I'm off day after tomorrow, and Mishka has asked

me to the movies again. You remember Mishka Yegovov, the redhead. You introduced us at the New Year's dance, and we've gone out several times."

"Of course, I remember," muttered Yelena, stabbed by a sharp needle of jealousy. "Well, go then. He invited you."

"No. I won't go without you." Irina became suddenly serious – childishly serious, with an intent stare at Yelena.

"What are you, a child?" grumbled Yelena. "What do you mean, 'without you?' I'm working."

"Yelena, take a day off," Irina insisted. "The day after tomorrow is my birthday. Did you forget? I'll be twenty-four," she added with as much regret as pride.

"Oh, great," laughed Yelena. "Twenty-four! I'll be thirty-one this fall. I can't decide. Is anyone else going? Will Kostya be there?"

"No, and that's the problem," Ira answered regretfully. "Kostya left for the Baikal-Amur Mainline[25], didn't you know? Everyone says it's better than vegetating here. Out there are open spaces, adventures. Two years ago, they re-started construction. He finished technical school, and, well, Kostya left."

This information rendered Yelena even more morose. Unlike Misha, Kostya had never really appealed to her, but she was angry nonetheless that he had not said good-bye. Why did she have to find out from this new, empty-headed girl? Did the boys like only such witless beauties from the capital?

"So, what kind of idiot are you?" she asked, trying to conceal her irritation. "There'll just be the two of you. Mishka invited you, so go with him. What do you need me for? It's not your birthday yet. We'll find a minute to talk the next day."

---

25 The **Baikal–Amur Mainline** (Russian Байкало-Амурская магистраль (**БАМ**), Baikalo-Amurskaya magistral', **BAM**) is a 1,520 mm (4 ft 11 27/32 in) broad gauge railway line in Russia. Traversing Eastern Siberia and the Russian Far East, the 4,324 km (2,687 mi) long BAM runs about 610 to 770 km (380 to 480 miles) north of and parallel to the Trans-Siberian railway. Wikipedia

"But that's the thing – I don't want to go on a date with him." Irina was becoming impatient with her obtuse friend. "That's why I want you to come along. I like Mishka, but only as a friend. With you along, he won't try anything. I want to go to the movies on my birthday and I can't use that as an excuse not to go out with him. And it's a good movie – *The New Adventures of the Untouchables*. It was released at the end of fall, but I didn't have time to see it because it was final exam time, and I had to defend my diploma. Come on, Lenocha, say yes. Don't you remember the first movie? It was very good. 'Pursue, Pursue in Hot Blood,'" she said with an ingratiating smile.

These words provoked in Yelena neither envy nor jealousy but real hatred. So, this educated upstart didn't care for Misha! The best man in the village had begun to court her, but she calls in her friend to spoil the date. It wasn't enough that she gets all the best, and she's unable to appreciate it. Such thoughtless girls have it so easy in life and are handed everything. Why?

This question without an answer scorched her inside, and Yelena, powerless to resist her own envy, roughly shoved Irina toward the door while she spoke sternly, masking the hurt with friendly casualness.

"Go, go, and don't overthink it. Understand? When a guy like that asks, you simply must go. You'll see, and then you'll thank me. Don't grumble or act up. If he tries to kiss you, let him. If he asks you to spend the night with him, do it. Other girls spend their whole lives dreaming of such a man, but you … pursue it in hot blood! Can you guess how many suitors I had when I worked in the police? Real ones, not movie romances. I'll get along fine without your movie. Go with Mishka and stop being nervous, you idiot."

Yelena could have sworn that in that moment she believed what she was saying. She might really have been content with

Ira dating Misha. It seemed to her that it would be easier. It would be easier to know that her friends were together, that they made a great couple and loved one another. She could accept this and in time reconcile herself to it, just as she'd become accustomed to many worse things in her life. It was much more difficult for her to accept this oppressive ambiguity, the realization that Misha was still formally unattached, but his heart was taken, and not by her. It was unbearable to see that Ira did not appreciate Misha while he wanted her in vain. This left Yelena some room for hope, but he would surely continue his pursuit of Irina. No! She could not abide this. Yelena had no intention of tolerating such monotonous, melodramatic torture and therefore rudely commanded:

"You'll go alone with Misha, and that's it. I'll be at work. Is that clear?"

"I don't enjoy being with him," Irina essayed her final argument.

"And don't you make fun of him. This is no circus. A man needs someone at home," she grumbled, jostling Irina out of the apartment. She shut the door on her friend and leaned against the door as tears welled in her eyes ...

Chapter 9

Two Years Later

It was a normal summer day, sunny and a bit chilly, like many others. Already half gone, the short Ural summer no longer inspired joy but rather had become as routine as winter. The large, dark green leaves were covered with dust and some already had begun to yellow, hot days were no less exhausting than cold ones, and only the long, cool evenings and the beckoning sounds from the city parks reminded one to appreciate the season, so short in this region.

It was Irina's twenty-sixth birthday, and as was her wont, she took the day off and travelled to Sverdlovsk with Misha and another couple. Mikhail inspired her sympathy but was not an object of passion.

Maybe Yelena was incapable of such passion. Yes, she liked Misha, but she survived his loss, ungracefully but not as tragically as it first seemed, and she put it behind her in short order. She simply did not permit herself to dream or think about him, and in time concluded that failure itself was more painful that the loss of any particular person.

And today she was not thinking of Misha. Yelena was happy not to have gone with Irina although she had been asked, as usual. This was a special day for her, exciting and spiced with a tart, almost painful foretaste of hope, and Yelena would never have let it go by. Over the many years of her difficult life she had forbidden herself to dream, forbidden herself the consolation of hoping for a miracle. She had armored herself with callousness and resentment, worked hard, lived from day to day, and tried to be satisfied with simple pleasures. Free days. Holidays. Dances at the club. Rare visits to Sverdlovsk. A new movie. She held onto the faint hope that something would come her way and she would be able to convince her superiors in the police to send her to the training courses in Sverdlovsk that would qualify her for promotion. In the city she could start making useful acquaintances and somehow distinguish herself. Yelena was unsentimental; she had no dreams of a Prince Charming and had learned not to regret it. But even so, on this day she was having trouble coping with turbulent emotions.

Volkova had informed her yesterday that a KGB Major from Moscow would visit the SPB today.

"Be on your best behavior: fast, efficient, no personal questions, and don't talk too much. Just do as he says," had been the Chief Medical Officer's instructions. "He wants to see one of the patients."

"Butko?" guessed Yelena. It wasn't hard to divine the reason for the Moscow Chekist's visit: two weeks earlier the Chief Medical Officer for unknown reasons had ordered that the Ukrainian receive no more injections or any other medication. This could mean only one thing – he was to be released soon, and this rarely occurred without KGB sanction.

"Yes, him," shrugged Volkova. "So be here a half-hour early tomorrow and be prepared."

Yelena didn't have to be asked twice. A KGB Major! She'd never had contact with such a person. An adrenalin driven whirlwind of feelings that she had kept locked away for years suddenly engulfed her in a jumble of emotions. Hope, rapture, fear, anger, pain, and joy swept over her in an incoherent flood of sensations that simultaneously heated her blood and jangled her nerves. A KGB Major was the successor of those same Chekists who had so long ago ruined her life and family, and she should have despised them all. But at the same time this was the apex of the system to which she herself belonged as a police officer.

Chekists were close to the police but at the same time unattainable, desired but unreachable, just like Moscow. Yelena's colleagues harbored a traditional dislike for them, but in the depths of their souls the envied the special privileges of this mysterious estate. Yelena felt like a scorned and forgotten poor relation faced with meeting a real *KGBshnik* who might in spite of everything remember their kinship. She wanted to scream at him: *"I'm one of you. I'm an officer, a colleague. I'm the same as you. I work against crime, too, and I know about duty and orders. I too can be merciless. I'm no worse than you."*

She repeated these words to herself; the sense of worthlessness and deprivation she had experienced since youth seemed swept away be a huge, destructive wave. It was as though after becoming so accommodated to the unfairness of life she suddenly felt it so sharply that tears started in her eyes fueled by anger and powerlessness. Years of hidden feelings spilled forth forming all sorts of combinations. Yelena hated this yet unseen Chekist – but she could avoid being attracted to him no more than she could deny the blood ties that were unknown to him but obvious to her.

She feared that she would be unable to conceal how much she resented being unrecognized and undervalued, that she might allow such inappropriate hostility to show. Yelena wanted more than anything for the *KGBshnik* to see her value, to understand their unconscious but deep kinship, to reach out and help her – her, a person whom no one ever had helped. Such unexpected vulnerability frightened her, but she could no longer repress the hope that infected her hardened heart with such sweet poison. This was her chance to break out of this hole, perhaps her only chance. She had no right to let it pass. But what could she do that might interest this Moscow Chekist?

Hope for a better life seized her. Yelena saw with sudden clarity her past life of deprivation and desperation and nearly cried out from the nearly physical pain it brought her. She regained control and suppressed the scream. She mustn't permit herself to hope. Never. She must be prepared for this meeting to bring nothing new into her life – for this sleek Muscovite to pay her no attention, not to give her a second glance, not to sympathize, not to notice …

Yelena was prepared to carry out any order from this unknown person – and at the same time unhesitatingly to betray him if only to achieve the desired result. Faithfulness, infidelity, NKVD or KGB, the truth or lies – anything seemed possible to her to extend the boundaries of her disgusting little world, to grit her teeth and move toward those stars shining atop the Kremlin towers, toward the red battlements of those walls, toward the broad avenues of the Capital.

It seemed that all that was needed was to take a step on those stairs and begin to climb. Maybe she would fall, bloody her hands, her blood and that of others, leaning against the concrete walls with reddened palms, silently groaning before again beginning to climb, always upward. She would make it to where rich and scarce goods awaited in the stores, where people more interesting than Misha strolled, where like a New Year's fairy tale the Capital bustled, the Capital as cruel and cynical as Yelena herself …

She didn't sleep that night but nonetheless was refreshed and enthused by her heated blood. The night sky was not yet lightened by the first signs of dawn, but Yelena rushed into the street unconscious of the cold and nearly ran to the bus station. She saw the first pink and orange break the horizon through the bus windows, and she felt as though her heart

was filled with fire, as well, unable to extinguish the treason-
ous, naïve belief inside.

Svetlana Eduardovna greeted the Chekist herself and
guided him immediately to her office where they discussed
something alone. Outside, Yelena dared not try to eavesdrop,
but disappointment and anger slowing filled her. Now he
would come out of the door and walk past without even noticing her – or maybe he would cast a cold glance in her direction and try to escape the dark walls of the psychiatric hospital
as quickly as possible to return to his world, to the spacious
offices at the Lubyanka.

"Yelena!" Volkova's voice broke the silence, and Yelena
swallowed hard trying to assume a calm demeanor as she
opened the office door.

The Senior Medical Officer quickly introduced her. "Major
Rakhmanov, this is Junior Lieutenant Butenkova, our nurse."
Rakhmanov turned to her and courteously extended his hand.
Yelena now got a good look at him: tall and broad-shouldered,
he did not look like a cold-blooded monster. He was a quite
presentable, with black hair and a face that was neither remarkable nor repugnant, although his chin was too narrow
and expressive of secret thoughts or maybe ruthlessness. He
maintained a guarded mien, or so it seemed due to his small
eyes. He might have been handsome had it not been for those
eyes that were unusually unexpressive and lent him a de-
tached and impenetrable appearance.

"Yelena, take Dimitriy Yevgenevich to the ward, to Butko," ordered Volkova.

"Of course." Yelena nodded eagerly. "Let's go, Comrade
Major."

They walked silently along the corridor, and Yelena understood that each step distanced her further from her trea-
sured goal. They would arrive at the designated cell, and she

would have to turn back. He would nod slightly at her, and after a second wouldn't even remember her name…

"We stopped medicating him two weeks ago," she ventured, desiring at least to say something.

"Yes, I know," said Rakhmanov. "Your chief informed me. I wrote to her about this."

"Butko was stubborn, conflicted, argued with the doctors and nurses. I didn't know, to tell the truth, whether he was getting any better," continued Yelena, stressing the last word.

The KGB major slowed his pace a bit and gave her a hard look, as though only now he was taking note her presence. He hesitated a moment as though he were deciding whether it was worthwhile to share information with her. Rakhmanov understood that he was not dealing with a simple nurse, but with an officer of the Militia or Internal Forces. Normally, members of the KGB had a low opinion of the Militia ranks, and even joked that MVD stood for "the illiterate grandchildren of Dzerzhinsky." (малограмотные внуки Дзержинского) But instincts developed over the years suggested that in this case he could take a risk and toss the girl a bone, not in the form of a secret, but something that would lay a foundation for trust. There was something about her that suggested a readiness for unconditional devotion – or at a minimum a hunger for such devotion which could be triggered at the slightest signal. So, Dimitriy began carefully.

"I understand your feelings. His former lover rushed to marry a Jew shortly after his arrest. They applied for travel to Israel. The reputation of this couple was so low that we didn't especially care. She had another friend in the Mordovian camps, and we wanted her as far away as possible where she couldn't pester us about his well-being. But we miscalculated. She and her husband went to America, and there this girl raised hell about her former lovers. You must know that Western intelligence services adore loudmouthed traitors like her. They got her included in some important conferences where she ranted about 'punitive psychiatry,' as they like to call it. In a word, she made a lot of rather serious trouble. As you probably know, there are some serious talks with the Americans now about limiting anti-missile defense systems. And on the margins of these negotiations it is necessary to make concessions to one another. The most important issues of state security can be threatened by American quibbles about things like the well-being of dissidents. Sometimes you have to give something up."

Yelena nodded in agreement, encouraged by his openness.

"What a shame that you weren't here two years ago!" she blurted. "One of these types was ready to cooperate. He wanted tell everything he knew."

"And?" The Major could not hide his interest.

"He stupidly revealed his desire to a new nurse, and she decided he was delirious and did nothing. Then he attempted suicide. He didn't survive," she finished with evident bitterness.

"And what sort of nurse was this?" he asked suspiciously. "Why didn't she report this?"

Yelena perfectly understood the subtext of the question. For a second, she was tempted to play to his professional suspicion, though with a hint of meaningless intonation which could slightly strengthen his suspicion and maybe make her, Yelena, irreplaceable in the eyes of the Major from Moscow. Instead, she pulled herself together and gave him a firm answer:

"She was a common person just out of the Institute. I think she acted innocently. Afterwards she realized what she had done and would never repeat it."

That was all. Hoist on her own petard, she averted her eyes. She had just destroyed a once in a lifetime opportunity out of stupid decency, out of an illogical pity for the empty-headed upstart. But most vexing was the fact that Irina was incapable of understanding the damage she had done! Now the Chekist from the Capital would lose interest in her and continue to Butko's cell.

But instead, Rakhmanov seemed to like her answer.

He unexpectedly asked, "Where did you work before the mental hospital?"

"In the Militia," she answered with renewed hope. "I participated in work against the Karimov Gang. Maybe you heard about it. After the war they were active here. They plundered entire villages."

"No, I didn't know about it," replied Rakhmanov with a touch of sympathy in his voice. "I work in a somewhat different section."

"We were unable to finish them off," she said, "The plundering stopped, and some of the bandits went underground. We suspected they were connected to a certain suspicious fellow from the village of Malakhovo. He had a strange background. He was taken prisoner during the war, and the Americans freed him. Then, when he returned home, he was immediately arrested and sentenced to ten years in the camps. But he was released after five by the amnesty and settled here in the wilderness and caused no trouble. But you understand, he was in prison, socialized with the Americans in Germany, and here the bandits never touched his village. We watched him at home to find out if they were there."

"And how did it end?" Rakhanov seemed interested in what she was saying. Yelena was bursting with joy.

"Nothing," she replied in frustration. "Our main investigator was transferred to Sverdlovsk and replaced by someone who dropped the case. We never got to the bottom of it. It's been about five years now."

"Well now, Junior Lieutenant Butenkova," pronounced Dimitriy Rakhmanov as though he had made some sort of decision. "I see that you are a serious person, a responsible and honest person. Here is my phone number. Should something interesting happen again, whether with this nurse or your bandits, or should one of the patients want to cooperate, you may call me at the Lubyanka. Do you understand?"

"Yes, Comrade Major," she said, unable to conceal her pleasure. No, she had been mistaken only in that she was not ready to deceive this man, at least not yet. She held the card he had given her clasped tightly in her hand as though it were the richest treasure, and her eyes gleamed with pure devotion. Rakhmanov noted this and nodded with satisfaction.

When Dimitriy arrived at the cell two burly orderlies already had brought Viktor Butko out. Major Rakhmanov involuntarily froze, amazed at the changes in the Ukrainian. In place of the tall, fair haired, handsome man, before him now stood a scrawny, haggard person with yellowing skin, suggesting a serious problem with his liver. His cheek bones stood out sharply, and his dry, yellowish gray skin stretched over them like cigarette paper, making his dark circled eyes even more expressive.

"Is there someplace we can speak privately?" asked Dimitriy, trying not to stare at the prisoner.

"Of course. Come with us." The orderlies headed silently to the end of the corridor unceremoniously shoving Butko ahead of them. Rakhmanov dismissed Yelena and followed them. They stopped at a door at the end of the corridor which led to a small room which had at one time served to store records. There were shelves along the walls covered with dust, and in the corner beside a small window high in the wall stood a dirty, wooden desk that looked like it belonged in a secondary school.

Dimitriy ordered the orderlies to leave them before turning to Butko. "Sit down," he said, still averting his eyes from the prisoner. They sat facing one another on benches on either side of the desk while the room filled with an oppressive silence. For a long time, Dimitriy did not break the silence as he chose words that would elicit an answer from his interlocutor. At last, he cautiously began.

"Can you guess why I came?" he asked, and after another long silence continued, "It's because of your friend, Natalya."

In the empty, colorless eyes of the prisoner something resembling interest appeared. In a dry, voice unfamiliar to himself he asked, "What about her?"

"She's making some very big problems for our country," replied Rakhmanov with a heavy voice. "She ran an unprecedented campaign against the Soviet Union and openly works with our enemies. In short, this is not simply another 'dissent,' as you like to call it. This is pure treason against the Motherland. She does not conceal her connections with our enemies."

Dimitriy purposely withheld any mention of Natalya being in America to plant unease in his enemy's mind. And he hit the mark: Viktor Butko shivered, leaned slightly forward and whispered: "What do you want from me?"

"I want to offer you a task," replied Rakhmanov. "I forgot to mention that your girlfriend is now in the USA. I can offer your only chance to get to your much-loved West - unless you prefer to rot away in the East for the rest of your life."

"To the West?" Butko was dumbfounded, but enormously relieved to learn that Natalya was living abroad. "And you will simply set me free?"

"Of course," answered Rakhmanov with a patronizing smile. "The Soviet State is more humanitarian than you think. Just agree to what I say, and you'll be released. There is only one condition." He paused for a few beats. "You must find your girlfriend and convince her to stop working against her own country. Don't forget that besides you, another of your friends is in the camps, and should she continue to make trouble, believe me, he'll never get out alive. And you also have a brother. By the way, he and his wife adopted a girl from an orphanage in order to somehow compensate for losing their child in that tragic flood. And right after that your sister-in-law became pregnant, which means that the former orphan will soon have a sister or brother. So, you see, your relatives have a happy life."

Viktor listened to him with unconcealed disgust. This was blackmail – banal, unvarnished, vulgar blackmail. It was revoltingly clear that this man, intoxicated with his own omnipotence, this worthless man who sat before him and played with the fates of his loved ones, shamelessly touching them with his filthy hands, bandying their names about, could decide their fates, and there was nothing Viktor, isolated in his imprisonment, could do. Such scum held absolute power to debase and threaten, and now were trampling under their filthy leather boots his very soul, fully cognizant of their impunity. This was their country, their time, their epoch. Despite the revulsion that Rakhmanov inspired, Viktor understood that getting away was the best, indeed the only possibility he had. But he did not wish to escape under the KGB's conditions.

"I can't impose on the freedom of another person," he said. "Can't you understand that this is her decision? I can't force her to do anything. She's trying to defend others as well as me…"

Rakhmanov interrupted him. "Believe me, at the bottom of it all she's defending you. Almost everything she does is for you. Apparently, she means more to you than your accomplice." He gave a poisonous smile and added, "What is more, you are responsible only for yourself. Promise me now that if you go to America you will not make any statements or start any campaigns and the like. No public activities against the Soviet Union. Do you agree? If you give me your word, you can be free today."

Under any other circumstances Viktor would not have agreed to such a proposition, but he remembered all too well that he had something to do, an important mission on which the lives of millions of people depended. And no public action was required to carry out that mission.

"I promise," he answered, looking the Chekist straight in the eye. Dimitriy Rakhmanov held his eyes as if trying to ascertain whether the prisoner was telling the truth. He came to a decision, opened his small attaché case, and laid some papers on the desk.

"Your medical record. Documents. Pass. New clothes have been placed on the cot in your room."

"There are other things I need to collect," said Butko, and for the first time there was uncertainty in his voice.

"Yes, of course." Rakhmanov looked at his wristwatch. "Your cellmates have been sent outside. No one will bother you. Someone will escort you to the exit. You'll receive permission to travel in a few days, I promise you."

Viktor said nothing. He could not force himself to thank this person who had made his life a living hell for the past two and a half years. They stood and went out into the corridor without speaking. The KGB Major escorted him to the open door of the empty cell, waved farewell with a slight smile and walked away down the corridor. A vigilant orderly stood at the door. Viktor knew they would no longer detain him. He went into the cell and for the last time looked around the wretched and cold tiny living space, sagging bunks and the permanent puddle in the middle of the floor. It was hard to believe he had spent two years of his life here.

He carefully closed the door behind him and went to his bed. He had only a few belongings, but he was not interested in them. Kneeling beside the bed, he ripped open the hiding place in his mattress, and slid his hand inside. His fingers wrapped around tightly rolled up sheets of paper he knew were covered top to bottom with nearly microscopic, barely legible letters. He held them as one would hold something of great value and began to scatter them among his other things.

Having changed clothes and assured himself that he had all the necessary papers, Viktor went out into the corridor and walked to the iron barred door at the end. An orderly followed without touching him. As if in a fairytale, some amazing pipedream, he stepped across the threshold of one iron barred door after another. Corridors, flights of stairs, bars. No one stopped him for a search or to check him over. Massive, merciless locks opened before him, each step taking him closer to freedom. Viktor regretted only that he had been unable to say good-bye to Golubov, to see for the last time the unfortunate Vasiliy and the other patients. They were all behind him now, and ahead was the interior courtyard filled with Autumn sunlight. The barbed wire, communications lines, the guard towers at the corners. He showed his pass at the sentry box, and after a few minutes' wait the gate opened before him. Viktor took a step and filled his chest with late July air warmed by the sun. Freedom!

Chapter 10

In this place the years changed nothing: not the neon letters on the opposite wall, not the selection of drinks, not the steely glint of the pipes mounted just under the ceiling, deliberately placed on view, not the shabby green felt of the pool table. Opposite the bar, across the road in the small hotel everything also was as it had always been: the huge, stuffed brown bear in the foyer with its paws resting on the branch of a shriveled tree, the rustic decoration of the rooms and the massive beds with headboards of asymmetrical lacquered logs. The aroma of wood hung over everything – a miraculous and slightly fabulous interweaving of woody scents. Rough and gracefully finished, uneven and polished, dark and light, plain and painted in natural patterns of interwoven shades, the tree reigned here, filling this cozy, old fashioned place with a sense of purity. If he were not on another foreign mission, Patrick did his best every year to come to this place if only just for a few days, and his hometown enveloped him in the aromas of a serene childhood, the taste of honey, and the eternal symbols of the bear.

Only the youngish girl behind the bar was new. She took his order and turned to the rows of bottles on the mirrored rear wall. Patrick wondered if she would have been here had he come at his usual time in June. It had not been possible to take a summer vacation this year – there had been too much work that could not be postponed, and then there had been an unexpected trip to England. The British colleagues had generously offered their "younger brothers" the opportunity to participate in the debriefing of member of the Soviet Trade

Mission in London, Oleg Lyalin. This hapless KGB officer had been caught in romance with his own secretary and the was detained for drunk driving. The price for his carelessness was cooperation with MI-5 to whom he provided copious information on the make-up of the KGB and GRU *rezidenturas* and everything he knew about KGB operations in Great Britain.

His information proved accurate. In exchange for political asylum the defector gave the British the Soviet plans for sabotage in London, revealed what he knew about the network of Soviet spies in England and leads to Soviet illegals in other Western countries, including the USA. Patrick extracted everything he could from Lyalin, including personal details about KGB and GRU officers known to him at the Center and in the US, especially those susceptible to recruitment. After returning home and finishing his voluminous reporting on his conversations with Lyalin, he learned that the British had taken the unprecedented step of expelling 105 Soviet diplomates. This did not especially please him because he understood that such actions always result in reciprocity, but at least in this instance the repercussions would fall only on his British colleagues while Lyalin's information helped foil the activities of Soviet *rezidenturas* in many Western countries. You had to give the Brits their due – this had been a spectacular recruitment.

He recalled how the defector had marveled at his fluency in Russian – almost perfect, but with a barely detectible accent which nonetheless did not betray the fact that he was an American.

"If I didn't know you were from the States, I would think you were from some Baltic country," confided Lyalin. And so, getting rid of a slight Baltic accent would be his next language improvement chore.

It had been a successful trip. Patrick loved the UK, her enchanting antiquity, the medieval beauty of her palaces and the grandeur of her history, but wherever he travelled, he was always glad to return home to America. He carried her with him wherever he was, he would regard the most deserted corner of the world through American eyes, confident that she would transform the world while he paved the way for her to walk the planet, as always – triumphant. He was young and full of enthusiasm, but now after six years with the Agency, he felt the need to rest.

The sound system filled the bar with the familiar sadly sentimental strains of "Danny Boy." Patrick loved the gentle motif of this unofficial Irish hymn. He was not recognizably Irish, having inherited his American father's dark hair and smooth, slightly dark skin. He had inherited only the eyes of his Irish mother – clear and crystal blue in the sun, and dark with gray highlights in the shade.

Patrick Corn was ten years old when his family moved from Montana to West Virginia, but he would never forget the friendliness of provincial towns and unmatched beauty of Glacier National Park which he had visited with his parents from early childhood. He remembered the pine forests with their crystaline streams and the blindingly blue mountain lakes that seemed to absorb the blue of the sky. Their smooth surface slightly disturbed by ripples, they stretched to a distant, fine line from which rose the forested hills. And behind them rose the sharply defined peaks of the mountains and the sparkling snow on their slopes.

He loved going up to the glaciers when the mountain slopes with each twist and turn provided wonderful glimpses of hidden valleys. They revealed themselves slowly, growing in all their majesty – from the forests below to the clouds above. From the glaciers narrow streams flowed into waterfalls and, in spite of the scorching sun, carried into the valleys the taste of cold, just melted snow.

A wonderful, miraculous world stretching between heaven and earth helped Patrick forget the eternal stress and at times exhausting sense of the importance of his work. Here in the mountains was revealed to him something truly important and unchanging, that it is possible to survive human vanity and replenish what remained of his soul with strength. Closer to the mountain peaks all of nature seemed drawn to the sun, and the fir trees reminded him of arrows rather than drooping tents. rivulets cut through the bright, green carpet of grass. Rivulets cut through the bright green carpet of grass as he approached the large blocks of snow. They emanated cold, as if from a freezer, and Patrick recalled how as a boy he had happily run up to the ice to touch it with his hand to feel the melting water and place his face next to it to feel the frosty air.

This time, with the few remaining friends he had in town, Patrick once more spent an entire day at the park. And now, having absorbed natures freshness, he was at last alone in the painfully familiar bar of the small hotel listening to a favorite song of his childhood, his being filled with long awaited contentment. In this moment he needed to forget about the dangers of the hostile external world, not to think about past victories and new assignments, to know nothing apart from the twilight, the bar, the sound of music, and the aroma of wood...

"Patrick!" He was startled by a voice that was unmistakable even through the loud music. He had worked with Richard Hood for almost three years in an Eastern European Station. Rick had recently returned to Headquarters, but Patrick had hardly expected to see him here. He had not told anyone where he was going on leave, and the fact that they had searched him out (not a difficult task for professionals) suggested that something serious was afoot. Any thought of his long-awaited vacation disappeared, leaving him bitter and displeased. He had been here only a day, and they would not leave him to spend the evening in peace.

"What happened?" He turned on the stool without standing or offering Richard a place at the bar. He felt no need to hide from his old friend that he did not welcome his appearance.

"They want you at the office. It's very important." Hood had the decency to inject a hint of regret into the words. "They're planning an important mission and only you can carry it out. And there is little time for preparations."

"And they couldn't wait another three days?" asked Patrick, nearly in despair. He gave the darkened bar a farewell glance.

"They couldn't wait even until tomorrow. Let's go to your hotel and get your things and head to the airport. You must be at Headquarters tomorrow morning." Hood gave a longing look at the rows of bottles behind the bar.

"Are they nuts?" asked Patrick, but only for the sake of decency. He had been in the CIA long enough to understand that something truly extraordinary was afoot for them to have searched him out in Montana...

Next morning, he was in a small conference room at Langley. It seemed almost a dream that only yesterday he had met the dawn on the serpentine path leading into the foothills of the mountain glaciers. Now he would have to forget the park, the bears, and the bar.

His boss, Christopher Groves was not a despot. Before heading the CIA's Soviet/East European Division he had served as Chief of Station in Moscow. Patrick himself had never been in Russia and so there had been no opportunity to work with the Chief in the field, but Groves' professionalism was legendary.

"So, who exactly gave us the documents?" he asked again.

"A well-known Soviet dissident, an engineer by profession," replied the Chief as he handed him a file folder. "He was released from a psychiatric hospital this summer."

"Where?"

A corner of Groves' mouth lifted in what might have been a smile. "A special kind of Soviet camp where they use psychotropic preparations to suppress the minds of prisoners. This is necessary if the KGB wants to completely destroy a man. You haven't heard of punitive psychiatry?"

Of course, Patrick knew about this. A few months earlier he had asked an analyst for documents from a London psychiatric conference on this problem. But the recent trip to England and the interrupted leave had nearly made him forget.

"The source says he shared a cell for over two years with a military engineer, Colonel Aleksey Golubov, the former deputy director of a secret Moscow research institute. We confirmed the information about Golubov. Included in the material he provided were unique plans for a new A-35 thermonuclear warhead and important information on the USSR's anti-missile defense. This information was so valuable that Pentagon specialists sent it directly to the White House. It might be used in anti-missile defense reduction negotiations with the Soviets. The Department of Defense values Golubov's information highly and appended to its analysis a list of questions they say are vital to answer.

Patrick said nothing, anticipating what would come next. The outlines of his future assignment were beginning to take shape, and frankly speaking, they were not very encouraging.

"The source who provided the documents thinks he gave us everything Golubov had. Most of the material was written by Golubov, and some parts were written by the source according to what Golubov told him. Following his release, the dissident managed to get to the US thanks to the efforts of his girlfriend who lives here. According to him, Aleksey Golubov remains in a so-called 'closed psychiatric hospital' near the village of Medinskiy in Sverdlovsk Oblast, and at the time he wrote the documents he was still in good mental health with a fine memory." Groves paused.

"Sverdlovsk Oblast? That's in the Urals," began Patrick.

"Sverdlovsk is a closed city. No foreigners allowed. Our diplomats aren't allowed there."

"Quite right," sighed Groves. "That's why you'll be going there as a Soviet citizen."

"But they'll figure it out right away ..." began Patrick.

Groves interrupted him. "We've tried to anticipate every possible risk. We were able to pull together a detailed biography of Colonel Golubov, as well as information on his relatives. First, his parents passed away, unable to survive what happened to their son. His father committed suicide, and his mother died a year later. Golubov's wife and child remain free. They returned to Kharkov, to his mother-in-law, but that is not important. Our colonel's father, Matvey Golubov, went through the entire war and participated in the liberation of the Baltic countries from the Nazis. You've mentioned several times that Russians think your accent is Latvian or Lithuanian, right? Latvians are quite like us. At least, they love good beer and know how to brew it. And they are great basketball fans. And consider their flag – it's similar to the Irish flag." Groves smiled slyly.

"Apart from the accent and basketball, it's important to have the right documents," said Patrick.

"Without doubt," said the Chief as he handed over a passport. "These documents are in the name of a real person who was born in Vilnius in 1945. Yurgis Gintaus. The child died when he was five, but his birth certificate is valid. He was born out of wedlock, probably the offspring of some Soviet soldier.

His father's name is unknown, and his mother, Edit Gintaus, disappeared. After the death of her child it's possible she joined up with the "Forest Brothers" or some other rebel outfit."

Patrick remained dubious. "In any case there would have to be some biographical background in Latvia, friends he grew up with, the school he attended. There must be some witnesses to his life. Should the legend be checked out, it would unravel pretty quickly."

"The legend of any illegal will unravel if checked out," answered Groves, annoyed by Patrick's objections. "This is unavoidable. The one thing that an illegal must hope for is that no one should check him out. We've checked, and it turns out that the security system of Soviet Special Psychiatric Hospitals is not as good as you might think. For example, when an inmate is released, they allow not only his relations in, but also his friends. Once, when a well-known rights defender was released, a man unknown to the prisoner showed up saying he was a doctor when in reality he worked as a first aid nurse. Our tame dissident provided several such stories that were confirmed by other sources. Medinskiy probably doesn't have its own KGB unit. You'll only have to convince the medical personnel to permit you to meet with Golubov. Of course, there are risks, and that's why it's important to focus on these people and try to use personal contacts. I don't have to teach you how this is done."

"Let's talk a little more about the legend." The assignment in all its absurdity and obvious danger was beginning to appeal to Patrick. It was important, really important. To judge from the Pentagon's response, the United States had never before had such a source in the Soviet Union. The idea that a great scientist should be left to rot in a psychiatric hospital was monstrous and absurd, and Patrick instinctively wanted to strike a blow against this insane system.

"It's very simple. You, Yugis Gintaus, are the illegitimate son of Matvey Golubov. Your father died a year ago, and your mother somehow learned of this and for the first time told you about him. You looked into it and learned that you have a half-brother who is now in Medinskiy. You decided to try to find him, even there."

"If Yurgis was born in 1945, he should be 26 years old," said Patrick, "I'm 31, and I've never been to Vilnius ..."

"You look younger than you are, and the difference in age is not so much." It seemed that the Chief was convinced that Patrick was the ideal candidate for this mission and was not about to change his mind. "We'll give you a crash course about Vilnius and the rest. But inasmuch as the disarmament talks are in full swing, the information is urgently needed, and Golubov's condition and his imprisonment are of major concern, you'll have about two months to prepare, not more."

"I can't learn to speak Latvian in two months." This was Patrick's last possible objection.

"You don't have to. According to the legend, you were born after the war, and in Soviet Latvia not everybody knows their own native language very well. Don't forget that the Communists oppose every manifestation of national culture. The only remaining trace of their native language for many children today is their accent. We'll give you some language basics, of course – it would be strange if you knew nothing at all. But you will know Russian better than Latvian, and that won't seem out of place. It would be more complicated if you had been born before the Soviet occupation."

"Looks to me like you've already thought this through," smiled Patrick. He picked up the new Soviet passport and saw that it bore evidence of light use, just as it would be if it belonged to young Yurgis Gintaus. Only yesterday he had been surrounded by Montana's mountains and their forests and crystal streams. Now he would go to the grim, frigid Urals, a desolate land of frost and prison hospitals where no foreigner was allowed. How would he communicate with his own people, with the Station?

As if reading his thoughts, the Chief smiled. "You won't be on your own, Corn. We have a man even there."

This raised Patrick's eyebrows in astonishment.

"Nikolay Kondratyev from the village of Malakhovo. We recruited him in 1945 when he was liberated from a German prison camp. But you know how the Russians treated their soldiers who had been captured by the Germans. He was sent immediately to a camp where he sat for five years, as I recall. This experience deepened his hatred of Soviet power, and he started helping anyone who opposed it. After a few years he re-established contact with us, though he's gone quiet of late, and hardly anyone around here remembers him. That's good for you. He must still have the radio set we gave him about eight years ago. It was the latest technology at the time. You will give him instructions to open a commo channel. In an emergency we have agents who could get another commo device to him. We'll notify him in advance, so he'll be expecting you. He's well acquainted with the local situation and can brief you once you arrive. You'll be staying with him."

"I've dreamed about something like this my whole life," muttered Patrick, although the existence of a "sleeper agent" was encouraging.

"And do you know what? When I was your age, I dreamed of something like this, really." Groves' tone was grave. "To have the opportunity to do something so important and grandiose, something which truly might save the planet from destruction – how many people ever get a chance like that? Your trip to Great Britain was important, but the results were nothing extraordinary. Do you understand what I'm saying? The names of a few illegals and the members of *Rezidenturas*, and a few agents is standard fare. But a source inside the USSR who worked on the development of Soviet anti-missile defense, we never had. In the event of war..."

"I understand," said Patrick. The importance of this mission was clear and had already pushed thoughts of Montana from his mind. Before him was an unprecedented mission, one which Patrick could not refuse.

Chapter 11

She woke up late, nearly noon, and stretched, enjoying the sweetness of a lazy morning. The miserly November sun had already reached her window and slowly warmed the air with a narrow beam that looked like it came from a projector, illuminating drifting particles of dust. Irina turned away from the light and planted her head back in the pillow. Even the landlady had become used to the girl sleeping in on Sundays following tiring work shifts and five A.M. wakeups and did not disturb her. Irina had carefully plugged and sealed the cracks in the window in September, and now enjoyed the heat slowly accumulating in the room from the sunlight.

But her pleasure was short-lived. Unpleasant thoughts again made their way into her head, like lights in the middle of the night – one after another. How many days until the long-awaited deadline? The count had come down to days rather than months, but Irina kept her hope in check, not daring to permit herself the sweet illusion of a dream. Soon, she will have spent three years in Medinskiy, and the period of required post-graduate internship would come to an end. Finally, she would be free to find her own employment.

Of course, one needed to begin a job search earlier so as not to be considered a parasite, and Irina knew quite well what she would do. Toward the end of her three-year service, she would go to the Sverdlovsk psychiatric hospital because she had trained there, and they knew her. She would find out if there were any vacancies, and even if there were none, she would go to her faculty at the medical institute and ask for help. If forced to do so, she would try to find work in her hometown where her parents still lived. It didn't matter where, so long as it was far away from here.

She had told herself many times that it was useless counting the months because constantly living in the future prevented her from enjoying the present; enjoying the good that could be found even here. However, this morning Irina understood with unexpected clarity that there was absolutely nothing here to enjoy. All along she had done her best to suppress such thoughts in the depths of the moment at hand, proceeding from one small goal to another. From the next weekend or holiday, to the next date with Misha, to the movies or dances, to spring, to summer. She had managed to scrape out such an existence month by month and year by year only in the end to face the unavoidable fact that all this time she had been living another's existence, an empty illusion in which nothing was real.

Now, lying in bed watching the bright, microscopic crystals of dust motes floating in the sunlit air, Irina realized with crystal clarity that for all this time it had been as if she were playing a role in some ridiculous play written especially for her. She had tried to be the ideal tenant, of the sort Maria Innoketyevna imagined her to be, all the while in the depths of her soul she abhorred this town and this apartment. He had a friend who envied and disliked her. Ira did not feel close to Yelena and felt she could never reveal her true thoughts to her. She tried only to treat Yelena amiably, doing her best to bury the mutual hostility and was relieved when it appeared that she had been successful.

She had a strange sense of guilt toward Yelena, her hard life and the indelible stamp of orphanhood which marked the entire being of this young woman with such hard corners. It seemed to Irina after a while that behind the cynicism and vulgarity of her colleague there existed an overshadowing vulnerability. Yelena had the air of a puppy thrown into the street which concealed behind the ugliest mask the desire to whine, snuggle up to someone's feet in canine devotion in exchange for only a single intimation of intimacy. But even if this were correct, Irina was not the person to break down Yelena's barriers so instead she could only put on her own mask – that of a carefree and affable girl capable of providing at least a ray of warmth for her friend's rough heart.

Just as true friendship, Irina had never experienced true love. She was going out with a man who demanded nothing of her beyond friendship and brotherly affection whom she tried her best to love. That she was unsuccessful, Irina had acknowledged only the day before when Misha finally proposed. She didn't understand why he had waited so long and promised to think about it in hopes of putting off an unpleasant explanation, ideally just before her departure from Medinskiy. She did not deny to herself that this was cowardly and that in truth she had simply used Misha to brighten her loneliness in this unbearable place. She had only one justification – she had really tried to fall in love with him. She had visited him, met his family, simple, nice people. But again in their cozy wooden home she realized that she was only playing the role of a well-mannered, nice girlfriend but that this was not the life she wanted.

And even more alien and strange was her work. She had never dreamed of this when studying at the institute – not about filling unfortunate patients with neuroleptics or, even worse, healthy people simply because they had permitted themselves to think differently from the majority of their fellow citizens. To pretend there was nothing wrong, that she tried only to do her job well and display some minimum of humanity in the midst of terrible, inhuman conditions – this was the sum of her long workdays during which she felt like a patient herself …

From childhood Irina had been interested in the depths of human consciousness, what moved human souls, the interaction of noble motives and base passions, the complex mechanisms of thought from which are born conclusions and errors. Why, for example, if the Soviet system were so beautiful, could so many people around the globe not recognize it? Why did so many people continue to live under oppression and believe in lies? Little Ira thought about this but could find no answers.

In her senior classes she read Dostoevskiy and dreamed about becoming an actress as a way of penetrating the consciousness of the people whose roles she played. It seemed to her that if she could project herself into another personality, the normal world would assume new colors, open her soul to others who may be unlike her, but still possessed such interesting and complicated souls. Different characters attracted her more than places and picturesque landscapes. For a time, she participated in school plays, playing roles quite unlike herself. Ira came to realize that playing a part was not enough to understand the essence of another person. She could only imagine herself in the other's place, different with a different fate and different principles, while still in her own skin. This curious combination of the real and the imaginary both attracted and frightened her and offered no definite answers. Finally, Irina discovered psychology and the related discipline of psychiatry.

No less so than with medicine, psychiatry related to psychology, and this gave students the unique opportunity to discuss topics that verged on the forbidden. The KGB was suspicious of student philosophers or writers and zealously tracked various "unreliable" circles of philosophizing youth. However, the ubiquitous State Security thought of student psychiatrists the way they thought of medical doctors and did not consider them especially free-thinking as students in other disciplines.

At the institute, Irina eagerly studied different psychological theories and memorialized details of those that interested her most in a notebook, hoping to gain a better understanding of the intricacies of the human psyche. Occasionally she came upon quite seditious things that had nothing to do with psychiatry or psychology, but rather lay in the sphere of philosophy or religion. For example, Irina was surprised to learn that Karl Gustav Jung once quite accurately noted that from the point of view of psychology as a science we cannot prove or disprove the existence of the spiritual world. He believed that since there are imprinted archetypes in the psyche, we may assume the presence of prototypes that made the imprint. Thus, wrote Jung, the presence of the archetype "self" indirectly suggests the existence of God. Such thoughts were completely inadmissible, and Irina was so frightened she tried to put them out of her mind.

In her first year, she reviewed an essay on how various Western schools of psychology relate to the moral codex of the builder of Communism and what Soviets might accept and what they could not. That psychiatry is the criterion of morality was her greatest takeaway from her studies. Unlike psychology, overflowing with philosophy and relativism, psychiatry is a more exact science with strictly defined norms and pathologies.

Serious violations of societal mores and taboos invariably lead to pathologies. The intimate connection between her work and morality inspired Irina for a long time. What had now changed?

"How did it happen?" Irina whispered to herself as she pulled the covers over her head, feeling as though indolence and emptiness were wasting her last free day. How did it happen that instead of helping people return to full lives full of health and joy, instead of guarding societal morality, she had become and executioner taking part in the slow, torturous, daily march toward death of healthy people? How had she come to this?

She sat up on the bed with a groan. She had learned as a student that gestalt therapy included an understanding of "introspection" through which a person internalizes feelings, views, convictions, norms, and forms of the behavior of others. These alien attitudes, called introjects, conflict with one's own experience, are not assimilated by one's personality and lead to discomfort or even illness. And now, Irina felt engulfed by these very introjections – alien stereotypes, alien concepts which she involuntarily followed.

She sprang from the bed, noting that the beam of luminous dust motes had narrowed. It was almost noon, the sun departing, and she still had to clean the room, go to the store, and she wanted to go to the dance tonight. Misha was going away for the weekend for his aunt's birthday in Kamensk-Uralskiy and would not return until late. This meant she could simply rest this evening without suffering through another excruciating date. Until now she had been uncertain about refusing Misha. She had become accustomed to him over the past two and a half years and wanted to put off to the last possible moment responding to his proposal.

Yes, that day would come, but not now. In the meantime, she did not want to go with Yelena. She decided to go to the dance alone, at her own risk, as though she expected some sort of miracle. But she knew that miracles did not happen, at least in her own life, and in Medinskiy in particular. She nonetheless decided to break from her joyless routine in search of momentary, illusory, light-heartedness...

The village club exuded its normal atmosphere of hot clay

and coziness. Outside it was snowy and wintery cold in contrast with the warmth inside. The decorated holiday tree had been taken down leaving the dance hall seemingly more spacious. There were few people today with the looming prospect of a new work week. It was livelier on Saturdays than Sundays. But she had no desire to dance. It was enough to sit at a table and lean against the wall and watch a few couples sway to a simple melody, their silhouettes moving in the dim light, and the restful atmosphere in this tiny corner in the midst of the severe Ural winter.

"Excuse me. Would you like to dance?" An elegant, dark-haired young man bowed slightly to her with an expectant smile. He spoke with a slight accent, maybe Lithuanian or Latvian, which she found charming. Irina could not believe her eyes. What was such a polite and attentive young man, so different from the simple village boys, doing in this backwater?

"Yes, of course," she answered, unable to conceal her nervousness. She stood, perhaps a little too eagerly, and shyly accepted his hand, fearing her impulsiveness might scare off the stranger. It would not do for him to think she was one of those girls ready to pounce on any boy and attach herself to him from the first minute. No, she was nothing of the sort. His sexual attractiveness did not affect Irina – at least, she hoped so. But he was clearly someone of her sort, the kind of person she had hoped to meet in the forested wilderness.

The stranger took her in his arms and began to slowly circle the hall. Irina feared that he could sense the way her heart was racing. She suddenly, irrationally, wanted to tell him everything: about the limitations of Western schools of psychology some of which had too primitive an understanding of people and some of which exaggerated the importance of individualism. And about how she, Irina, had taken from each of them a bit that she could use in addition to the school of Soviet psychology. But instead, she had come up against the terrible world of the SPB, leaving her feeling she had betrayed the essence of her profession and herself. So much that she had repressed raged inside, and Irina wondered at how it seemed she had waited all this time for the slightest contact with someone who might understand.

Her head began to spin. In the embrace of the stranger she felt a special tenderness, and the aromas of wood and clay became so intoxicating that even the scent of a thousand flowers and the most expensive perfumes could not compete. Could all the smells and feelings of this world cover the freshness of the snow, the astringency of pine resin, and the heat of the hot stove? And in this small corner of the world, in the disarming simplicity of chintz dresses on the streets under heavy fur coats, Irina suddenly feared that her unexpected cavalier might turn out to be just another empty-headed Lothario who would have no interest in whatever she had to say. Sure, he might be of similar background, but who said he was like her? Why did she think he considered her an equal? He might think her a country girl he could have a good time with on a boring evening while on assignment. What if he took her for someone else, for a common, illiterate, flighty idiot who knew nothing of life apart from village dances?

These thoughts frightened Irina so much that she involuntarily pulled away from her partner. Catching her movement, he opened his arms. His hands fell away from her like a downy shawl falling from her shoulders, slightly brushing her skin. Irina smiled, nodded at a door and headed to it. The door led to an old reading room which had grown from a hut that served as a library. Later, when Medinskiy received settlement status and started to grow, other, newer libraries appeared. The room with a couple of tables, books and news bulletins on the walls with portraits of Lenin was dark. Sometimes modest couples came here for a kiss or young people might circle one of the tables to sing songs with a guitar. On Saturdays or holidays, when dances lasted long into the night, everyone served tea from thermoses. During the day, it was used by various circles from singing to knitting.

Fortunately, the room was empty now, with someone's boots drying on the radiator, probably they belonged to someone who had arrived late and found no space in the cloakroom. Irina switched on the light, amazed at her own boldness, and confirming that the young man had followed, firmly closed the door. She had not expected such chutzpah from herself. Taking an unfamiliar man to an empty room? What had she been thinking?

"I'm sorry..." she began, somewhat embarrassed, as she sat at one of the tables. "It just that I don't know you, and it was too noisy out there to talk. I've not seen you around here before, so I decided we should become better acquainted since we had danced together..."

She fell silent and blushed, mentally cursing herself for her awkwardness. Was she doing the right thing? Did this fit into his rules of decency? Where had he come from, and why had he approached her? Was a single dance enough to justify subjecting him to an interrogation? "You're a fool. After this, no one will ever ask you to dance again," she said to herself. What was it, really? The strange accent, the gallant manners? And because of this she decided that this man would understand what was important to her? What did she think she would do – tell him about psychology and psychiatry? Lord, she didn't even know his name. And she could have asked while they were dancing without getting him alone.

But it seemed he found nothing odd in her behavior. He looked around the room with interest and cast a slightly ironic glance at the portrait of Lenin. He sat down and said, "It's cozy in here."

"My name is Irina," like a Young Pioneer she extended her hand only too late realizing that a handshake would now just look stupid and yanked her hand back with another blush. When was the last time she went on a date with someone other than Misha? Only at the institute, but there it had been somehow easier, much easier.

"I'm Yurgis, Yurgis Gintaus. Just call me Yura," he smiled.

"Are you Latvian?"

"From Lithuania."

"I… I'm from Chelyabinskiy Oblast," she said. "If you want to dance some more we can go back. It was just unusual to see you here, and I wanted to find out who you are, but it was uncomfortable out there." She was repeating herself and decided to drop the subject. "This used to be a reading room with a library. But now it's a place for young people to relax. Sometimes they play the guitar or prepare club bulletins," she said, waving an arm at the walls.

"Club bulletins," he repeated with a look at the walls before turning back to her with a sly look. "Do you write them, too?"

"No. I don't often come in here." Her mind went blank. "There was so much work."

"So, where does such a charming girl work, if it's not a secret?" he asked with genuine interest.

"I work at the psikhushka, where I fill the lives of people with suffering and lead them to an animal-like existence. I have a fiancé, Misha, whom I do not love, and a girlfriend whom I cannot stand. I'm stupid and traitorous and have done nothing to change my life. I immediately understood that you could save me from all this, from myself. I wanted to pour out to you all sorts of nonsense because here there is no one else who could bear to hear it. But I won't tell you any of it because you would soon stand up and leave and go to your Lithuania while I remain here. And it would not be worth your while to give me any hope that things could be different."

She pronounced these words carefully, mentally beating the rhythm of each syllable and perfectly understood that she would not say any of it aloud. He remained silent, waiting for her answer.

"I'm a nurse," she said quietly.

"A fine profession," he nodded respectfully. "I'm a historian. I've always envied those who do something concrete. Makes no difference what it is – moving furniture or healing people. Your life has meaning, real usefulness. But I work with the past, with impersonal papers. But the past fascinates me. Silly, eh?"

"No," Irina felt as though her heart would stop. "No one knows what is best. A bad doctor could kill a patient, but a good historian can tell us about our life in a way no one else could. Are you here to research something?"

"No, I have a very personal connection here … But you could not possibly help. I won't bother you." He smiled broadly and glanced in the direction of the door. "We could have another dance if you're OK with it."

"Let's go," said Irina, slightly disappointed that he lacked confidence in her."

"Just one question," pronounced Yurgis as he stood. "Could you tell me what bus I take from the town center to the psychiatric hospital? If you know, of course."

"The 130." She grew cold, frozen to the spot.

"Thanks." The Lithuanian smiled again, but the smile was mixed with sadness. "Well, let's put a happy end on the evening, and tomorrow we'll go our own ways."

"Wait!" She had come to a decision and took his hand, holding him back. His fingers were cold despite the warmth of the room. "I'm sorry to be nosy about your business, but if you have someone close…" She hesitated. "They have fairly strict rules about visiting the patients."

"Wait." Yurgis seemed only now to understand something. "Do you mean to say that you work as a nurse there? For some reason I thought you were talking about a regular hospital … I really didn't know."

There was so much confusion and even guilt in his voice that Irina had no doubt he was telling the truth. Yurgis sat down again, uncertain of how to extract himself from an uncomfortable situation.

"I had no idea," he began. "And to think I walked right up to you… just a silly coincidence. For some reason I couldn't imagine you and such a gloomy place together."

"Don't worry. I believe you," muttered Irina, also taking a seat. She was experiencing a colossal sense of guilt. Why did everything have to happen like this? Why did the first man who had appealed to her in years have to be a relative of one of the patients she tormented?

Yurgis interrupted her painful silence. "It's my first time in this part of the world. I didn't know where to begin. I found the address and decided to go Monday morning. And, well, in my rush I forgot to find out the number of the bus. I came to the dance only ask someone about the route. Everyplace else is closed. I thought maybe I could find out at the station tomorrow, but it's so busy… I was afraid of losing time and missing the bus. I saw you, and … well, I sort of lost my head. I didn't want to ask you about anything, but you invited me in here, and we talked… I almost forgot. I didn't want to tell you why I was here…"

Irina was recovering from her embarrassment, "Don't worry," she said. After all, she could try to help him, and maybe somehow ease some of her chronic guilt.

"You say that even if I get there, they won't let me in?" asked Yurgis.

"Is it a friend or relative you have there?" she asked, adding, "A lot depends on this."

"A relative, a very close relative," replied Yurgis bitterly. "But the trouble is, I have no documents to prove it. I use my mother's family name... our father died recently. We have a common father. Shortly before his death, he found my mother. For the first time since my conception," the Lithuanian laughed mirthlessly. "I had never seen him before. He and my mother had an affair at the height of the war, in Autumn 1944 when Soviet troops entered the country. He already had a family, but you understand, no one on the frontlines at that time thought about this. I was born shortly after the victory.

"Me too," echoed Irina, grateful for his openness, even if involuntary. "Summer of forty-five."

"Me too," laughed Yurgis. "So, we're contemporaries? My father found us," he continued, "and told us that his legitimate son was a very smart and talented military engineer but ended up here without hope of returning. Soon after, father died. This is rather strange. I gained a father after I grew up and not long ago. But now I know I have a brother. It's important to me to see him if only one time, Ira. And the worst part is that he knows nothing of my existence. Even my father didn't know all the time. Only after he understood he would never see his son again, he began searching for my mother in hopes that she had become pregnant by him back then. I can't forgive him to this day for having no interest before that... But my brother has no guilt in this. The damned war – there were a million such stories. A common wartime romance ... I don't know what happened with him, but he is my older brother, Irina. I can't pretend not to know of his existence."

Irina felt as though her eyes overflowed with tears. This

was what brought this unusual man to Medinskiy. Why hadn't she thought of this immediately?

"What's your brother's name?" she asked.

"Lyosha. Aleksey Golubov. I don't think we look much alike."

"Yes, I know your brother." Irina hesitated. The military engineer. She knew only too well how strict his confinement had been. Volkova had even warned her about him, calling him a "dangerous prisoner." But could she tell his heartbroken relative?

"We have a visiting day for relatives," she began cautiously. "I can try to arrange a meeting for you. Normally, the names of patients permitted to see relatives are agreed with the Chief Medical Officer. But if I'm on duty that day I don't think it would be a terrible thing to just this once write out a permission slip for you to see Golubov. Meetings are normally on Saturday, and the Chief Medical Officer is rarely present. She gives the list to the duty nurse who writes out the passes and gives them to the guards. The guards take the relatives to the meeting room, make sure all is in order, and later escort them out. The orderlies bring the patients. If there is no incident during the meeting, no one checks anything later. I can try to retrieve your pass from the guards without notice.

"But you'll be taking a chance." Yurgis gave her an alarmed look.

"A little," she agreed, "but I'm planning to get out of this place soon, so ... why not leave a good deed behind?"

She was seized by a strange conviction bordering on recklessness. Hadn't she just this morning wished to change her life, even reproached herself for what she had become. And now as if in answer to her thoughts she had been given the chance to grant at least one victim of the SPB a morsel of happiness – a bit of news, a half-brother, the continuation of the blood and flesh of his dead father. She felt she would never forgive herself if she refused to help this handsome, dark-haired, gentle and a bit distracted man, which only added to his charm. Yurgis had seduced her with his attention, touching honesty, and concern for her well-being. This was the first time she had seen a real Lithuanian, and maybe because of this he seemed a little foreign, like a fairytale prince from another world.

"May I ask one more thing?? Yurgis leaned toward her studying her eyes. "Warn him about me, please. He doesn't even know he has a brother, and I don't know how he'll react."

"Yura, I..." she began. How could she tell this slender intellectual that Golubov more than likely would have no feelings about him for the simple reason that he could barely think under the influence of drugs.

"His condition is quite complicated," she carefully selected her words. "The hospital has a strict regime, very strict. Medications are required. The pills relieve stress and other symptoms, but ... there are certain effects ..."

"I understand." Yurgis leaned back in the wooden chair, and his previously bland expression became serious. "I'm not a child, Irina. I don't know what happened to my brother; I don't know what he did. But tell me frankly, does he still resemble a human being? Is he capable of speaking with me?"

Irina was filled with thick, painful shame. Guilt, like a fluid flooded her lungs and prevented her from breathing, poisoning her blood from within, turning it to fire.

"It depends on the medication." Her voice was hard, too, as she tried not to surrender to her burning conscience.

"Medications that *you* give him?" asked Yurgis.

This was fated to happen. What had she expected in such a situation? An invisible wall grew between them. She, Irina, was on one side of this wall, and her Lithuanian friend on the other with the prisoners. The very prisoners Yelena had taught her to hate...

"It's my job," she answered quietly.

"I understand completely," he sighed and rose. "In any case, thanks for your warning. But if Aleksey can't even speak with me, there is no point in the meeting. Why should you take a risk for nothing?"

"Evening and morning," she said quietly.

"What? Excuse me?"

"He won't be given his evening dose Friday or his morning dose Saturday. I'll do it for you. You'll be able to talk."

"How can I thank you, Ira?" Yurgis' look told her he was impressed, and maybe embarrassed over his recent unspoken reproach.

"It's nothing," she answered drily. "You dance beautifully and provided a wonderful evening. Consider me thanked. Where are you staying? Do you have a telephone? How can I get in touch with you to let you know if I'm successful in setting things up?"

"I don't have a phone," said Yurgis. "Let's meet Friday evening after your shift. Just tell me where, and I promise to be there."

"I'll write the address. It's the new library. It's normally closed Saturdays but is open Fridays. The locals seldom go there other than small schoolchildren. We'll meet Friday at six, and I'll tell you everything. The library closes at eight."

"I owe you." Yurgis stood and bestowed her a smile of gratitude.

"Next time bring a few cans of Lithuanian sprats," joked Irina. "But remember, only one meeting. Do you understand?"

"Of course." He nodded his understanding and then smiled at her so warmly and benignly that Ira felt her guild-weighted heart rise to the starry, winter Ural sky...

Chapter 12

If there existed somewhere on earth a place more depressing that Medinskiy it was the village of Malakhovo. At least this was Patrick's thought as soon as he arrived there. Surely, the road to a bright Communist future should at least have some streetlights. However, in the absence of anything resembling a road, the absence of streetlights was completely logical.

"You should be happy that you came in winter. In spring there is such flooding that there is no way you can get here. The pools sometimes last until the first snow," said the owner of the safehouse, Nikolay Ivanovich Kondratyev, upon his arrival. Patrick thought the old man bore a remarkable resemblance to the way Russians are depicted in Western cartoons – shaggy beard, faded padded jacket, *shapka* with earflaps, and felt boots. Only a balalaika and a bear were missing. But he was far from a caricature. From under the *shapka* the old man studied the American with clever, piercing eyes filled with profound sorrow. Sorrow had attached itself to Nikolay Ivanovich's soul. His every move, his every glance carried with it a suggestion of pain, and it was uncomfortable to be so close to such pain. Patrick stared at him mutely.

"Just call me Uncle Kostya," the agent continued. "Don't concern yourself with the way I look: I live like everyone else and try not to look any different. I live alone, and no one visits me, so you'll be safe. You speak Russian, don't you?" he asked as an afterthought.

"Yes, of course," Patrick suddenly found his tongue. "Don't worry. I'll try not to embarrass you. I only have to meet with someone a few times."

"Your Russian is good," said the old man. "But around here you'll arouse attention. We don't have many visitors here from the Union's western republics."

"I understand."

They had barely passed through the gate when a dog lunged at him barking loudly. Patrick involuntarily recoiled as the huge animal got nearer, but then he noticed it was restrained by a long chain.

"Don't be afraid. She can't reach you," said Uncle Kolya as he calmed the dog. "*Druzhok*, sit. This is a friend, *Druzhok*."

Druzhok? This meant "friend" in Russian and seemed to Patrick to be particularly inappropriate for such a vicious beast, which now whined in resentment before barking a last time. He didn't return to the kennel but stretched out on the ground and watched Patrick until he and Uncle Kolya climbed onto the porch and disappeared inside the house.

The old bachelor's hut was small, but cozy. It had two rooms, one of which served as a kitchen while the other did double duty as living room and bedroom, separated by a curtain. The hut's windows were small and low and allowed little light inside.

"Not exactly what you're used to in America, eh?" said Kondratyev with a slightly guilty glance around.

"No," admitted Patrick, and decided to ask the question which had troubled him the whole way here. "Uncle Kolya, it it's not a secret, why didn't you stay with our troops? When they freed you in Berlin... would it have been possible?"

"This, Yurgis, is one of those things you regret your whole life," sighed the old man. "It's the way it is, when for the single, solitary time in your life a possibility presents itself, a single chance, and if you don't take advantage of it, you'll never see another. A day doesn't go by that I don't return to that moment. And the funny thing is, when I relive it, I remember why

I did what I did. I couldn't leave then, I just couldn't. Russia was my homeland. I wasn't prepared to turn my back on her. I was born before there was a Soviet Union. Now, of course, after the hell we've lived through, after the camps, after everything I've learned and seen, I would have. But who needs me now? But then, I'd gone through the entire war dreaming of home and the comforting thought that I would return there. I had nothing then besides my native land, nothing, at all. I loved her and wanted nothing more. If I had abandoned her then, I would probably be quite a different person – worse than now. Now, such a step would be justified, but then it would have been shameful. I was a soldier, I'd taken an oath, and I was an officer. And so, I preferred stupidity to shame. I did what I thought was right. Maybe it's hard for you to understand."

"No," replied Patrick. "it's not."

"It's a vicious circle, isn't it?" the old man laughed mirthlessly. "If I had known then what I know now about the cursed Soviets, I would have left with barely a thought, and it would have been the right decision. It's paradoxical, isn't it? I know that at the time my conduct was correct, but all the same, I can't forgive myself for it."

Patrick remained silent. There was nothing he could say. But he understood how fortunate he was. He didn't have to choose between what was best and his country because they were one and the same. He did not envy those confronted by such an inescapable choice for which there was no right decision. This broken old man was guilty only of having been born in such a country as Russia, and Patrick could not offer him exfiltration. Uncle Kolya was right – no one in America needed him now.

"Let me fix you some dinner." Kondtratyev broke the silence. "I have some eggs."

Patrick had no doubt. Throughout his travels to get here, he had become convinced of one thing: if there was enough of anything in Russia, it was eggs. To avoid attention at airports, he'd made most of the journey by train and had learned to regret it. Narrow bench seats, loud snoring throughout the night, constant noise, and the odor of the toilets that filled the whole car – he'd had enough of this Soviet exoticism. Apparently, the collectivist way of life that was to lead to a celestial Communist society was well on its way.

And after several days' travel, the train car had become a small commune. Children raced through the aisle, in one compartment someone produced a bottle of vodka, and anyone who wanted to join in crowded around. Those with better luck with their fellow passengers conducted long conversations and laid out their simple food for all: smoked chicken, dripping fat onto copies of "Pravda" that served as wrapping, black bread, withered cucumbers and invariably boiled eggs with blue yolks.

Patrick prudently bought several cans of sprat in Moscow, thinking it would help him pass as Lithuanian, and his fellow passengers happily took their share, offering cold eggs in return. No one wanted the eggs, and they lay spoiling on the table, rolling against the glasses. Out the window lay endless forests and fields, flickering as they passed. He was amazed at how, on one hand, the Russian countryside was so like the American, and on the other quite different. Unlike his native Montana, Russian forests did not inspire thoughts of grandeur, but gave a sense of long neglect, sadness, and desolation.

In the American countryside with all its naturalness, there was always some man-made beauty. It was unobtrusive, but decorated every detail of the landscape, bringing it nearer to perfection. Each cherry tree, each stone-lined front garden, a tastefully conceived flower bed and trimmed trees in his home country reflected the residents' care for the land on which they lived. Such manmade details did not spoil the greatness of nature but framed it like precious stones.

In Russia, the land seemed abandoned and lonely, repulsively wild, although at times the breadth of fields laid out on squares with wooden houses at their edges fascinated with their innocence. The closer the train approached the Urals, the more often snow appeared outside the window, and finally the weather turned to winter before his eyes, as if in these parts January ruled year-round. Patrick was getting closer to his goal.

"Uncle Kolya, I have a small favor to ask," began Patrick after dinner, having delicately rebuffed the old man's offer of eggs. "There is someone I need to check out, a girl. But, as you said, I would stand out here. It's a small settlement where everyone knows everyone else, and if I start asking questions about her, someone is likely to tell her about it."

"Quite right," nodded the old man. "Don't worry about it. What girl is it?"

"She's a nurse at the SPB. Her name is Irina. I don't know her last name, but everyone calls her 'Irochka.' According to our source, she was the nicest person in the facility, so I think it best to begin with her. I need to know where she lives, what she does in her time off, where she goes, her private life – in other words, those opportunities that might present themselves to initiate personal contact. It would be great if I had a photo of her."

"That's a complicated task," Uncle Kolya rubbed his chin. "I know a few of the boys. Some of them are former prisoners, and some the children of the exiled Volga Germans. They are trustworthy. The Soviets were so hard on their families that they simply hate them. A while back they organized a sort of 'band of avengers' and robbed collective farm management and Party bureaucrats. I nipped it in the bud, but the Militia got interested in them, and some of them turned to real crime. This was after I retired and cut contact with you. I had no access to anything important, so why stay in contact? Then I tried to help these youngsters. I thought I had nothing to lose. Things calmed down after a while, but I'm still in touch with a couple of them. They're common village boys, but I think they could get away with finding something out about your Irochka. Every village has a club where the youngsters dance, and they will know if she goes there, whether she has a boyfriend ... Such things get around. Of course, I'll tell them nothing about you, and they won't ask any questions."

"Thank you." Patrick was truly grateful "You're a champ."

"And what do they call you, Yurgis?" The old man's question was unexpected, and in his eyes momentarily appeared a crafty glint.

"Yurgis Gintaus," repeated Patrick with a wide smile and the same crafty look.

"Understood," Nikolay Ivanovich quietly laughed. "Probably something like Mike or John. Am I close?"

It took three days to gather the information on Irina, and Patrick learned she had been assigned here from Sverdlovsk, rented a room near the bus station, had been going out with a boy called Mikhail Yegorov, and attended dances. She seemed to be a normal Soviet girl from a small provincial town.

Patrick decided the simplest approach would be to begin with the dances. If that failed, he would try the bus station where he would wait for her to return from work when she would not be in a rush and pretend he had just arrived in Medinskiy. He had a more complicated third alternative: start a friendship with Mikhail, hook up with a girl and go to the movies or the dances with them. But this plan was too time consuming, and it would seem odd that an anxious younger brother would be starting a romance instead of trying to see his imprisoned relative. So, that left the dances or the bus station.

He devised two courses of action, depending on whether Misha was in the club or not. Best of all would be if Misha were not there, Patrick would play it by ear. He would invite Irina to dance in hopes of making an impression on her. His natural charm never let him down. The girl had a higher education, so the image of a shy intellectual in sharp contrast with the village youth seemed the most likely to succeed.

He would not say a word about his reason for being there and pretend he was interested in her. He would ask if he could walk her home and, on the way, ask how to get to the psychiatric hospital, as though the question had just occurred to him. He would have to do this when they were half-way there so she would not be able to avoid the question. The plan would develop from there. Should she reveal where she worked, he would pretend surprise, embarrassment, and tell his story convincingly. Should the girl be reticent, he would ask her out again. This would have to be done right before they parted ways so that any mention of the SPB would seem to be a separate matter.

To his amazement and relief, everything turned out to be easier than he could have imagined. Irina herself out of the blue invited him to the dusty room right after their first dance. The room was badly maintained, like everything in the Soviet Union, smelling of drying boots, cheap tea, and hot clay with the bearded, Octobrist profile of Lenin displayed proudly on the wall. He was accustomed to seeing this profile in the most unexpected places. Lenin seemed to observe the all-encompassing wretchedness with satisfaction, ensuring that his life's work was successfully put into practice.

When Irina silently nodded at the door of the former reading room, Patrick mentally prepared himself for a kiss or unplanned sex. But the Soviet girl was the embodiment of communist chastity, and the American belatedly remembered that there was no sex in the USSR. It took him a moment to understand that Irina was shy and complicated and behaved accordingly. He was even pleased. He'd never resorted to the bedroom in his work and did not like the method because he considered it cheap and immoral. He liked the intellectual approach, attuned to the nature and psychiatric type of the target.

Clearly, she liked him. So, he had to overcome her reticence and create rapport. After a few meaningless words and some thoughtful comments, Patrick realized that the girl yearned for intellectual conversation. From then on, the American did not doubt that he would succeed. It was just important not to frighten the prey.

Following the question about the psychiatric hospital, Patrick decided to take a chance and pretended to end the conversation so they could return to the dance. If that tactic were unsuccessful, he had no doubt that he could find a pretext to return to the subject later. But there was no need. Irina pursued the subject and convinced him she was on the level. The rest was just technique.

Irina kept her word and appeared at the library on Friday. She confirmed that he could come to the SPD the following morning to see Golubov.

"But there be only one visit," she warned him again.

"Of course," Patrick agreed. But he knew he would have to convince Irina to arrange more meetings. By then he was 70 percent certain she would agree.

"Irina, how and where can I find you after the visit?" he asked. "I must thank you for everything you're doing. And I'd like to discuss how the visit with my brother went."

She was obviously flattered by his trust.

"My landlady gets upset when I bring a visitor home," she replied with some embarrassment. "But we can meet at the 'Hedgehog' restaurant. It's behind the supermarket. Do you know it? I can see you early on Sunday, around four P.M. when I have more time. Will you tell me about Lithuania?" She suddenly posed the question with childlike naiveté.

"Whatever you like," he promised. He wondered why they seemed to like hedgehogs as much as eggs in the Soviet Union.

Now, back from their meeting, sitting near the dark window of Uncle Kolya's hut, the American caught himself thinking about Irina. His conscience was clear. He did what he had to do. He could avoid any romantic entanglement and keep the relationship platonic. Patrick had no sympathy for anyone working at an SPB, which he likened to a German concentration camp. But Irina did not seem to be a bad person. She felt guilty about where she worked, and that guilt could be manipulated. But, in truth, he felt pity for her, pity mixed with that sense of responsibility so familiar to any CIA officer. It was his professional duty to minimize any risk to this girl, but he knew how very little it would depend on him.

Through the window he could hear the unlovable *Druzhok* whimper from time to time from somewhere in the yard where the hens roosted in the chicken house. He was mentally going over the questions he would pose to Golubov the next day, and thoughts of the danger to Irina were pushed to back of his mind. He was worried about what was to come, fully aware of how much hinged on it. Was it possible that tomorrow's meeting in a chilling prison hospital in a snow-covered Ural village at the edge of the world could alter the course of history and prevent the nuclear destruction of the planet? Who knew how much really depended on his meeting with this psychiatric hospital patient?

During his initial years with the CIA Patrick suddenly realized something he had never considered before. The world which had seemed so simple and one-dimensional in childhood contained endless possibilities, alternate realities that border one another closely in ways invisible to man. Only he and his colleagues knew of the existence of these possibilities while most saw only that which touched their daily lives. The world is blind and unaware that without the efforts of hundreds and thousands of unknown people, terrible things could come to pass. Now, the world was heading toward oblivion with no warning to its blithe inhabitants, while only a few heeded the small clues and felt the hot breath of the hidden threat bearing down on them.

A war not unleashed. No thundering explosion. Myriad deaths avoided. Millions of people took this for granted, without the slightest suspicion that everything could be different. And only Patrick saw how the wheel of fate turned daily and set into motion the gears of delicate mechanisms as one possibility took the place of another to determine the course of history. Revelation of Soviet missile defense plans could demonstrate the futility of the nuclear arms race and the frenzy for mutual destruction, and possibly prevent a nuclear war. Could there be anything more important and nobler than this? Tomorrow he would do everything possible to ensure that millions of people could live in peace.

Chapter 13

This was not a hospital, but a prison – a real Soviet camp, the sinister GULAG of which so much was heard. Now all the terrifying power, soaked with the blood of millions of suffering people, became real for him as he stood before the high walls topped with barbed wire, in the barren courtyard sandwiched between them with mute guard towers at the corners overlooking this dreary place with thin communications cables between them, like ivy crawling along the walls. Patrick shuddered involuntarily at the sight of this merciless, inescapable machine. He, an American, a staff officer of the CIA, now walked voluntarily into a Soviet concentration camp and heard the heavy gate clang shut behind him, cutting him off from freedom.

The guard glowered at him with contempt, as though he were a pestering insect, and drily demanded his documents. Patrick handed him the passport, the Soviet passport of Yurgis Gintaus, and looked the guard square in the face – without excessive insolence, but also without fear, calmly and respectfully so as to offer no provocation. The man at the checkpoint looked so long and hard at the documents that Patrick became concerned, but at last he produced a piece of paper that contained the handwritten Lithuanian name, brought out a hand stamp and pressed it with a bang to the paper hard enough to shake the counter. The American took the pass, wondering that the wooden counter could endure such attacks every time a pass was stamped, and finally entered on of the worst places in this country.

Several people already were milling about at the entrance. They looked worn out and unhappy, but still hopeful as they waited to meet with their loved ones. Separated from the real world by two fences - external and internal - they avoided conversation among themselves, united by a common, unstated grief. The sky matched the color of the walls - gray and gloomy, lowering over the psychiatric hospital like a lead ceiling. But even here Patrick was buoyed by the invisible strength of his country.

He composed himself and banished emotion - the way he normally prepared for an operation. In this mode his thoughts came clear and fast, reducing his world to a black and white chessboard. Only ends and means existed in this reality, targets and resources, problems and resolutions, and each step had a specific reason and purpose. Gestures, looks, words, the smallest intonation - all were dictated by the goal, implanted in his mind. This gave him strength, flexibility; by strength of will he suppressed all fear and doubt, which permitted him to view the worst places as little more than different parts of a labyrinth, part of a puzzle that must be solved. At such times his professionalism became almost physical - cold calculation, sharpened senses, control of a fluid situation, the constant search for the optimal reaction.

His task was great, and he had memorized all the questions - bringing a written list with him would have been suicide - and now he again and again mentally reviewed them. Of course, he must get the details of everything concerning the missiles, their launch, guidance mechanism, and destructive capacity. Some of the questions came from the Pentagon which was especially interested in the construction of the A-350zh anti-missile defense system, its velocity and maneuverability characteristics, angle of launch and guidance. Including, of course, the make-up and characteristics of the military unit. Separately, the military was interested in the composition and characteristics of the on-board equipment and missile launcher, the characteristics of the detection and tracking radar stations and the algorithms for generating control commands. Some of the questions concerned the ability of the A-35 system to hit ballistic targets with multiple warheads, as well as how it counteracted interference and false targets.

The CIA was more interested in anything concerning the developers of the missiles, the design bureaus, manufacturers, and test sites. It was very important to find out the time and place of the of the installation of anti-ballistic missiles for combat duty, and preferably information about military personnel. Patrick understood that an engineer who had not been involved in missile defense activities for two years might not have all the answers, and yet he hoped that Golubov retained some essential knowledge from his work during the developmental stage.

But something else concerned him: the amount of damage wrought by the medications. Had he understood who he was going to meet when Irina told him about the appearance of his "brother?" Would he believe Patrick was who he said he was and not a KGB provocateur?

After a time, a young man in uniform appeared out of the building and took them inside to a large hall where the patients waited. Patrick searched for the face from the photo of Aleksey Golubov they had shown him at the CIA – the same photo that at one time had hung on the board of honor at the Moscow scientific research institute. With some difficulty he recognized him in a gaunt man with trembling hands and an unhealthy yellowish complexion suggesting liver problems. A wave of sympathy momentarily engulfed him, penetrating the armor of his professionalism. He approached and quietly addressed the patient.

"Aleksey?"

The man flinched with the look of a hunted animal – a

look that might be pregnant with meaning – and took a step towards a long table at which other patients were already sitting with their relatives. Without a word, they sat in the corner away from prying ears.

Golubov remained silent, staring at his visitor from under his brows.

"We were told you wanted to contact us," Patrick began cautiously. "Our common friend, Viktor Butko. He gave us part of your materials, and I assure you that they are of great value. I would say tremendous value."

"I don't understand what you're talking about," said Golubov in a dry voice. Clearly, he did not believe him. It was obvious that the scientist was lucid, and Patrick approvingly noted that Irina had kept her word and not medicated him. A hunter's instinct replaced his momentary sympathy. Patrick felt that he must at any price wrest the truth from this unfortunate man.

"Aleksey Matveevich, we don't have much time, and I'm taking a great risk. Believe me, the KGB would not do all this, considering where you are. They don't need courts and proof to make the people in this place disappear forever. Had the documents you gave Butko fallen into their hands, they would have killed you. But you had some luck – Viktor made it to the United States and immediately told us of your request. Your information was valuable, but we need more. And what we need is so important that it brought me here."

Golubov stared mutely at his face until something like long-delayed joy sparked in his eyes.

"You're taking a real risk," he began. "And your Russian is very good."

"Aleksey Matveevich," Patrick gently but with quiet insistence got to business. "Right now, our countries are engaged in negotiations regarding the limitation of anti-missile defense. But it's complicated because the Soviet Union denies it's working in this area and insists that the USA is too aggressive. You understand that it is impossible to reach agreement on the limitation of certain programs if a country denies their existence. Your leadership demands that we make serious concessions while they make none. The negotiations are heading for a stalemate. Of course, thanks to your information our side can be more certain and force the Soviet Union to live up to its obligations."

"Or, at worst, it is important that you know how to counter this system should the negotiations remain stalemated?" Golubov's lips twisted into a sour smile.

It seemed incredible, but this Russian apparently cared for his country even after all it had done to him. The American felt nothing for Russia: neither love nor hatred. She was an external threat – an ominous and dangerous one, which had to be neutralized. Emotion was a detriment in this business. He was interested in Russian culture, in her people – it was easy to admire some of the qualities of Soviet citizens. But it didn't matter when it came to defending his own country. It would be pointless and disrespectful to lie to Golubov about his priorities, so he answered with as much diplomacy and candor as he could.

"I do not hope for the destruction of millions of innocent people, regardless of their nationality. No one in their right mind wants that. So, together we must do everything possible to prevent a stalemate in the negotiations. Don't forget that it was you who came to us."

Golubov nodded and without wasting more time began: "Construction of sites for the A35 system with A-350zh were begun in 1962 and completed while I was still working in 1967. I was part of it all. At first it was planned to expand eighteen 'Yenisey 8' launch complexes with eight launchers each. True, the projects were substantially reduced. Tests of the first line A-35 system were planned for this March. You must understand, I don't know if they were successful, but in the event that no deficiencies were found in the system, they should have been put into service in the same year – at least that was written in the plans."

"As far as we know, the missiles were tested," said Patrick in a quiet voice. "That's why we have questions for you about them..."

Three hours later, Patrick Corn impatiently paced the trodden snow around the "Hedgehog" café as he waited for Irina, doing his best to contain his excitement. Golubov's information was so valuable that the American was ready to hurry through impassable snowdrifts to Uncle Kolya's hut so he could contact Headquarters. But the communications link would not be available until dark, and now he had other no less important business – to convince Irina to set up more meetings with the engineer, and especially not to medicate him.

That one meeting would not be enough had been clear from the outset. The scientist could recall some information immediately, but some he would have to exhume from deeper memories, and that would take time. The American did not doubt that, now armed with the questions, Golubov would be able to reconstruct important pieces of the overall picture, especially if his mind were not fogged daily by the effects of anti-psychotics. The engineer would be able to make notes for their next meeting, and then Patrick would try to set up a deaddrop with Headquarters. In the worst case, he could always ask Kondratyev to go to Moscow and make the drop...

His mind was filled with plans, and blood pounded in his temples. He was ripping important information out of the very heart of the Soviet GULAG in the midst of oppressive suffering and torture. But it was too soon to congratulate himself – there were long weeks of high-pressure work ahead with ever-increasing risk of discovery. He scanned the area for the thousandth time fearing surveillance. Despite the cold, he felt hot. It was not the first time working in intelligence that he did not try to suppress his emotions. He understood that feelings should not be avoided, but rather embraced for inspiration. Patrick knew he could divert his passion to other uses.

"Sorry, I'm late!" Irina rushed toward him, wrapped in a short, fur coat. Her tender face, big eyes, light brown hair, the snowflakes on her collar, the confused smile at their first meeting. A grand Soviet girl unaware of his true identity. Patrick's operational coolness returned combined with recent emotions to form a dangerous mixture ideal for creating the most subtle, believable lies.

They went inside the classic Soviet café, its walls covered with drawings of smiling hedgehogs that seemed to be completely satisfied with life in Medinskiy. The menu was sparse: sausage, fresh salad, vinaigrette, soup of a suspiciously unattractive color, potato puree with a cutlet, weak tea and compote.

"The sausages are best," confided Irina. "And the salad is OK. The tea is tasteless, but the compote is palatable."

When they were seated at a rectangular table with a blue, unattractive surface that looked like it belonged in an institution, Irina finally asked the question.

"So, how was the meeting with your brother?"

She was tense, and Patrick understood immediately that the success of his operation depended on his answer.

"I don't know how to thank you..." he began with feeling. "He understood where I came from and believed who I am. It's so strange to find a brother as an adult. We had so much to say to one another. I wanted to know about my father most of all..." his voice faltered.

"Did Golubov tell you about him?"

"Just a little," he answered guiltily. "There was so little time."

Irina said nothing. She opened her purse and rummaged through it to find a crumpled piece of white paper. Patrick immediately recognized it – his pass into the SPB. "I was able to retrieve it from the trash with no one noticing, and I replaced the list of today's visitors, too. There is no trace of Yurgis Gintaus having visited the hospital." Her words were bitter, as if she were talking about herself instead of the hospital. This did not escape Patrick's notice, and he decided to pursue the topic.

"I'll return to Lithuania soon, and there no trace of me will be left behind in Medinsky. My brother will die slowly here, and I'll never see him again. I counted the minutes today and wished for only one thing – that our meeting might never end. His every word was unbelievably meaningful."

He wasn't lying. Golubov's every word was, indeed, unbelievably meaningful. It was possible that even Golubov did not fully appreciate their value.

"Traces of you will remain here," said Irina. "I will never forget our meeting at the club."

"I didn't ask if you were married," he said with a slight smile.

"I have a fiancé," she answered and impulsively added, "But I don't love him."

"Then why…?"

She didn't answer, but asked him instead, "Are you married?"

"No, and I don't have a fiancée either."

"I'm getting out of here soon," added Irina. "They assigned me here to intern after I graduated, and my three years are up soon. I'm thinking about looking for work in Sverdlovsk. But do you think I might have success in Lithuania? I was trained as a psychiatrist. Do you think it would be hard to find a place to live and work in Vilnius?"

"I've never had anything to do in that area. I couldn't even suggest anything." This was slightly alarming. The conversation wasn't going according to plan. "But the city is certainly charming."

"Yes, so I've heard, but I've never been there. My parents and I never travelled anywhere besides the Crimea and Kislovodsk." Irina looked at him with disarming naiveté. "Yurgis, tell me about Lithuania."

He was ready for this question. Over two months he had mastered the local geography, scenic places, and folk legends. He had planned that when things got to this point, he would tell her a few lovely Lithuanian stories, and he had several to choose from. But now he could think of nothing except the story of Aigle, the queen of the snakes. No, this fairytale was too risky, and despite its allegories, too close to the truth of his own secret. But he had to say something deep and meaningful, something that would lead Irina to give him just one more meeting with Golubov.

"In the western reaches of Lithuania is the city of Palanga, on the shore of the Baltic," he began. "It is a well-known resort now. There is a botanical garden, and in it a sculpture of Antinis, 'Aigle, queen of the snakes.' I saw it for the first time in 1960. Have you heard the legend of Aigle? In Russian, her name is El'."

"No, I've not. Tell me!" Irina was spellbound.

"The three daughters of a peasant were bathing in a lake. When they came out on shore, the youngest one, the most beautiful, Aigle, saw a snake coiled on her dress. The oldest sister tried to shoo it away, but the snake suddenly spoke to Aigle in a human voice. He said he had fallen in love with her and demanded that she promise to marry him. The girl had to agree. At home, her parents tried to hide Aigle from the snake's messengers, and instead of sending the girl, they sent various animals dressed in veils, but each time the deception was detected. Aigle had to leave her home. On the banks of the lake she was amazed to find a handsome prince named Gilvinas. He said that only she could see his true nature while everyone else saw only a snake..."

"She got lucky," smiled Irina with a tender look at him.

"Aigle fell in love with the prince, married him and had three sons: Ažuolas, which in Lithuanian means "oak", Wasis, or, in Russian, ash, Berzhas – birch, and a daughter, Drebule, which means aspen," he continued. "She did not think of her own home until the children asked about their grandmother and grandfather. Then she asked her husband to permit her to see her parents. Gilvinas very reluctantly gave his permission but asked that she and the children remain with her parents not longer than nine days and insisted that she should not tell her parents his name. Her parents greeted her with joy. But her brothers did not wish to let their sister return to the snake and began to pry out of the children the name of their father."

"And what did the children do?" asked Irina. She listened to the story as if she were a child: interested, immersed in the subject as though he were talking about real people.

"Despite severe threats the boys did not give Gilvinas away, but the little daughter of Aigle was frightened that her uncles would tie her to a tree in the forest and leave her for the animals to eat and told them everything. That same night, the brothers lured the prince to the shore and cut him into pieces. When Aigle returned to the lake and called out for her husband, bloody foam appeared in the waves, and she realized that Gilvinas was dead. She heard the voice of her husband who told her what the evil people had done and that their daughter was responsible. Aigle cursed her daughter who changed into a trembling aspen. Aigle herself became a spruce, and her sons, an oak, an ash, and a birch... in short, this story is about how important it is to keep other people's secrets," Patrick concluded.

"I don't have children yet," Irina replied seriously, "but as for me, I won't give you away, Yurgis, or is your real name Gilvinis?"

He laughed quietly and changed the subject.

"You are so nice... Irina, I don't like that you must work in this damned place. But I know that for people like me, you are our only hope. And for the prisoners, too. You are the only person able to ease their suffering. But it's too much for you. Do you understand what I'm saying?"

She gave him a look full of classical Soviet fear, the way citizens of the "socialist paradise" react when someone touches one of those forbidden topics that everyone knows, but no one dares mention. The silence stretched out, loaded with fear and embarrassment – all of which betrayed the fact that Irina understood the dark side of her work. This was the moment to win her cooperation regardless of how unpleasant it might be for Patrick.

"My brother is perfectly healthy. You know he is."

She hung her head.

"I asked him what had happened. He said he had only expressed some doubt about the need to increase the number of lethal weapons in a conversation with his superior. That's all he did. And you see how he paid for it."

"I can't help him, Yura." Her voice was strained, and her eyes filled with tears.

"I know. You've already done more than enough," said Patrick. If she didn't suggest another meeting with Golubov, he would have to ask her directly. He hoped she would get the idea.

"Do you want to see your brother again?" She read his thoughts.

"Is it even possible?" He was incredibly pleased.

"Well," Irina smiled again and shrugged her shoulders in surrender. "At least this means you'll be here a little longer."

"We can meet again." It was half-statement, half-question.

"Do you really want to?" She looked straight into his eyes. He withstood her examination and answered as convincingly as possible. "More than you can possibly imagine."

He could not help but see how her eyes overflowed with joy.

He escorted her home, parting with her at the entrance. He tasted bitterness, as though he had swallowed poison with the compote. But the American understood that the meal he had consumed had nothing to do with what he felt. He had first experienced the idea of how poisonous his own words could be during his first overseas tour in Poland in the mid-60's. That first lie ignited an unaccustomed fire in his heart, producing a slight nausea and dizziness. But he thought he had inured himself against it. So, what had changed now?

Maybe during the time spent at CIA Headquarters he had become accustomed to honesty and forgotten how to lie? Or was it the purity and disarming credulousness of the Soviet girl? No matter how hard he tried, Patrick could not escape a sense of guilt concerning Irina. He told himself it was not his fault, given the circumstances. He had not forced this nice, Soviet girl to commit crimes for the Soviet regime. The merciless and hateful communist system had turned yesterday's student into an unwilling executioner. Those to blame were the ones who sent her here, those who placed a syringe full of anti-psychotics in her hand, who were the reason for her eternal, chronic feeling of shame.

"At least I'm helping her shed some guilt by doing something redeeming, something good. Without me, she would just be another one of them," Patrick said to himself. But the bitterness did not go away. He went through the motions of checking for surveillance, but his thoughts returned to Irina. He would be home soon with Uncle Kolya and late that night would contact Headquarters as planned. But, strangely enough, his former enthusiasm had dissipated. He was just doing his job, and who ever said it would be easy?

Chapter 14

December always brought to Medinskiy frost and the familiar Winter melancholy in anticipation of long, dark, and cold months. The melancholy was mostly from a sense of despair that grew with each day. It had been nearly six months since Major Rakhmanov's visit to the SPB, but nothing in Yelena's life had changed. The spark of hope which had appeared so bright and tangible had faded without a trace, and her existence which had shone so clearly in its glow now grew dark. It was as if an alluring, blinding, and unusually beautiful light had for a moment pierced her gray village life and detested job, flashed and cast a treacherous spark into her heart and then disappeared somewhere beyond her reach.

Yelena once again felt like the little girl standing at the window throughout the long winter evenings waiting for her mother. They had told her many times that her mother was dead and would never come, but Yelena would not cease her vigil watching the snowflakes sparkle in the light of the streetlamps. Her mother came later, when Yelena had finally lost hope.

Hope for nothing! This was the lesson she learned from childhood, but she had broken her own rule and permitted the Chekist from the capital to create an illusion of hope that this time it would be different. This illusion until now had simmered somewhere in the depths of her frozen soul, and now, left to herself, she found the small calling card with the telephone number – her pass to a new life. She told herself that she must not use it unless she had something serious that might truly interest Rakhamov. But there had been nothing, at least until recently.

The inhabitants of Medinskiy in hopes of somehow injecting some color into their severe winter began preparations for the New Year celebration early, saved their money for oranges and went to Sverdlovsk to buy presents. There was no one to whom Yelena would give a present, but in mid-December she was stunned to learn that Irina had broken up with Misha.

Unable to pretend any longer, she cried out angrily when Irina confirmed the news. "What have you done, you fool?"

"I just couldn't do it, Yelena, can't you understand? I don't love him. I don't want to ruin both our lives."

"So, why did you encourage him for so long? Why didn't you turn him down immediately?"

"I tried... I really tried to love him, and it even seemed that I had succeeded. But when he proposed I realized I couldn't do it."

Irina paused with an expression of guilt mixed with some sort of unexplained horror as the realization hit her. "You like him?"

Yelena wasn't prepared to admit anything. Yes, once she had liked Misha, but over time she had stopped thinking about him. But it was unbearable to think that she had been prepared to let him go without a fight, to sacrifice her own passion in favor of an unfamiliar and ungrateful city creature. And now her gesture had been in vain. The coquette from Sverdlovsk had played with Misha for a couple of years and cast him away like a doll which no longer interested her. It was unbearable.

"So, whey did you insist that I go with him?" asked Irina, no longer able to bear the long silence.

"Because I wanted you, you idiot, to be happy. But I see that you are incapable of it," hissed Yelena through her teeth.

"But I will be happy," Irina answered softly. "We just have different ideas of happiness, can't you understand? You can't find your own happiness through someone else's, you just can't. Misha is your happiness, your fate. Mine is something else entirely. I should have understood this from the beginning. I'm the guilty one, I know. But I hoped it would somehow work out... And I didn't know that you liked him. You never let on..."

"You have no idea what happiness is to me or what fate has in store," said Yelena, her jaw clenched. "Now get out of my sight."

They avoided one another after this, but one day Yelena heard a rumor: Irina was seeing some handsome, black-haired fellow, clearly not a local, and they had been seen together several times. Oh, the whore! Then Yelena thought of her conversation with Rakhmanov and how she, at the risk of losing the KGB officer's interest, had protected Irina and told the Chekist that she had not reported the repentant prisoner only out of ignorance and inexperience. Maybe her honesty had given the Major the impression that she was a gullible simpleton incapable of recognizing a potential enemy. And so, even if Yelena could not conceive of Irina as a real enemy, she could have demonstrated to the visitor her readiness to always be alert. Irina from Sverdlovsk had no idea what Yelena had done for her and would not have appreciated it any more than she could appreciate anything else.

Overcome with blind rage, Yelena waited until Irina made her usual rounds before searching her personal locker in the office. She had no idea what she was looking for – a photo of the mysterious, dark-haired man, letters from home, whatever. Yelena was almost certain that a girl like Irina could never be seditious. She simply wanted to know how the object of her smoldering hatred lived and breathed, with whom she was meeting, whom she had chosen over the best man in Medinskiy. In the depths of her soul she hoped to find forbidden literature, *samizdat,* or suspicious poetry – anything that would provide an excuse to call the magic number and correct the stupid, sentimental sacrifice she had made six months ago. Yelena did not find among Irina's things forbidden manuscripts or photographs. A duty book, a pair of notebooks, glass flasks. The notebooks contained only medical notes and no seditious poems. Then, a square of white paper slipped out from between the pages. Yelena recognized it easily – a pass given to outsiders, more often than not relatives of the patients. The characteristic seal driven deeply into the paper was easily recognizable. But the strange thing was, what was it doing among Krasilnikova's things?

Her hand shook as she read the name on the paper – an unknown, non-Russian name – Yurgis Gintaus, and the date of his visit. Then she resumed rummaging through Irina's things, redoubling her effort. Nothing interesting. Needle and thread, a shoebox. Yelena shoved the box to the corner of the locker, and something clinked softly inside, sounding like coins. With a quick glance over her shoulder at the door, she tried to control her excitement as she opened the box. Her fingers would not obey her immediately, wasting precious seconds. Finally, the lid came off to reveal ampoules of medicine and pills. This scum was not administering medication to the patients and keeping it for herself! She was a thousand times more dangerous than she seemed.

Yelena scurried to the door to check the corridor. It was empty. She turned the lock and returned to the box, full of indignation mixed with delight. She felt like she had that first day when Rakhmanov arrived at the SPB. She had discovered more than she could ever have hoped. Krasilnikova was sabotaging the treatment of dangerous psychopaths and for some reason had stolen a pass from the guards. This was criminal behavior, real sabotage, and much more serious than *samiz-*

dat books. And who would have thought that this naïve, perpetually sweet kid might be capable of such things?

Yelena could feel the professional instincts of a member of the Militia rising in her again after all her years at the psychiatric hospital. She had become a real bloodhound. Obsessed by her new ambition, she pawed through the box again and again, like a dog catching scent of its prey. She belatedly realized she could not remember the exact position of the things in Irina's locker. The years had robbed her of old skills. She did her best to remember as she replaced the objects. The box with the medications, notes, the paper with Yurgis Gintaus's name – everything must remain in place without the slightest alteration. Finally, she closed the locker and without waiting for Irina to return, rushed downstairs and out to the guard booth at the check point, pulling on her coat as she went, the frost stinging her face with a million icy needles.

"Hallo, Vanka," she cried before she got there. She would wait until she was inside before stating her business.

"Is something wrong?" asked Vanya. He was only an enlisted man, and he was respectful toward Yelena. She may not have been high ranking, but she was still an officer.

"Vanka, show me the list of patient relatives from last Saturday. I have to check on something," she ordered.

"Yes, ma'am," Vanya didn't question her and produced a folder, a bit worried that he might be in for a scolding. Yelena tore it from his hand. Inside was a single sheet of paper which she carefully scanned line by line, name by name. There was no Gintaus on the list.

"Yurgis Gintaus," she said, her voice hard, "Does this name mean anything to you?"

"Yes," Ivan replied with no hesitation. "It's an unusual name, Lithuanian, I think. It caught my attention."

"Did you give him a pass?" Yelena's voice shook.

"Well, yes." Ivan was becoming alarmed. "But he was on the list."

"Look again." Yelena shoved the list at his face as a feeling of triumph rose within her. "There is no Yurgis here. The name doesn't appear anywhere."

"What the shit," murmured Vanya as he looked over the list of names. "But his name was here, I swear it. I saw it with my own eyes. Why else would I have let him pass? I would never have given him a pass if his name were not on the list," he cried.

Yelena could sense his fear – viscous, nervous, imploring – all combining to give her the sweet feeling of power.

"How many times did you give him a pass?" she demanded.

"I don't know… Well, maybe a couple of times when I was on duty."

"Do the nurses come by often to see you?"

"Every day," Vanya seized upon her question like a trapped animal seeing a way to escape. "Nurses, doctors, and orderlies. Sometimes to get the key to the pantry or return it, sometimes to pass on some orders or check the shift schedule. You can't remember everything…"

"Are you ever absent?"

"Hardly ever," he muttered guiltily, "there's dinner and shift change. Sometimes you have to go to the toilet. Once in a while to drink some tea with the guard inside the building, when no visitors are expected. It's hard to sit in this booth alone all day."

"Comrade lieutenant!" Vanya could no longer hide the desperation in his voice. "It's not my fault. The name was on the list. Your colleague gave me the list."

"Do you want to avoid blame for this?" Yelena frowned at him, putting her face close to his. "Then forget this conversation – speak of it to no one. Act normally. Accept the lists without question and show no suspicion, voice no objections. Read them carefully, and if you see the name Yurgis Gintaus, call me immediately. If I'm not on duty, call me at home. I'll write the number down for you. Is that clear? This is a matter of State security."

"Of course," Vanya nodded, swallowing hard. "And the Chief Medical Officer?"

"I'll inform her myself."

She returned to the hospital not even noticing the cold now, still unable to believe her luck. Her hatred for Irina, so recently erupting within her like a volcano, had taken an unexpected turn, transforming into something like gratitude. Tomorrow would be December 20th – the Day of the Chekist. Earlier, she had had the idea to call Rakhmanov to congratulate him and remind him of herself. But now she had something to tell him. She had an unquestionably valuable gift for the *KGBshnik* and even managed to conduct her own investigation. He had to appreciate it.

Her hopes for a new life regained strength, and though much was left to be done, she thought she could discern a dim light at the end of a long, dark tunnel. She was herself again, entirely herself – an intelligent, industrious, tenacious professional prepared to destroy any enemy, regardless of how she might have felt about them before. It cost a great deal of effort to speak with Irina as she had before without betraying the blazing tension that seemed to have turned all her nerves into a single, tightly stretched string. She would make it through, she would wait for the next day. And Yelena was wreathed in smiles, unable any longer to deny herself hope ...

The 20th of December she rose early and remembered that the Moscow time zone was two hours behind. Sleep would not return, and she wandered aimlessly around the apartment counting the hours. Finally, with trembling hands she dialed the coveted number, making sure of each digit. On the third ring, a male voice answered. Rakhmanov was there.

"Dimitriy Yevgenyevich, this is Junior Lieutenant Yelena Butenkova from the SBP in Medinskiy. Do you remember me?"

"Yelena, of course I remember you." She imagined that he was pleased.

Trying to conjure up a dry, official tone, Yelena told him everything that had happened: her discovery of the pass and the medications among Irina's things, her conversation with the guard, the rumors about Krasilnikova's new boyfriend – someone recently arrived for whom she had broken up with Misha.

"It gives the impression that Krasilnikova struck up a romance with one of the prisoners' relatives and arranged for them to meet in secret. So that her lover's relative would appear to be sane, she withheld his medications," she summed up.

"Very interesting," Rakhmanov was undoubtedly interested. "Yelena, do you know which patient this Gintaus came to see?"

"No, not yet," she answered guiltily. "Of course, the list of visitors shows the names, but this viper seems to have exchanged the list after each of Gintaus's visits. But I warned the guard that the next time he sees the name, he should contact me immediately. This means that the next time Gintaus comes we will know exactly who he is seeing.

"Very good," approved Rakhmanov, and after a few beats added, "I'm not sure we are actually dealing with a relative. The friends of these so-called dissidents often deceive hospital personnel so they can meet with their accomplices. But as a rule, they limit themselves to one-time meetings in different institutions, visiting nutcases and criminals all over the Union. The don't risk hanging around in one place very long. They even romance the nurses. Relatives don't normally act like this. You say he has visited the hospital at least twice?"

"According to Ivan, twice while he was on duty. Tomorrow morning someone else will be on duty, and I will tell him to show me the lists," she said.

"You are a real professional," approved Rakhmanov.

Flattered by his trust, Yelena squeezed the receiver, proud and thrilled, her heart in her throat: whether from joy or in anticipation of the investigation ahead. It the same for both, answering to the same calling. Their thoughts were one; they pursued the same goal and understood one another without words. He appreciated her and even permitted her to enter his holy of holies: his very deductions, thoughts, and suspicions. And she was certain she would not let him down.

She risked asking, "You think Ira is letting someone into the hospital who is not a relative but one of these pro-Western traitors? Why would he act to atypically?"

"We'll know that, Lenochka, when we find out who he came to see. Is this your number?"

"Yes, my home number. I only recently got it," she answered proudly.

"Excellent. Let me have it. I'll give it to my colleague in Sverdlovsk today so he can get in touch with you. Set up a meeting with him, and when he gets there have a full report on Krasilnikova ready. The hospital will have her official file, but we need to know what only you can know. Her likes, her habits, any details of her life she may have shared with you, the names of her acquaintances and friends, anything she may have said or done that seemed suspicious. Can you do that?"

"Of course," said Yelena, somewhat disappointed. He's not even coming himself but shunting her off to some Chekist of lower rank. Didn't he trust her yet? Was he testing her, or did he think that anything happening in such a remote place was unworthy of Moscow's attention?

As though reading her thoughts, Rakhmanov reassuringly added, "In the meantime I'll check on this Yurgis Gintaus. If something interesting pops up, I'll try to get there as quickly as possible."

Yelena smiled sadly at the phone. Well, of course, a Major from Lubyanka behaved the way a high-ranking chief should. He would not travel across half the country just because she called but would begin by sending a colleague to check things out, and if everything checked out would decide if the matter were serious enough to require his presence. It was the same with the Militia – the same bureaucracy everywhere. Of course, nothing changed Yelena's opportunity to prove herself – the Sverdlovsk KGB would surely appreciate her merits. But she hoped most of all that Major Rakhmanov himself would come.

"Oh, I almost forgot. Have a happy holiday," she added, aching at the thought that the conversation was at an end.

"Thank you, Lenochka," replied the Major. "Thank you again for your vigilance. I will take personal charge of this matter. My man from Sverdlovsk will be there today. How long will you be at home?"

"Until eight this evening."

"Excellent. Be ready."

"I serve the Soviet Union," she said the words with a light irony so that she would not appear to be a fanatical fool, but also to demonstrate that despite the irony, the words held meaning for her.

"We all serve her, Comrade Butenkova," was Rakhmanov's serious reply. "Only her. So long, and thanks for the congratulations."

She replaced the receiver and smiled in the empty chill of the apartment. What was Irina it had once quoted? "Pursue in hot blood." Exactly what Yelena now felt – the heat of the chase, the increasing tempo of hot blood, the desire to find the truth, to track down the prey and finish it off once and for all, to force her to confess all her frauds and tearfully beg forgiveness which, Yelena was certain, would not be forthcoming. She gloated. She would do everything possible and impossible to carry on to the end, not only for Dimitriy Rakhmanov, but for herself, as well.

Chapter 15

The weather before New Years turned unexpectedly sunny and clear to the amazed delight of all. Against this backdrop, a light frost no longer seemed daunting but instead an inevitable but pleasant attribute of winter. In a word, the conditions were ideal for forays into the countryside, and it was unsurprising that Irina invited him on a hike to a mountain they called "Ursa Major."

The mountain's uneven slopes, steep on one side and level on the other indeed resembled a bear emerging from its den. It was covered with blindingly white snow, and the only color in the landscape was provided by the eternally green firs. Snow reigned everywhere here. It enveloped the forest and sparkled underfoot erasing the contrast between bare stones and grassy meadows. It covered the earth and accumulated in the lowlands, settling in drifts around each tree and trembling on branches – white on green. The winter forest opened around them like the fairy tale garden of the Snow Queen. A narrow path, trodden by previous visitors, led to the pinnacle of the snow-encased den of the bear.

"You don't have such mountains in Lithuania, do you?" she asked solemnly.

His response was evasive. "Why not? There are mountains everywhere."

He would not have said that the Ural forests and hills, even if covered deeply with snow impressed him greatly. The diversity of nature and the height of the mountains here were inferior to his native Montana, and yet he had begun to appreciate the differences between Russia and America. The wild, unclaimed and harsh landscape of Russia offered a special, illogical appeal, perhaps because it seemed to express a longing that the people concealed. It was the embodiment of a profound, unconscious, human isolation. The snow-covered landscape evoked this feeling, which was hidden under the veil of everyday life here, an unconscious melancholy, a sort of internalized orphanhood. It exposed innermost human nature, naked and helpless, and having drawn him in, he could not draw back because it had implanted in his heart an irradicable memory.

They reached the summit, and Irina sat on a fallen pine. Patrick pulled a thermos from his backpack and handed it to her. She gratefully removed her mittens and wrapped her hands around its warmth as she admired the panorama that opened beneath them – an expanse of snow with occasional brown and green splotches where the trees showed through.

Patrick sat next to her and was sad to think this would be one of the last times he would see her. It was clear that he could not meet with Golubov again. The risk was too great, and to risk more was unacceptable. Patrick had detailed all of this in his last communication, and today Nikolay Ivanovich was to return from Moscow with a reply from Headquarters, which should have been left in one of the CIA's carefully chosen deaddrops.

Patrick had met three times with Golubov, and each time his information had been more valuable than the last. Free of the destructive effects of the anti-psychotics, the engineer could remember more and more details, recreating structural drawings from memory, as well as information on military personnel, their names and even habits and vulnerabilities. He recalled details of the preparation of the missiles for tests, the order of approvals, plant locations and designations, their specializations, and much more. A picture of Soviet military industry so carefully concealed from prying eyes was now revealed piece by piece, becoming clearer with each meeting.

It seemed that the meetings with the American had become Golubov's main source of strength. He anxiously awaited them and spent all his time between meetings preparing for them, making notes and mentally reviewing details of his previous work. Everything was going well, but Patrick realized it was time to call a halt. At any moment the guards might remember his name and notice that it was missing from the new lists. Irina could be caught when she switched the papers. His every appearance in the small village increased the chances of attracting attention, and that would mean an inescapable death sentence not only for him, but for the girl he had dragged into espionage. The charming story of the Lithuanian prince must come to an end regardless of the pain it would cause him.

The unsuspecting Irina gave him a serious look, and swallowing hard, said, "You know, it's been three years since I came here."

"Yes, you said you wanted to look for work someplace else," he responded cautiously. "In Sverdlovsk?"

"No. In Lithuania," she exclaimed with an imploring look. "I'll go with you to Lithuania. Would you like that?"

It was hard for him to lie to her. When Patrick agreed to join the CIA he had been certain that he would deceive only merciless and cold-blooded enemies, not a nice girl he had involved in a crime against the Soviet authorities. But he knew that he could handle it – he must handle it. He had to look into her trusting, lustrous eyes and with all the conviction he could muster say, "Well, of course. It would make me happy."

She smiled thankfully, and Patrick felt his heart shrink in his chest as though it were in a crushing grip impossible to escape. He knew he would suffer after this meeting, knew that each lie he uttered would pour poison onto his soul, knew that the memory of this conversation would make him shudder.

But he was doing everything as he should – that which was necessary and nothing more. Too much was at stake.

The gratitude that filled Irina impelled her to openness, and she found herself saying something she had long wished to say but had never dared.

"You know, it sometimes seems I'm living someone else's life. I'm playing a part according to a script, someone else's part, I talk with people I don't understand and who do not understand me. I go to work I hate and always pretend ... I pretend that I don't know, that I don't understand that some of the people in this cursed psikhushka are perfectly healthy, that we are killing them every day, that we are making worse even those who are really sick. I pretend that this is ... just work like any other, that I can simply complete my duties and pretend everything is normal. And everyone else also pretends, also lie as though they were in the same insane play. And I lie to them, I lie to myself. I've become so much a part of this filthy lie that I no longer understand what normal life is or what is real in it. You probably can't understand."

"Oh, no. I understand you perfectly," he answered bending his head so she would not notice his sad smile. This girl would tell him about lying and playing a role? What did she really know about it?

She looked at him in surprise, and Patrick hurried somehow to explain his comprehension.

"You know what history is about in the Soviet Union? I'm constantly forced to avoid facts, to bury them under the Party line, to hide inconvenient details from students. I don't want to lie to them, and so I try to stick to subjects from long ago, far from today's world. But even those are not immune from modern clichés. And it's not only history. My life is a lie, do you understand? I always do what I'm supposed to do. I live by the rule 'do what's required,' every day I convince myself that I'm behaving correctly, and as a result I never do what I really want."

"That is called 'introjection,'" said Irina with an unhappy smile.

"What?" Patrick was non-plussed.

"In Gestalt therapy this is called 'introjection' - assimilation of other people's attitudes that conflict with your own. And these conditions themselves are called 'introjects,'" she explained.

"And do you know how to avoid introjections?" He leaned close, embraced her and kissed her – burning and passionate, as though it were the last thing he would do in his life. She responded eagerly, trembling whether from the cold or her unexpected audacious frankness, and then, overwhelmed by her own decisiveness rose and pressed her hand against the tree trunk, and there on the summit above the empty forest declared:

"What is happening in our country, Yura? We declare people mad when they simply dare to say aloud what we all think. Sometimes I think that it's we, not they, who have gone mad, that of us all it's them who are the most normal while we are the psychotics. The whole country has gone mad and all of us with our heads trapped in this web of common insanity. And no one except them had the strength or courage to break free. They are free, but we are not. We live in constant fear. You only wanted to see your stepbrother. Is this a crime? Why do we have to keep it a secret?"

"Because you are dear to me," Patrick stood and put his arms around her. "Because I don't want anything to happen to you. You deserve better than to rot in this hole. You deserve better than to rot in this country. We can try to go far away, farther than Lithuania. To a place where this web does not exist. To a place where we can be ourselves. Just be a little patient, OK?"

Did he believe what he was saying? Patrick didn't know. Headquarters would never permit him to bring Irina with him. It was simply impossible. They could not escape the Soviet Union together. He shouldn't go so far. It would only complicate everything. The memory of Oleg Lyalin in London having an affair with his secretary swam before his eyes. This had put Lyalin in such straits that he had to work for a foreign intelligence service. Did he want to chance ending up like this? No. The very thought of working for the KGB was so repulsive that even the threat of death would not convince him, especially now that he had seen the horror of the Soviet camps. But that which attracted him in Russia had nothing to do with Communism or the KGB, and he couldn't understand what it was.

The Soviet people without realizing the wretchedness of their lives, eked out their gray existence despite everything and were not discouraged. They received their miserly salary and on Saturday before dawn and rushed to the collective farm market in hopes of buying meat which was available only once per month. There was no good meat, only heavy, gristly bones, but they gladly snapped up even these.

Large women, many of whom had never been in an automobile and knew only crowded public transport, bent under the weight of two bags of goods from the store tramped through heavy snow and impassible drifts. Pulling off their mittens at the door, they dug out their heavy keys with blue fingers that became instantly prickly from the frost, and then climbed several flights of stairs because the buildings seldom boasted an elevator. They brought home chickens of an unhealthy blue color, poorly plucked with feathers sticking out in all directions, and placed them in boiling water to finish plucking, and then with the dexterity of a butcher, carved the small carcasses.

They had primitive gas stoves, and young girls fearlessly opened the valve to release the colorless, poison gas and struck a match to light it. Patrick was amazed that cooking could be so dangerous. What if a girl were overcome by the gas before she could light it? Or what if the gas did not ignite immediately or the girl should burn her fingers and drop the match, all the while breathing the gas? Even the preparation of meals in this country seemed to be a life and death balancing act. What were these people preparing for? To life in a nuclear winter? To a zombie apocalypse? To the special requirements for survival in a "bright future?"

And Irina, too, was a product of her country, meekly and unconsciously bearing the weight of Soviet life all the while remaining friendly, conscientious, and childishly naïve. Maybe because of this she was unlike all the girls he had known before. They had known one another for a month and their affection had not gone farther than a kiss. Patrick had not forced the relationship for good reasons, but it was unclear why Irina held back inasmuch as she did not hide her love for him. Living conditions? A harsh landlady? But they could go to Sverdlovsk and spend a night in a hotel. Even in the Soviet Union such things were possible.

"You know I refused Misha after I met you. Right after we began to see one another," she said. She had up to now left her former fiancé unmentioned, and Patrick never asked about him so as to cause her no discomfort. It was important that she help him see Golubov, and so he wanted nothing between them that could harm his mission.

"How often did you see him?" asked Patrick because he felt he had to say something.

"A little over two years."

This stung him a bit, either because he had upset this girl's life, or because he was jealous of the unseen but incredibly fortunate Misha who could be with Irina for years with no secrets and no fears.

"Don't punish yourself," he said, "Lots of things happen in life. Obviously, he wasn't the man for you. It's a good thing you didn't marry him, and fortunate you didn't get pregnant."

"That would have been impossible," she replied, immediately understanding his inquisitive look. Embarrassed, she continued, "There was never anything between us."

She sat on the tree again and explained. "Don't think I'm a prude. It's not a matter of 'socialist morality' or anything like that. Not because the Party would not approve. I don't care about that anyway. It's just that ... it's the way I am. I believe that one must be in love, really in love. I believe in it, in true love. I never felt that way about Misha and don't like casual relationships. I didn't want to allow someone I wasn't sure of to get too close. I'm serious about this, Yura, really serious."

Patrick nodded, trying to hide his surprise. She was unlike any girl he had met before. In the States he had come across 26-year-old virgins, but they were from deeply religious families ruled by strict Puritan morality. When things got hot they were seized by an almost panicky fear of breaking a Commandment that had been hammered into them since childhood. But he saw no such irrational fear in Irina. Nor was it some sort of hypocritical Soviet rationalization. Her chastity was natural, simple, and conscious and therefore even more attractive.

A voice in his head said, "You'll never find another girl like this, no matter where you are."

As if in answer to his thoughts, Irina again looked at him and added simply and seriously, as though speaking of work rather than pleasure, "I would with you."

"Later," he took her hand and smiled tenderly. "After we get to Lithuania."

When he heard the slow, deliberate steps and the scrape of snow, Patrick was not startled. He knew it must be old Kondtratyev returning from Moscow, hopefully with a response from Langley about the advisability of prolonging the operation. Regardless of the importance of Golubov's information to date, he was nearly certain they would recall him soon as he had suggested. The game had gone on for too long, and to continue would be nearly suicidal. He mentally accepted this, but in the face of logic he couldn't stop thinking of Irina. He would leave forever and never see her again, embrace her, or just take her hand. She would wait for him, maybe even travel to Lithuania and look for a man who had never existed. What would she think when she figured out he had betrayed her? Would she think he had never really loved her?

Patrick was long accustomed to the fact that it was nearly impossible for normal people to understand what was natural for intelligence operatives. Most people could never realize that it was possible to lie to someone and love them at the same time, to use them but really care for them, to trust them but still conceal from them truly important things. In the normal world love was built on trust and generated openness while a lie could destroy the closest of relationships, but in his world, these were mutually exclusive parallel manifestations. Irina had grown dear to him like no one else ever had, but he could not reveal the truth to her, and he could not take her with him. Such thoughts were unbearably painful. He hated himself because despite his professionalism he had permitted himself such deep feelings for a Soviet girl, and because he could change nothing.

He realized that success was separated from failure not only by the knowledge, labor, and feats of many thousands of people, but also by pain as deep as a knife wound. Among myriad scenarios there was space filled with persistent quotidian pain, which doomed one to loneliness and yearning for the life unlived, as unseen and unknown to anyone as those very unrealized possibilities. He and Irina had their own web of madness from which there was no escape ...

"I brought everything." Uncle Kolya appeared at the door, breathless but satisfied with himself. The first important mission after so many wasted years had revitalized him, and he took his duties seriously.

"Thank you, Uncle Kolya," replied Patrick. "Believe me, America will not forget you."

It was a catch phrase, and Patrick knew it would affect the old man, and it did even though Kondtrayev knew he would never see America. He handed Patrick a crumped cigarette pack from a cheap brand and the American carefully extracted his instructions. When he had decoded them, he sat for a moment before quietly calling to the old man.

"Uncle Kolya... they agree it's time to wind down the operation, but they would like more. They suggest that we consider a possible exfiltration, an evacuation," he explained.

"You want to take him to America?" Kondratyev was incredulous. "And how would you go about that?"

"I don't know," said Patrick. "We've never successfully exfiltrated anybody out of the Soviet Union. Even if we come up with a plan, how do we get him out this damned nuthouse? Even if Irina could get the keys, from what I've seen of their security, it would be impossible to get him out."

"Maybe we could organize a fire," suggested Kondratyev as he took a seat next to Patrick. "A long time ago, to be honest, I dreamed of burning this camp to the ground. I could bring my boys in, if necessary. They didn't do so badly finding out about that girl." He winked at Patrick.

"A fire?" Patrick was doubtful. "The other patients could die."

"Why do you think that?" Kondtratyev was insulted. "We'll set fire to the storage buildings. Everyone will rush to put them out, and you can release your engineer and open everyone else's cells. They'll scatter to the four winds. Maybe some of the most hopeless will perish, but Yurgis, you must understand that if the doors are open and they don't run from a burning building, they already have lost their reason. They are empty shells, and their lives are torture worse than death. Forgive my cynicism, but I saw worse in the war ..."

"I understand," sighed Patrick, "and I agree with you."

He couldn't deny that the idea of taking Golubov to America and destroying the concentration camp and setting its victims free was incredibly attractive. Those unfortunates who had been deprived of their basic survival instinct, might burn, but he was prepared to pay that price. The ones who could still be helped needed saving – this he understood. But the main thing was that the idea of an exfiltration made it possible for him to propose to Headquarters that Irina be included because she had to be part of the plan which would put her in danger.

"So," he began, thinking quickly, "right now, it's best that I disappear from view for a while. I'll tell Irina that I have to return to work in Lithuania, but that I'll come back. There will be no more visits to Golubov. We'll have to lay low and make our plans. Such things aren't done in a single day. I'll get Headquarters' consent to the basic evacuation plan, and you work out how to burn the SPB with your boys. If we're lucky, this will be the most amazing operation in the history of intelligence."

"The main thing is, we'll be helping some good people," added the old man.

Patrick nodded, conscious of the overwhelming responsibility. At the same time, he felt a strength born of hope that would allow him to overcome any obstacle.

Chapter 16

A February blizzard beat against the windows, and it seemed as if the voice of the wind alternated between a piteous whine and an impatient threat to shatter the glass. Restless and vicious it raged for a third day, sweeping across the streets and piling the snow in dirty gateways, covered already narrow paths, and attacked those unlucky enough to be outside making their way against it with resentment and hopelessness. Major Rakhmanov looked wistfully out the window, turned, and retook his seat behind the desk trying to concentrate on work.

Over and over again he tried to understand where he had made a mistake, what he had done wrong. He had been in Medinskiy two months now, but there was no trace of the illusive Yurgis Gintaus. Yet again the nettlesome thought that it was too late haunted his thoughts. The mysterious visitor, whoever he was, had left Medinskiy forever, and the KGB had missed him.

Immediately after the call from Yelena Butenkova, Rakhmanov sent a request for information on a man named Yurgis Gintaus. It turned out that there was no one in the Soviet Union with that name who could have visited the Ural SPB. There were four similar names in the report he received. One was a senile old man who hadn't left Vilnius in ten years. Another, a professor of biology, also was old and lectured every day in one of the Leningrad institutes. The third had been sent to prison three years earlier for anti-Soviet propaganda. And finally, the fourth would have been the same age as Krasilnikova's young man had it not been for one important fact – the unfortunate youngster had died when he was five years old.

Given such results, Rakhmanov reported immediately to the Department Director and was sent the same day to Medinskiy. In the meantime, his colleague in Sverdlovsk met with Butenkova, listened attentively to her story and read her report on Krasilnikova. He gave Butenkova a miniature camera to collect evidence. But again, they were too late – by the time Yelena received the equipment, Krasilnikova's box no longer contained the incriminating pass or the medications, and there was no proof other than Butenkova's word.

They were not overly concerned at first and waited from week to week expecting the mysterious "Gintaus" to re-appear at the SPB. Yelena, inspired by the arrival of the *KGBshnik*, tried so hard that Rakhmanov feared her excessive zeal would betray her. She checked her colleague's locker several times a day, verified the visitors list every week both before and after visiting hours, consulted with the guards and even, displaying considerable adeptness, tried to wheedle information out of Irina on her personal life. But it was all in vain.

At one point Rakhmanov suspected that Butenkova had imagined the whole thing in hopes of somehow winning his favor. However, subsequent investigation confirmed that a man with the same name had indeed purchased a train ticket to Sverdlovsk in mid-November. This information combined with the data on the dead child who had been born in 1945 led to an undeniable conclusion: someone was really trying to pass himself off as Yurgis Gintaus, and this someone had access Soviet civil records. It was clear that this matter exceeded the competence of the Fifth Department. Real counterintelligence work was required.

All points bulletins were sent out soon after confirmation that an unknown person was using a false name. But nothing turned up. "If we are dealing with a real spy, he likely has documentation for several false identities," thought Rakhmanov. The matter was complicated by the fact that there was no opportunity for him to conduct full-fledged interrogations in Medinskiy and could not even organize permanent surveillance on Krasilnikova. The village was too small, and any strange activity by outsiders would attract attention immediately. A professional intelligence operative would be alerted by the slightest rumor, the slightest hint of danger. "Gintaus" would disappear forever without leaving a trace of his presence in the Urals.

"Who do you think he came to see?" Dimitriy asked Yelena upon his arrival in Medinskiy on New Year's Eve. Rakhmanov took careful note of the fact that she presented a rather dangerous mixture. On the one hand, Yelena was the ideal person for the job – disciplined, idealistic, devoted and conscientious with well-developed habits. On the other hand, her excessive enthusiasm and clearly overstated expectations from their cooperation could give rise to problems in the future.

"I can't be completely certain, but I can make a few guesses. One of our patients, Aleksey Golubov. He's been here nearly three years. Like many of the patients who have been here that long, he developed liver problems. You can tell by the color of the face – the skin turns yellow. But I've noticed that for the last few months his skin color has markedly improved and he became healthier. He does his best to pretend he's taking his medications and almost succeeds. But there are things he can't conceal, the size of his pupils, the condition of his skin. None of the other patients have exhibited such changes. If you were to ask me which of them has stopped taking medications, I would point only to Golubov."

Cold, precise phrases. Professional focus and well-concealed anger toward the enemy. She did her best to emulate him. She dreamed of speaking with him as an equal. This woman hungered to be fully involved in the operation – she wanted to be trusted, to be consulted and included in discussions of the next steps, to have information shared with her and plans made with her. Rakhmanov guessed that in exchange for this emotional gift she was prepared to conquer mountains, and he saw no reason to deny her what she wished. After all, she deserved it, and the future course of the operation also depended greatly on her.

"Golubov is a military engineer. He was sent here because there were strong reasons to suspect him of being unreliable. In his job he had high-level access to our military secrets." He paused for emphasis.

Yelena's eyes blazed. "You mean to say..." She also did not finish her sentence.

"Yurgis Gintaus does not exist," continued Rakhmanov. "Or rather, those who do exist are of no interest. The only person of such a name and age died when he was five years old."

Her professional restraint momentarily forgotten, Yelena nearly choked, and lowered her voice to a whisper, eyes wide. "You mean to say that Krasilnikova is a foreign spy?"

Dimitriy chose his words carefully. "I said only what I know. Now you understand why it's so important to find him."

Rakhmanov tried not to show it, but Yelena's suspicions affected him no less than her. Someone using a false identity had been here to meet the disgraced military engineer. The idea that it was espionage was no longer as farfetched as he had thought at first. The signs suggested this was the work of a professional, and had it not been for Yelena's vigilance, it would have escaped notice. Until this moment, he had discarded the idea that here in the depths of the Soviet Union a real spy had been at work and uncovering such a spy had seemed almost a fairy tale that no one could imagine.

In 1972 Dimitriy expected to be promoted to Lieutenant Colonel, and now he dreamed of what would happen if he, practically on his own captured a foreign intelligence operative red-handed. What if behind the identity of Yurgis Gintaus was hidden an operative of the CIA or MI-6? Rakhmanov was nearly dizzy with the thought of fame, honors, promotion to full colonel, and the enormous damage that would be done to the enemy by such exposure. Extreme caution was necessary. New Year's celebrations passed, and he hardly noticed. So, what if he had missed a carefree rest, had not enjoyed the comfort of his family, but rather had been on the outskirts of civilization in this frozen Ural village – the game was worth the candle.

Immediately after New Year's Dimitriy flew to Moscow to personally report Yelena's suspicions to his leadership and thoroughly check all possible connections to Golubov. No friends of Golubov could be found in any of the Baltic states. The engineer's only living relatives were his family in Kharkov and his younger sister, Darya. Oksana Golubova was interrogated by the Kharkov KGB at the beginning of January: they coaxed her and threatened her, reminded her they controlled the fate of their child, alternated "carrot" and "stick," and finally gave up – the engineer's wife had never heard of any man named Yurgis Gintaus, and she had never seen her husband in the company of foreigners. The interrogation of the sister yielded a similar result.

Animated by the results and even more strongly convinced his suspicions were correct, Rakhmanov returned to Medinskiy. He hoped he had arrived in time to prepare for a new meeting between Golubov and his secret acquaintance. He met daily with Yelena, ever hoping for new evidence or the appearance of the desired name in the lists of visitors. But time passed, and Gintaus did not appear.

A dark premonition of failure grew within him. At the beginning of the investigation he had debriefed the guards and with their assistance put together an artist's sketch of the false Yurgis. The sketch was distributed to all traffic police posts, but none of them had seen the strange "Lithuanian." The KGB's Sverdlovsk operational group conducted a secret search of Krasilnikova's apartment which required a sub-operation to lure Marya Innokenevna to the Social Security office. The search turned up nothing, not a piece of paper with a name, not the substitute lists, no antipsychotics, and moreover, no instructions from the CIA or other foreign services. Rakhmanov understood that failure proved nothing: Irina rented the apartment from the old woman, and probably would not have kept such objects at home. Each day gave him less to go on.

He could not simply arrest or call Krasilnikova to a conversation with the KGB; this would only scare Gintaus away, and they would never catch him. A vision terrifying in its clarity appeared before Rakhmanov: the enemy had completed his mission, and they were too late. Possibly, the man they sought had long ago left the USSR. After a while, Dimitriy no longer thought of an early promotion to full colonel and instead began to fear that his inglorious failure might deprive him even of a lieutenant colonel's stars. They were so close to unraveling the puzzle, but it seemed the enemy had outsmarted them.

Yelena understood this, too. The enthusiasm in her eyes turned to dark disappointment. Still, she rummaged through Irina's things with the same intense rage, continued her work with the guards, and on Rakhmanov's instructions tried to determine Golubov's circle of contacts inside the hospital. This also yielded no results: the former engineer maintained no relationships with anyone. Moreover, by all indications he had begun again to take his medications, and his skin, which had so recently begun to look healthy, now was a ghastly yellow.

Her helplessness tortured Yelena. The impossibility of doing anything that might serve her new boss enraged her and gave birth to a mass of complexes. She tried to resolve the problem on her own, trying to renew her friendship with Irina and spend as much time as possible with her. Rakhmanov feared that her inexperience in matters of espionage might lead to her giving herself away. It didn't take him long to see that Yelena had always underestimated Krasilnikova, thinking she was a naïve little fool.

"She is a psychiatrist with a higher education who was able to lead everyone at the hospital by the nose after just a few months," Dimitriy explained to Butenkova during one of their regular meetings. "She will notice right away any change in your behavior. Unexpected friendship, exaggerated amiability – all of this will immediately strike her as strange. Any odd question will put her on guard. Your behavior must change very slowly, imperceptibly, naturally. This is one of those situations it's better to underplay than overplay."

"Do you think we're too late?" she asked him frankly. They had not noticed when they had begun to treat one another informally, but it had seemed so natural that neither of them could now return to dry officiousness.

"Yes, I've thought about it," admitted Rakhmanov, lowering his head. "I've thought about it a lot of late. But what's left for us to do? We don't have a single clue, no proof. Even if we interrogated Krasilnikova, we would probably have to let her go. And this would mean losing any chance of catching Gintaus. Irina is our last hope. We can't surveil her in the usual way – any outsiders would be noticed. You are our only hope."

Yelena broke out in smiles at these words, flattered by his trust and the responsibility he had given her. She nodded solemnly so he would see how much this mission meant to her. Every time she began to have doubts about the advisability of continuing the operation, Rakhmanov reassured her there was still hope and that he could not continue without her. He knew that such words worked magically on this woman, instantly concentrating her thoughts and course of action. But by the end of February even the magic had begun to lose its effect.

"Three visits to the SPB over less than a month and a half and none for the last two." Yelena sat on the edge of her bed in her small apartment and cast a despondent look at her boss. "I was at a dance with Krasilnikova yesterday evening. She sat in a corner nearly the entire time by herself. She didn't speak to her former fiancé. And yet again she said nothing about Gintaus."

Dimitriy thoughtfully rubbed his slightly protruding chin and cautiously asked, "Yelena ... are you certain she suspects nothing?"

Such a suggestion was incredibly painful for Yelena. She jumped up, angry, and flared, "You can't even imagine how well I can pretend. Even I didn't think I could do it so well. Don't forget I was in an orphanage, and life taught me how to lie better than any of your special training. I played my part with her like I was working from a script. I manipulated the whole thing to seem like an open conversation. I admitted to her that I used to like Misha, but I refused him because I wanted her to be happy. She was so moved that we hugged one another and cried. After such 'revelations,' becoming closer will seem natural. She believes we made up and understand one another..."

"But in reality, you did not forgive and forget," he said with a smirk.

Yelena frowned. "What does that have to do with anything. There's nothing personal here, you know. I pass the time with her only because we know she's connected with a spy. Should we turn a blind eye to espionage?"

Dimitriy grew silent. To argue with her would be useless and maybe harmful. He saw that in the depths of her soul his helper understood his words had been correct and were the cause of her zealousness. Clearly, this was a habit acquired at the orphanage: don't admit to anything under any circumstances and stubbornly deny any accusations because any admission of guilt was followed swiftly by severe punishment. Nevertheless, the reason for their failure must be determined whether Yelena liked it or not.

"I'm thinking about where we might have made a mistake," he began. "Is it possible that some information about our investigation somehow reached Krasilnikova or Gintaus? It's quite possible, of course, that it's just a coincidence. They might have completed the operation shortly before my arrival, and we can't be blamed for that. If we are dealing with a professional spy, he might have professional instincts. I know I do. It's hard to explain, but when you gain such a level of intuition, you can sense the smallest intimations of danger, sometimes out of thin air, in the street, in the city which surrounds you. Of course, I'm not a real operative, but when I first started, I worked under cover in the GDR, and I know how it works."

"It's called 'the sixth sense.' I know," Yelena perked up. "I remember when I worked in the Militia and I had such a feeling, our colonel expressed special thanks to me. He said everyone develops this over the years. He was in the war and told me that experienced soldiers and commanders relied on it. They changed reconnaissance missions if even just one of them felt something was wrong. If even just one of them had a strong feeling, they would change all the plans, and only thanks to this they survived. But I didn't think these giggling imperialists had this, too."

"Oh, they have a lot of it," Rakhmanov laughed mirthlessly, seeing that his story about 'the sixth sense' failed to convince Yelena. No matter what she said, it seemed she took his every word to heart and was asking herself if she might inadvertently have frightened their target. The thought that she was helpless and unable to help her beloved boss was driving her crazy. It was clear to him that Second Lieutenant Butenkova was ready to conquer mountains for him, and the lack of results was unbearable because she thought she had let the KGB down. She was ready to declare her innocence to everyone but herself.

Rakhmanov understood that regardless of the results of the operation, such devotion should be encouraged. As a superior officer he was obligated to provide moral support to his agent to continue working. Two months had gone by, but he was not ready to give up.

He looked dubiously around the apartment. "Is it too dangerous for us to meet here?"

"I live alone." Yelena gave him a slightly frightened glance, hoping he would not curtail the meetings he knew meant so much to her."

"I know. But you have neighbors on the other side of these cardboard walls."

"So, what do you propose?" She was unhappy. "It's cozy here. I baked fish for you."

"You're not obligated to feed me. Someone should take care of you for a change. Here's what I propose. When is your next day off? We could go to Sverdlovsk. I have an official car, and it won't take more than an hour to get there. We can go to a good restaurant where we can discuss things quietly."

"A restaurant?" She could barely believe her ears. From her reaction one might guess she had never been in a restaurant. "Are you serious?"

"Absolutely."

"Boss, you are a wonder!" And, casting professionalism aside she flung herself at him and wrapped her arms around his neck.

Three days later found them seated at a table covered with a neat, white tablecloth in the "*Bol'shoy Ural*" restaurant while Yelena delightedly studied the menu.

"Chicken soup, spicy meat stew, broth with dumplings, steamed fish in sour cream or battered, perch in a white wine sauce, steaks, meatballs, chicken croquettes, roast duck with apples. Dima this is fantastic. I can't believe my eyes. But the carp in Polish sauce at 92 kopecks doesn't seem too expensive, so I will order that."

"Order whatever you wish. Forget how much it costs. It's not a problem. The office will get the bill."

He watched her with a satisfied smile. This girl needed so little to be happy, and he could effortlessly provide it. Rakhmanov knew that a single evening like this would be enough for Butenkova to work for him a few months more to wind things up.

"I wanted to tell you ... ," he paused for effect. "This spring, in April, they'll be giving some training courses to raise the qualifications of militia officers here in Sverdlovsk. If we manage to finish our operation by then, I will gladly recommend you. A great future awaits you, I'm sure. We'll get you out of that hole and then, after some time, you could come work in the KGB."

"Boss ..."

She couldn't speak. She looked at him with delight and obvious love, and Dimitriy was flattered. His wife had thrown a fit during his last visit to Moscow because he had missed the New Year's holidays, but Yelena was prepared to accept him and his work to the end without the slightest hint of displeasure.

"You can't imagine what a great help you are to me. True, we haven't caught the spy, but if it hadn't been for you, we would never have known he had been in Medinskiy.

"Are you married?"

Yelena's question was unexpected. He answered her with deliberate dispassion and exaggerated indifference. "I have a wife and a six-year-old son. He's not interested in counterintelligence but dreams like all boys of being a cosmonaut."

Yelena was disappointed. "Understood. You have a happy family life."

"With my work?" He laughed. "You can forget about any happiness. I don't get home until late at night. And it's the same for holidays and weekends. When all this mess with this damned Gintaus started, I went to Medinskiy at New Year's. There was nothing but complaints and scandals at home. But you understand the duties I have."

"I understand perfectly," she nodded eagerly. "But for me it was the best New Year's ever."

Rakhmanov did not hesitate for long. He knew how such conversations normally wind up. But on the other hand, why not allow himself a little pleasure while he was far from home with a girl who was very unlikely to be in Moscow any time soon and could not spoil his relatively peaceful though not ideal family life?

"You'll to the training course in April and will surely meet someone," he said.

"I don't need just anyone," she said with some feeling, then became serious. "I'll take the training if we find this damned Gintaus. But it's likely he's no longer in the country. You know I'll do all I can. But maybe it would still be worthwhile to interrogate Krasilnikova. You could beat the truth out of her. I don't think we have a choice."

"'The uneducated grandsons of Dzerzhinsky.'" The thought came again to Rakhmanov. "And she is not far from them." "Let's have fun tonight and forget about work," he said aloud.

"You yourself said that it's better to discuss work here, far from Medinskiy," she said.

"We'll talk about it later. In the hotel," he replied.

Yelena gave him a lazy smile and nodded her understanding. She needed no more words to understand him.

Chapter 17

It was cold at the end of March, not much different from the end of February. Patrick wondered if summer would ever make an appearance in these parts. If in Moscow the streams were running again, the snow swelled with moisture and blackened along the roadsides, and the incomparable, heady scent of spring was in the air, here north of Sverdlovsk winter remained dominant allowing only a barely perceptible foretaste of the warmth to come.

He had only just returned from Moscow using his back-up documents that had nothing to do with his Lithuanian legend. In the Soviet capital Patrick had conducted a rare and risky meeting with a colleague from Moscow Station. It lasted only 15 minutes but permitted an extremely important discussion of the plan's details, the people who would escort Golubov after his escape and help him get to Moscow, the required disguises and false documents.

They went over all possible delays along the route, checkpoints and how to avoid them, planned stops, and the legends of each team member. Someone from Moscow Station succeeded in obtaining a map showing the locations of all the traffic police posts, explaining in detail the way searches were conducted. It would have been nice to have access to the all points bulletins in the Militia's hands, but their Soviet sources could not obtain this information.

Patrick knew the exact time when a NATO military transport aircraft was to take off from Vnukovo Airport. It would arrive the day before ostensibly to pick up radio equipment from the Embassy. Golubov would be fitted out with a military uniform and would take the place of the co-pilot. According to his biography, he had once trained as a pilot. Now, he would have an opportunity to act as one.

Everything seemed well-planned, though the operation would entail great risk. Headquarters was well aware that the operation could fail, but they weren't ready to give up on Golubov without a fight. And only one thing bothered Patrick, searing his conscience. Despite all his requests and arguments, Langley flatly refused to exfiltrate Irina. She was not a valuable asset, and even though she could be arrested following Golubov's escape, there was nothing to be done. According to the plan, Patrick was to disappear immediately following the extraction of the engineer from the psychiatric hospital. A new disguise and documents had been prepared for this. His escape route would take him to the Finnish border where he would be picked up by a car with diplomatic plates.

"The wife of one of our guys will fake an illness – not a very dangerous one, but bad enough to take her to Helsinki for treatment. Another officer's wife will accompany her. The husbands will go, too, ostensibly to take some vacation days and do some shopping in Finland. They'll pick you up at the assigned spot, and you'll get into the trunk. Everything will be ready for you," explained his colleague during their short meeting.

"Judging from the way things have gone, the Yurgis Gintaus identity has not attracted attention, and the KGB is unaware of the name. They shouldn't be looking for you. But everything could change after the fire. You'll have different documents, and hopefully they won't catch on in time, even if they start an investigation into the fire. But this Irina is something else entirely. If she were to go with you, they would notice her absence right away. Her photo would be disseminated far and wide. If you were to travel with her, you guarantee both your deaths."

Patrick knew that his colleague was right, but he couldn't

make peace with it. When he told Irina about the plan, that his Lithuanian friends wanted to organize Golubov's escape, that they had proposed the idea while he was home, she agreed without the slightest hesitation. Patrick was amazed by how she had changed since their first meeting. Frightened and hesitant in the beginning, she had become desperately brave, ready to take an incredible risk. Irina loved him, and this love inspired her and gave her heretofore unseen strength.

"It's like stepping from the darkness into light," she said. "At first doing something that is right seemed very difficult, but then something happened. Step by step, in time you realize that it's the only thing to be done, that you cannot act differently. And, even if you're afraid, something appears in your life ... something real. You, your brother, anything I can do for you ... This is the only thing worth living for, the only thing. You saved me, Yurgis. You saved me from this wretched, gray existence, from myself."

He could say nothing, again seized by an invisible fist that shattered his heart. Could he live in constant pain, in intense, daily pain, in absolute powerlessness under an invisible hand which squeezed the life from his veins? Now, he knew it was possible. And as usual, there was nothing he could do.

Once again, she stopped giving the medications to Golubov and informed him of the planned escape. The engineer brightened at first then gave her a worried look as he whispered, "They'll come after you, Irochka. They don't consider us prisoners to be people. They think we're vegetables that no longer see or understand anything. But we see everything all the same. Your colleague, that bitch Yelena, has been asking the orderlies about you. I got sick during one of our outdoor periods and returned to the cell early and saw how she jumped away from my cot as though she had been searching for something.

Concerned, Irina reported this to Patrick when the met next. "I don't know why she's spying on me," she said, her voice thick with fright and guilt. "I thought we had made up and she was acting better toward me. Could she have been lying to me all this time?" Her eyes bored into his seeking an answer.

"You can't imagine, Ira, how people can lie," replied Patrick. "Could it be because of the medications you didn't give Aleksey? Where did you hide them?"

"I stopped hiding them in my locker," she responded, "After what Aleksey told me, I put the pills and ampoules in my pocket and destroyed them after leaving the hospital."

"That was smart. It looks like Yelena wants to cause problems for you," he continued. "As we agreed, we'll set the fire during her shift. You must have an airtight alibi for that time, do you understand? You have the day shift, during the guard change you will open the gate and let our man inside and give him the keys for the inner door. He'll wait in the back room until evening. You will leave, hand the shift over to Yelena, and go to the dance. You must be seen by everyone throughout the night. During this time our man will set fire to the outbuildings and take advantage of the turmoil to open the gate. Others will join him, and, well ... by morning nothing of that damned *psikhushka* will be left standing. Our Lithuanian friends will take care of Aleksey, and I ..."

"You will come for me at the dance and take me away while everyone is running around in the snow looking for the escaped prisoners," she finished for him. "Just as we agreed. Yurgis," she gave him a strange look as though sensing something. "You will keep your word? You'll come for me? We'll leave together?"

"Of course," he replied looking her straight in the eyes. But, of course, he would not be coming after her. She would wait for him, looking through the dirty glass of the window, searching the thick, March darkness for his arrival. He knew it would be difficult for her to see anything outside, and she would press against the window hoping to see his figure. She would feel the chill of the eternal Ural winter seeping through the cracks in the poorly glued windows. She would wait for him, certain he would return for her ...

His answer reassured her, and Irina, forgetting her momentary fear, perked up.

"Until now it was hard to believe that your Lithuanian friends could do all this. Take us to the West, out of the Soviet Union. Impossible. We will be free, truly free, right? We won't have to lie and hide anymore. We'll see the whole, wide beautiful world. We'll be happy, Yura. We will, won't we?"

"I'm already happy whenever I'm near you. But are you sure you want to leave? You could find a good job in Sverdlovsk or Vilnius. You'll have an unbreakable alibi. How can you leave everything behind: your country, your friends, your relatives? You'll never be able to go home again. Do you really want that? Defection is risky, very risky. You don't have to put yourself in such danger."

"We've spoken of this, more than once," she replied, annoyed. "I'm going with you no matter what. I won't take part in all of this if you don't take me with you. If these people can help you and your brother, why can't they help me? You said yourself that they're your friends, that they want your family to be safe. And I'm almost part of your family."

This was the way she had talked when he had first proposed the operation. He could find no reasonable explanation for not taking her with him. If he were really a private person acting of his own free will with help from personal friends rather than American intelligence, why would they refuse to take his fiancée, other than out of fear for her safety? But Irina would have none of it. He was forced to deceive her. He did his best to assure himself that it was for her own good.

Now on the eve of the operation he sat in Uncle Kolya's hut surrounded by several husky young men and again went over the details of the plan. A diagram of the SPB was spread across a large, wooden table. Patrick scanned the smooth rectangles symbolizing the reception and examination rooms, the contours of the room equipped for the reception of patients, the guard posts marked on the map, the black squares of the cells, a schematic representation of the punishment isolation cell.

"Kostya, do you understand everything? You'll set fires in this area and that, and then come back here. If you run into a guard, take care of him and open the door. And what will you be doing, Maksim?"

They all knew their roles. Patrick tried to get his head into the job, hoping his years of the cold, businesslike tenacity required of a spy would sooner or later take over, and he would be able to escape into the saving emptiness of emotionless professionalism. But he was unsuccessful as if some intricate internal mechanism failed to function. The invisible hands of a clock stopped, and all movement stopped, but the world stubbornly remained tactile and mutable, refusing to become a faceless maze of unfulfilled probabilities.

After the boys were gone, Uncle Kolya lay down in his place, but Patrick would not sleep that night. His primary responsibility was his own life, he knew – a happy, true life filled with moments that would never be – a life with Irina. The infatuated girl would wait for him tomorrow at the window, unaware that the world would change forever that night, that somewhere far away, the dice would roll, and instead of what she expected something entirely different would happen. Patrick knew all the possibilities. Like an Old Testament prophet, he could see events that had not yet occurred and knew that tomorrow could end with only one of several possibilities, and he knew which it was ...

That night at the end of March gave no hint either of the coming spring or a solution to their problem. Yurgis Gintaus was nowhere to be found – both had to accept it. Yelena's meetings with Dimitriy were becoming more difficult and pointless. He no doubt was homesick, tired of the fruitless waiting, and it seemed as though he blamed her for their failure though he tried not to show it. Yelena also felt guilty but could not determine why. If only she had checked Krasilnikova's locker sooner, if only she had tried earlier to find out whom she was meeting. Everything would have been different – in her work, and maybe her life. Now she checked the locker every day, but nothing suspicious was to be found. Sooner or later, Rakhmanov would return to Moscow, and Yelena would be left with only the hope that he would keep his promise about the training courses.

Normally, she preferred night duty – the cells were locked and nothing special ever happened. One of the patients invariably became ill, but Yelena was never in a hurry to respond to requests for help – let them take care of themselves. But now the silence was oppressive and there was nothing to divert her from her sad thoughts. With a sigh, Yelena stretched out on the couch and tried to take a nap. She fell into a restless slumber, and did not understand what had awakened her.

She went out into the corridor with the idea of visiting the orderlies for a chat but noticed an unaccustomed dryness in the normally damp air. Sniffing, she opened the door of the treatment room. The air smelled of something burning, and the light in the empty room was becoming brighter, as though amplified by flashes outside the window. She entered the room and looked out the window and stared. Tongues of flame, bright and greedy, licked the walls of the outbuildings. As though enraged, the flames burst through the whitewashed walls to attack the wooden beams, devouring them quickly. Small flakes of snow drifting into the fire and turned into sparks that scattered in a hot spray which vaporized immediately.

Yelena rushed to the closed window and watched with horror as the fire leapt to the hospital itself somewhere on the second story and now crept up the walls. Below in the courtyard figures scurried around, partially hidden by plumes of smoke. Struggling to understand what was happening, Yelena was struck by a single thought – Golubov.

She rushed out into the corridor where the smell of the fire was now pronounced. Quiet just minutes earlier, the place was now filled with the clanging of doors and something that sounded like shots. Belatedly, Yelena remembered she was unarmed. The orderlies had weapons, but where were they? Her eyes began to tear from the smoke, but she heedlessly ran toward the cells. A man appeared suddenly before her, a man she would have recognized out of a thousand. Tousled, out of breath, in a torn quilted jacket with missing top button, he glared at her with hatred as he saw who it was.

Semyon Kalashnikov was a member of the gang Yelena had been after five years ago. She was sure of his guilt despite a lack of evidence, and the most she could do with him was send him away for a year for hooliganism. Now he stood before her and recognized her, shot her a malicious grin and raised a sawed-off shotgun. Yelena backed away, her mind a storm of thoughts: the first meeting with Rakhmanov, the paper with the name she found in Irina's locker, dinner at a restaurant and a night at a hotel – her first night together with Dimitriy. Would it all really end like this, now, with a gunshot in a burning building?

Something cracked behind Kalashnkiov like an explosion. Fire appeared at the end of the corridor, encircled the walls and crawled forward like a cat after its prey, pushing clouds of suffocating smoke ahead of it. Semyon looked behind him, and Yelena saw her chance and darted through the emergency exit onto the stairs. She no longer cared about Golubov. The ghosts of the past, old enemies, were catching up with her here after so many years.

"I've got to get out of here and call Dima. I must phone Dima so they can find Krasilnikova without delay. She's the key. There's no time to stop this scum, so we must get ahead of the curve. Where is Krasilnikova?" Yelena muttered aloud, swallowing smoke and coughing. She had to get downstairs where the fire had not yet reached. The fire had jumped to the building upstairs from the burning outbuildings, and if she were in luck had not yet reached the lower floors. She had to get away and call the KGB. Without delay!

Stumbling down the steps, Yelena Butenkova went as fast as she could. Finally, at the ground floor she could see that the hall was empty. It was illuminated only by the glare of flame through the barred windows which cast bizarre shadows on the walls. From somewhere up the main staircase she could hear voices echoing off the walls. At the guard post at the exit lay a dead body. Gripped by panic, Yelena found a bunch of keys and with trembling hands unlocked a small service room near the exit which was normally used by the guards. She closed the door behind herself without turning on the light and groped around until she found the telephone. It was important that she notify Dimitriy.

There was no dial tone. Someone had cut the wires, or they had been damaged by the fire. Exiting the room, she knelt at the body of the young guard and retrieved his pistol. She could hear voices near-by, and through the veil of smoke discerned silhouettes on the stairs. She had no way of knowing if they were prisoners or bandits, and she didn't care. Without looking where she was shooting, blinded by the tears in her eyes, she began shooting, frantically, like a crazed animal driven into a cage. The bullets disappeared into the smoke. There were screams as bodies fell, and she continued to shoot until the magazine was empty. "If only Golubov and this Gintaus were in this group." The words rang in her head.

Fear took over, and Yelena ran from the burning building before her victims could come to their senses. Outside, she was accosted simultaneously by heat and cold. The hellish mixture burned her lungs and scratched her throat. "I must get to the guardhouse and try to call from there. Maybe his phone is still working. Krasilnikova must be found," her fanatical obsession sustained her. It seemed that the very air around her was on fire. The flames shot into the frosty night and mixed with the cold air to become some sort of new, unknown element of nature, no less distraught than Yelena herself, and swirled around the courtyard in search of new victims.

The camp gates were wide open, and she could see people running out of them – one after another. So, they are alive, and she hadn't killed them all? How many had she killed? She fell to her knees in the wet snow and scooped it up onto her face. The cold moisture felt good against her hot skin. She had only to take a few more steps to the guardhouse, her only chance.

"It's you, you animal." A heavy had fell on her shoulder and jerked her around. She confronted the hate-filled eyes of one of the prisoners. She couldn't recall his name or why he was here. He stood before her in the snow in his thin, cotton pajamas seemingly impervious to the cold. Thin hands, yellow face that in the light of the fire resembled a monstrous mask. The veins on his arms swelled as the skinny man clenched his fingers into a fist and struck her in the face.

She fell to the snow with the salty taste of blood filling her mouth.

"How many years did you lord it over us," shouted another as he ran up and kicked her in the side. Blow after blow fell upon her as if all the hatred she had poured over the patients all those years was now returned to her in the frenzied blows of these desperate people. She covered her face with her hands and cringed in horror.

"Dima," her scream was pointless, but whether it worked on the prisoners or someone reminded them they had to hurry, they disappeared out the gate after a few more blows, and someone spit on her in parting.

Groaning from pain and humiliation, Yelena lay with her face in a snowdrift. She had shot at these people as if they were cattle, but they had not taken the trouble to kill her. They just left her in the snow, beaten and despised. They gained their freedom, who knew for how long, but they felt it. She remained amid the flame and frost, hated by all and useful to no one. With a groan she rolled onto her back and looked up. The sky seemed to be on fire, and the stars were nothing but sparks from the storm of flames on earth. Had she lost, after all?

Snow crunched beneath running, and Patrick Corn leaned against a pine tree peering intensely into the darkness ahead. The footsteps neared, and finally male silhouettes appeared through the trees. This was his team, men sent from Moscow Station, and Aleksey Golubov pulling on a thick, fur coat.

"Yurgis!" he embraced him warmly. "And my family?" Golubov's eyes were filled with hope. "They are in Kharkov. Can you get them out, too?"

"Aleksey, if you remained here you would have no chance of ever seeing your family again. I can't promise anything, but maybe after a few years something can be done. Right now, you are our main concern. You know that as long as we're alive, there is always a chance ..."

Golubov gave him a grateful smile. "And what about you?"

"I'll take a different route. Don't worry about me." He gave sharp nod of farewell and the group disappeared into the forest as quickly as they had appeared. A load of worry lifted from Patrick's shoulders, and when he turned, he could see the despicable SPB blazing beyond the trees. Golubov would not be the only one leaving loved ones behind today.

Without warning everything around him was bathed in a bright glow, either this or the stars had merged with the earth, and in an instant, the world was transformed. Spellbound, Patrick stared at the fire as though time had stopped and space expanded to leave him in a black cosmos in which different possibilities intersected and sparked off one another, as bright as the Milky Way. He could see with amazing clarity that no alibi would save Irina. They would arrest her, certainly tonight, and it was so obvious that Patrick wondered how he might ever have thought otherwise.

He stood in the trees at the edge of the forest that bordered the village in the frosty Ural wilderness somewhere on the other side of the world and realized that he was at an intersection where history would be determined, and from the plethora of possibilities, only one was viable. But Patrick saw clearly that here in the silence, broken only by the crackling of the fire, it would be up to him alone to be true. He might still change something, take the scenario in a different direction.

He feverishly considered different possibilities. Irina waited at the club from which the towering flames could be seen. Even if her alibi held, what good would it do for Irina to remain in plain sight and vulnerable? He couldn't take her with him, but he could take her to Uncle Kolya and convince him to hide her. In these remote places you could hide for years with a little effort. If he could get her into hiding, when he returned to the States a hero following a successful operation, he would demand, beg, for his beloved to be exfiltrated. No, he could not simply slip away without trying to save her.

The same professional instinct which told him Irina could not escape arrest now said he could under no circumstances be seen again at the club. He knew this but told himself that he would be in time – that he had to be in time to spirit her away. The enemy could not get organized so quickly and he would get away as he had planned – alone.

But things do not always work out.

The village club was the same as always. For a moment Patrick thought he had succumbed to a false panic, and the operation was going well. He hesitated only a moment before going inside. The foyer, as usual, smelled of hot clay and wet boots. He continued into the hall, and the music as if on command stopped. Surprised, Patrick turned to discover a man with a strong, slightly protruding chin and small eyes standing behind him in the doorway.

"Well, hello, Comrade Gintaus," said the man with a grin.

Chapter 18

Winter stubbornly but without success resisted the onset of spring. The snow shrank and darkened, becoming heavy and crusted, but still melted. The soft sun of April gently but surely undermined the huge snow drifts. Spring was upon Medinskiy, and the village came to life, covered with broad, impassable puddles of dirty water, but still brighter and with renewed spirit. But for Dimitriy Rakhmanov the place was more unbearable than ever. The joy of victory that came with the capture of a spy had long vanished, giving place to routine work which still refused to yield the desired results.

First, a thorough search of the area after the fire turned up no trace of engineer Golubov. The search radius expanded every day all the way to the border of the Soviet Union. The KGB Major understood that time was against him, but the facts were clear: either the conspirators were hiding the prisoner, or, and this was more likely, they had succeeded in getting him out of the country. There was no doubt that a foreign intelligence service was involved. It was clear that Golubov on his own could not have disappeared into thin air in a region unfamiliar to him without considerable assistance. It was additionally frustrating that the instigators of the fire who had been arrested and brutally interrogated could not explain this and seemed to know nothing.

Secondly, Dimitriy had been unable to establish the identity of Yurgis Gintaus. Multiple interrogations had failed to extract the truth from the man he had taken into custody. He'd tried everything from tempting offers to threats, but without result.

"Listen, I understand you perfectly," he admonished the

prisoner, "You are a patriot no less than I. Of course, it's unpleasant that your failure should raise a diplomatic stink and damage the reputation of your country. But such things often happen on both sides. That's what diplomacy is for – to decide such questions. There will be negotiations after you confess that will result in concessions from your side, and you can return home safe and sound. But if you don't confess, whoever you are, do you understand what awaits you? You will be tried as Soviet citizen Yurgis Gintaus. That's who you say you are, correct? For a Soviet citizen espionage is a capital offense, let alone espionage which involved sabotage. What do you prefer – a safe and rapid exchange for some Soviet citizen held by your country, or a bullet from a firing squad in some squalid prison?"

Gintaus looked silently at the *KGBshnik* with a slight, mournful smile.

"Why should you die?" Dimitriy tried another approach. "For the sake of covering up an operation we've already exposed? Or do you think the United States will look like saints if you protect their foolishness? Forget it. The United States have committed so many crimes all over the world that yet another will make no difference. Or, is it that you're not an American? Maybe you're British? You don't want to bring dishonor to Her Majesty? Or is it West Germany? Perhaps the operation was sanctioned by the States, and you don't want to see your country suffer for their mistakes?"

He tried his best to uncover the smallest sore spot, provoke the slightest reaction, but the mysterious Gintaus was intractable.

Rakhmanov leaned across the table with a menacing smile. "You don't fear death? Maybe you're right. But no one will kill you because we know you're a foreigner. We are not such fools that we would deprive ourselves of a bargaining chip. They'll just send you to rot in the camps – to real Soviet strict regime camps that are much better protected than a provincial mental hospital. Believe me, a few weeks in such a place for someone from the West is more terrible than you can even imagine. After a half-year there, you won't only tell us everything we want to know, you'll beg us to listen to you. So, tell me, is it really worth all that? It would be simpler to confess now."

"You know my name," the prisoner said quietly.

"Stop playing the fool," Rakhmanov exploded. "Yurgis Gintaus died when he was five years old. You have nothing to do with either Golubov or Lithuania."

He stood and began to pace around the small interrogation room, impersonal and cold like the entire Sverdlovsk pre-trial detention center. Dimitriy hated this enemy who had won his unwilling respect. This was the first foreign spy he had encountered. This was not a foreign correspondent, not a diplomat sympathetic with dissidents, but rather a seasoned operative. And this spy would not give up even after suffering a crushing defeat.

The longer the stand-off lasted the more it seemed to Rakhmanov that it was he rather than Gintaus who was losing the battle. The spy's capture had given him essentially nothing. Golubov had disappeared, successfully secreted abroad, and the KGB had no proof of what foreign intelligence service the captured spy worked for, American, British, German, maybe Israel? The Soviet Union had many enemies, and the pseudo-Lithuanian could be working for any of them.

"Listen, if you are worried about some sort of diplomatic scandal which would damage your country because of your failure, we can avoid all of that," he insinuated, controlling his anger. "No one will learn of your confession or even your arrest. You can return home a hero who completed an intricate operation. Decorations and a head-spinning career await you. And for all this you must only share with us some of the information you possess. I'm not asking too much. You give us something, and we'll give you something. We could call it friendly relations, nothing more. I don't think it's a bad thing to have some friends abroad."

The prisoner smiled at this. "I don't think we're friends."

Coldly calm with an unbending inner core – how could such a person ever come from the greedy, spoiled, imperialist West? Rakhmanov could not believe what he was hearing and could think of no explanation for it. What defect could the prisoner find in the arguments he was making?

Seized by anger, he bent to the prisoner's ear and whispered, "Nothing matters to you? Fine. But haven't you thought about your accomplice, this nurse, also rotting in the camps to the end of her life?"

He could have sworn that a shadow passed over Gintaus's face. Maybe he had at last found his enemy's soft spot.

Patrick tried to remain calm. "You would be punishing her for nothing. She has no idea who I am. You have seen that I don't like this subject. Irina did nothing more than change the routine of meetings between patients and their relatives. Legally this is nothing more than a disciplinary offense."

Rakhmanov watched him through slitted eyes. "You only think it was a disciplinary offense. Believe me, I'll do all I can to charge her with conspiracy and espionage."

Dimitriy was not being entirely truthful. He had no intention of sending Irina to prison. But he was certain that this girl was the only key he could use to get the prisoner to open up. After the initial interrogations he had concluded that she truthfully knew nothing about the identity of Yurgis Gintaus. She liked the prisoner – this much was obvious. And now Dimitriy wanted to know how deep their relationship went.

"He only wanted to see his brother," she had told him. "He learned of the existence of his brother after his father died. It was natural that he would want to see him. They had so much to say to one another. I'm responsible for everything that happened. Yurgis didn't know I was breaking the rules. He didn't know I set up the meetings without the knowledge of the Chief Medical Officer."

Rakhmanov read despairing, irrational, courageous decisiveness in her eyes. She was ready to defend this spy at the cost of her own life, but that was not why it touched his hardened Chekist heart. He had seen a lot of enemies: fanatic, hard-headed, and cowardly ones. And it was not the first time he had come up against something like this – dark circled eyes red from sleepless nights, a burning expression of fear, and pain so strong that that it blocked the fear and gave rise to a special, passionate courage ...

Dimitriy closed his eyes and shook his head as if to drive away a vision. More than three years had passed but it was as if it had happened only yesterday. He had seen her body only in the photos Vadim had given him, and could even now hear his subordinate's words: *"She was abnormally fearless and ready to do anything for him. Dimitriy Yevgenyevich, we should have detained her, and nothing would have happened."* ...

"Take a look at this," Rakhmanov laid a yellowed piece of paper in front of Irina. "It's a death certificate for Yurgis Gintaus who died the fifth of September 1950 when he was five. The man you knew was either an American or British spy. He lied to you all that time and cold-bloodedly used you for his own ends. He played on your emotions, or your pity, on your simple feminine sympathy. He has no relationship to Golubov or Lithuania. And you directly aided an enemy of our country to gain access to a man who knew the secrets of our anti-missile defense. You stopped the prisoner's medications which helped him provide details affecting the security of our country. And, finally, you helped our enemy organize the escape of a man whose knowledge might gravely harm the Soviet Union – your assistance makes you an accomplice in an especially serious crime. If the Americans destroy our country in a future nuclear war, it will be your fault. Do you understand that this is a capital offense?"

She silently stared at the birth certificate.

"Maybe this is a different Yurgis Gintaus," she said at last, raising her eyes to Rakhmanov. The small spark of hope he saw in them was not so bright as before.

"Look at the date of birth," he said, "There is no other even close to that age. I know you don't want to believe that this scum used you, but it's time to accept the truth. He placed you in danger of execution. Without your knowledge he made you a traitor to your own country, and it didn't matter to him what might happen to you."

"No, it's not like that," she insisted. "He came for me…"

"Oh, yes," laughed Rakhmanov. "And so, now you're ready to forgive him for all the rest? You, a Soviet citizen, are happy that a foreign spy stopped by to say good-bye, and you're prepared to forgive him for condemning you and your family?"

"Yurgis didn't want to destroy anyone," she answered with stolid determination. "He only met with Golubov. He didn't betray our country. A meeting or even rescuing a man from a torturous death – this is not treason."

Dimitriy decided to change tactics. "I know you want to protect him. There is only one way you can help your spy friend and rid yourself of the label of traitor. Talk to him. Explain only one thing. If he doesn't confess who he is, he'll be executed or sent to the camps. I swear that there will be no leniency. Betrayal of the Motherland can be cleansed only with blood. We can understand how a foreigner might work against us, but for a Soviet citizen there is only one solution."

"And if he confesses..." Irina's voice shook with emotion. "Dimitriy Yevgenyevich, what then?"

Rakhmanov started, momentarily at a loss for words. The feeling of *deja-vu* which had haunted him throughout the interrogation became so vivid that it seemed real. For a moment it seemed that Irina's expressive eyes were rimmed by glasses with black frames. Or was it that the circles under them were so dark? Suddenly, another scene appeared before him: virginally white snow, an unnatural posture, a bright streak of blood, tangled hair...

"If he confesses and it turns out he is a citizen of another country, we'll contact his government and exchange him for some Soviet citizen. He will return home in a few weeks. For helping us, all charges against you will be dropped. Knowing for whom he works, we can take the necessary steps to prevent nuclear war. Everything will be fine, Nastya," he added with all the conviction he could muster, and as if through a fog he heard her somewhat surprising words:

"I'm not Nastya, I'm Irina..."

Upon learning that someone was coming to see him in this place, Patrick Corn could not believe his ears. He was suffused with a black premonition, and at the same time – hope. He knew that it could be only one person but did not allow himself to hope that he might see her again. They took him to a small, drab room with blue walls. It was bare and lifeless except for a table and small benches attached to the wall. The door clanked open, a sound to which he had become accustomed, and she appeared, the only girl he truly loved and to whom he had never revealed his true identity ...

"Yurgis..." She sat opposite him and stared into his eyes. Pain, love, terror, uncertainty – all were in this look. He didn't know how to answer. He had drawn her into crime and though he had tried to save her, had failed. Could anything justify what he had done?

"I'm sorry I didn't get there in time." This was all he could say. She did not reproach him, did not raise a fuss, did not attack him with fists or tears. Unusually stiff, she asked only: "Who are you?"

"Yurgis Gintaus," he answered quietly. "The man who fell in love with you with all his heart. Forgive me if you can for all that happened."

"Yurgis Gintaus died when he was five," she said without emotion, with appalling calmness. "Golubov was not your brother. You are not Lithuanian and not a Soviet citizen. You were lying to me all the time. You used me from the moment of our first meeting, didn't you? You are a spy," she said, her voice filled with conviction, not doubting the truth of what she was saying.

He said nothing. More lies after she had discovered the truth would be petty and useless. "I fell in love with you," he said at last. "If not, I would not have come for you that night."

"Why should I believe you when everything you told me was a lie?" Her face was so full of pain that it spilled over onto him. Let all the pain in the world wash over him now, scorch his heart with a red-hot iron, burst his veins and let him die, here and now. It was as if he were the driver of a train tumbling into an abyss who knew things couldn't get any worse and succumbed to the inexplicably sweet anticipation of death.

"You don't have to believe me."

How long could this conversation last? Ten, twenty minutes, a half-hour? This was a fraction of a day, negligible in a lifetime, and nothing in eternity. He would weather this storm like he had all the others. He must make peace with what he had known from the beginning.

"Tell me who you really are." She could no longer hold back. "Don't you understand they will kill you if you don't tell? They'll shoot you if they treat you as a Soviet citizen. But they would not dare kill a foreigner. You only have to say who you are, and they will let you go. What is your name, Yurgis? Your real name?

He smiled weakly. "Do you remember the legend of Gilvinas? He asked Aigle not to mention his name. As soon as his young daughter gave him away, their entire family perished. I didn't make it up, Irina. It's a real Lithuanian legend."

"Really?" she smiled through her tears. "And what else was true in what you told me?"

"The way I feel about you."

"Tell them who you are," she begged. "I couldn't go on if something happened to you."

"Nothing will happen to me, Ira," he tried to calm her. "No matter what they say, they know I'm a foreigner. They won't dare execute me."

"But they'll send you to the camps. Is that any better?"

"Who knows?" he shrugged.

"And what about me?" She used her last argument. "If I can't convince you, they'll send me to the camps."

He had expected her to say this but remained determined when the words came. Why couldn't pain kill instantly? Who could have imagined such torture?

"You're right to hate me," he said after a pause. "You're right never to forgive me. I love you, but there is something I love more. Maybe it's stupid or fanatical, I know. But if you had only once seen what I have seen with your own eyes, you would understand. Or I hope you would. I've said all I can. Not one word I've said to you today is a lie, but I can't say more."

"I love you," she said, unable to hold back the tears that ran down her face. "No matter who you are."

"I know." After a beat he asked carefully, "Golubov – they didn't catch him, did they? If they had they would long ago have beaten out of him what they want to know."

"I don't know." She shrugged her shoulders. "Judging from the behavior of the *KGBshnik*, they did not."

The escort arrived and without saying a word led Irina to the door. She turned at the threshold to cast a last pleading look before she disappeared into the corridor. Patrick stared at the blank walls. There was nothing he could complain about and nothing he could wish. Out of all the possibilities, he had chosen the one that landed him in this place.

Dimitriy Rakhmanov sat at the desk in the office set up for him at Sverdlovsk KGB Headquarters. Over the past months, the office had become a second home for him, and he detested it no less than the village of Medinskiy. Nothing pleased him. The trial of Yurgis Gintaus was to begin soon, and he still did not know the man's true name. He already knew the sentence – twenty years imprisonment for treason. The KGB could not be permitted to execute a foreign spy, although Rakhmanov doubted that long imprisonment would convince the mysterious spy to reveal his secret. He was a true patriot of his own country, and a Chekist could not fail to admit it. Happily enough, his temporary duty was at an end and in a few days, he would return to his native Moscow where he still hoped to receive his promotion.

The jangle of the telephone intruded on his thoughts, and the duty officer informed him that a woman named Yelena Butenkova wanted to see him. Rakhmanov frowned with annoyance and growled, "Let her pass." Butenkova was the last person on earth he wished to see. She would probably ask him to help her get into the Militia training courses that should begin any day now. Dimitriy had completely forgotten his promise, and even if he had remembered, it would not be a simple matter to organize protection for Butenkova after she failed to detect the start of the fire at the hospital when she was on duty, let Golubov get away, and had even shot four orderlies, two of whom had died. He could keep her out of prison and she would not lose her job. Couldn't she understand he could do no more for her?

"Dima," she greeted him as she entered, and he was incensed by her familiarity. Yes, once they had addressed one another that way, but he had long ago forgotten it.

"So, what do you want?" he asked, without hiding his displeasure. "If it's about the training courses, you should have reminded me sooner. Besides, after everything that happened that night at the hospital, it would be difficult for me to do anything for you. Do you understand?"

"I don't need any courses," she said with some heat. "I only wanted to say good-bye. When do you leave?"

"In three days. I'm finishing up the final reports."

"Right." She was silent for a few beats. "Will they shoot Gintaus? By the way, do you know what his name means in Lithuanian? 'Protecting the people.' He chose the right pseudonym, didn't he?"

"Yeah. He won't be shot. He's going to prison," he answered drily and dispassionately, doing his best to end the conversation as quickly as possible.

"And will they send Krasilnikova to prison, too?"

"She was fired, and a reprimand placed in her personnel file. That will be enough."

"No way!" Yelena could not conceal her shock. "She helped a foreign spy."

Dimitriy grimaced. He was not prepared to discuss with this evil woman Nastya and her remarkable resemblance to Irina, let alone his eternal and irrational feeling of guilt. "She didn't know he was a spy. And she agreed to cooperate in the investigation. That was enough. And she will have a sort of 'probationary period' of several years during which she will be forbidden to leave Medinskiy. She won't be able to harm anyone in that village.

"So that's the way it is," Yelena was staring at him, almost hating him. "You sentence her as punishment to live in Medinskiy for a few years? I've always served the Motherland, and yet I've lived in Medinskiy almost my whole life. Do you think that's fair?"

"What is it you want?" asked Rakhmanov, losing patience at last.

"Life!" She was nearly screaming now. "A normal life. Mine, yours, ours. I want to go with you to Moscow, work side by side with you, be with you like that time in the hotel.

"Calm down." Rakhmanov gave a worried glance at the office walls as though he could measure their thickness by sight. "I'm married, in case you've forgotten."

"But you said you were unhappy with your wife who only caused trouble. You assured me that she doesn't appreciate the importance of your work or the need for you to travel away from home."

"Nevertheless, I love her, and we have a son," he replied. "I'm grateful that you volunteered to help me, but I've thanked you already by convincing the authorities to close their eyes to your mistakes, your very serious mistakes. We're even now."

Yelena was thunderstruck, and her eyes darkened as she as her voice returned to the normal, glacial tone she used at work, "You think you can use me and then toss me away like a broken toy? If your wife learns what happened between us …"

"You dare to threaten me?" he interrupted her. "Remember this, girlie, if my wife learns anything, it will not be Krasilnikova who is sent to prison for betraying the Motherland."

Yelena was stunned.

"What? You're prepared to send to prison for treason a person who has devoted her life to the defense of this country? You know this perfectly well. I thought honor meant something to you. I thought you were a real patriot and the Motherland was important to you."

"I am a real patriot, and the Motherland is important to me, but my family is more important. Do you understand? Now get out of here and let me work."

On wobbly legs Yelena went down the stairs and out into lively Vayner Street. To the left, on Antona Valeka Street was a bookstore. To the right the street led to 1905 Square with its towering statue of Lenin. Sverdlovsk swirled around her, bright, lively, alluring, but still inaccessible. She wept as she walked down the street avoiding the looks of passers-by. She was alone again, absolutely alone. She walked along the cobblestones of the square and a solution suggested itself. It was so simple and obvious that she was amazed not to have thought of it before. She must find her mother.

The past did not matter, not her childhood nor whether her mother might have acted differently. If she were important to anyone it could be only to the woman who found her as a fifteen-year-old and whom she had cursed at first. Her mother still lived somewhere in Medinskiy, right? And maybe she's still waiting for Yelena to accept her. The thought gave her strength, and with each step she became more confident. Her tears dried as something resembling peace danced in the distance ...

EPILOGUE

20 June 1985

Irina Yegovova hurried home from work, worried that the stores might already be closed and the hunt for scarce goods would have to wait until tomorrow morning. But she was not one to complain. After what had happened 13 years ago and many years working as an ordinary nurse, the position of nurse in a children's clinic seemed a miracle that would not have been possible had not her husband unexpectedly found a bribable "connection." Her benefactor had not run much of a risk. Over time, Irina's misconduct had been forgotten, and no one would check the "trustworthiness" of such an insignificant person.

She glanced at her reflection in a shop window and saw the reflection of a woman whom life in the Soviet provinces had made prematurely haggard. But remnants of her former beauty still could be seen. Her eyes were beautiful and expressive, and her hair still framed the contours of her face. But time and the first wrinkles had done their work. She was nearly forty, an age that in these places was considered nearly elderly.

It was a hot summer and the coolness of the evening provided welcome surcease from the rigors of a long day. Irina climbed the sagging, wooden steps to her landing in the three-story building and recoiled, unable to believe her eyes. She would recognize him anywhere, even if he had aged and bore the special imprint of the Zone, a feature so common in these parts that it was unnecessary to explain.

"Yurgis?" She too a step backwards, still doubting her eyes. The dark-haired man took a step toward her and smiled.

His smile had changed – it had become secretive, restrained, and entirely Russian with no trace whatsoever of western luster. But in spite of it all, it was him, Yurgis Gintaus, the man who had left an irradicable mark in her life.

"You've changed," he said, and Irina heard no charming Lithuanian accent in his voice. He spoke Russian as easily as she and no longer looked like a foreigner.

"You, too," she answered, not knowing what else she could say to him after so many years. "How did you manage to get back? They sentenced you to 20 years."

"I would like to know that, too," he sighed. "For some reason, the KGB discovered my real name and a lot of other interesting details. I can't explain how they came by the information after all these years. It seems we have mole," he added in a voice tinged with worry.

"Maybe now you could tell me your name?" The corner of her mouth twitched upward. "Now that you say the KGB knows."

"Corn," he replied without hesitation. "Patrick Corn. You're right. It's no longer a secret. I've got to leave the country within 24 hours," he added, then fell silent for a few beats. "I came to say good-bye. I'm flying to the States tomorrow."

"You don't seem too happy about it," she said, putting the key in the lock and opening the door. Come on in, Mr. Corn. My husband won't be back until late today."

"You're married? Is it Misha?"

"What was I supposed to do?" She switched on the light in the entry and turned to him, shedding her shoes as she went. "I was left alone in that wilderness without the right to leave, without work, and barred from any government position. He was the only person who cared anything about me and who truly loved me."

"I know you have every right never to forgive me," he began. "I could not have acted otherwise. But I'm happy that you are alive, well, and free. I knew nothing about you all that time in prison and believe me when I say it was the worst sort of torture."

"I had a normal life," she replied evenly.

"Do you have children?"

"No."

"I would gladly stay longer, but I have no choice. I must be at the airport in Sverdlovsk tomorrow morning – those are the conditions of my release. I'm an American ..."

"I thought so."

They continued into the apartment without another word, and silence hung over them.

"When I return to Washington, I'll try to get them to give you permission to travel abroad," he began.

"That's not necessary, Yurgis ... Oh, sorry, Patrick. My life is here. I have a husband, a place to live, and a job. I don't speak English, and I won't throw away everything I have."

"But you've never seen America," he persisted. "You have nothing with which to compare it. I'm sure you would fall in love with it at first sight. You can learn English. It's only a matter of time. You told me yourself that Soviet life is a web of madness, remember? And I'll do anything to get you out of it."

"I'm sorry, but I no longer believe your promises."

The words struck him hard.

"I understand," he sighed. "You simply don't love me anymore. It's to be expected after so many years ...

"I love you, Yurgis or whatever your name is, and I'll always love you. But it changes nothing. My home is here. Misha forgave me once after I turned him down. He supported me during the most difficult time of my life. I simply can't abandon him. But I'm happy that you came to say good-bye."

She unexpectedly rushed against him and embraced him with a deep, passionate kiss, then began to cry silently, saying only, "We never made it to Lithuania …"

"That's not important. You said you would not refuse me …"

"And I don't refuse you. But this will be the first and last time. You must return home. It's what you always wanted."

Branches of the poplars knocked against the windows, while inside the closed room a cool twilight reigned. Patrick knew that in a few days he would see his homeland after a 15-year absence. The beauty and grandeur of the American capital, the alabaster brilliance of its memorials that infused the very air with the echoes of history, the carefree vivacity of the streets and the incomparable spirit of freedom would again embrace him as though he had never been absent. But for the moment he was surrounded by the musty silence of a God-forsaken Ural village. Below, under the poplars, the swings in the courtyards creaked, and a light blanket of summer poplar fluff lay on the green grass. In his life there was only one happiness, one joy, one pleasure. He had waited a long time for it, quite a long time, but Aigle and Gilvinas would be happy…

AFTERWORD

"In the Web of Madness" is a rare combination of an exciting plot, subtle psychology, deep meaning, and realism. Young CIA officer Patrick Corn is dispatched on a dangerous mission. For disagreeing with the Party line a leading Soviet military engineer is imprisoned in one of the worst types of Soviet camps – a special psychiatric hospital, a "closed" facility managed by the MVD. The engineer could provide important information to the West, and Corn must establish contact with him using a false identity. The intelligence operative turns for help to young nurse Irina who has long suffered pangs of conscience over her work. The girl falls in love with the foreigner never guessing with whom she is really dealing.

Unlike many "spy" novels, this one is distinguished by a detailed account of the realities of Soviet practices as well as the subtleties of spycraft. The terrible and tragic world of those trapped in the system of punitive psychiatry is shown with documentary accuracy but without overloading the reader with excessive detail. Descriptions of the SPB[26] are taken from the recollections of prisoners, interviews and personal conversations of the author with actual Soviet dissidents who spent several years in similar places. Therefore the external aspect of a Special Hospital, as well as the peculiarities of their routine and even the names of medications reflect the cruel reality of those times. The book will serve as a good "vaccination" for those who today are beginning to feel nostalgia for the Soviet past.

Fans of espionage novels also will find the book interesting, considering the fact that despite the fictional subject, many of the facts used in the novel coincide with actual historical events. For example the character of the military engineer is similar to the most valuable CIA agent in the USSR, Adolph Tokachev, and the plan to exfiltrate

---

26 SPB - СПБ – спецпсихбольницу – Special Psychiatric Hospital

Golubov reflects the actual CIA operation to exfiltrate former KGB major Viktor Sheymov from the USSR. The historical context of the events described in the novel also is accurate: at the beginning of the 1970's in the background of arms reduction negotiations, the Soviets actually were working on a thermonuclear anti-missile system, the PRO A-35[27], the technical characteristics of which are precisely described in the book.

Another quality of the novel is its psychological depth. For all the attractiveness of the plot, this is a story of forbidden love capable of undermining an important mission on which hangs the prevention of nuclear war. The torturous choice between duty and sentiment, truth and falsehood, patriotism and conscience is a question without a clear answer. The hero of the book is not depicted in black and white tones, and the author reveals the need for inner peace even in characters guilty of terrible things who consciously partake of evil. Of course, one should not ignore the professionalism of the author: the book is richly and artistically written in the best traditions of classical literature, but at the same time is very easy to read. Not only frozen landscapes of a Ural village, but also Kiev, Leningrad, Kharkov and even the United States are presented as they were a half-century ago, as well as authentic Lithuanian legends.

And, of course, it may be important for Ukrainians to read about the Ukrainian nationalist movement of the time which also is depicted in this novel. Namely the Ukrainian dissident who does not shrink from his convictions even under threat of the Gulag is my favorite character. It's thanks to him that the military engineer establishes contact with the CIA.

The novel makes one think about what the world might be like were it not for the efforts, risks and suffering of tens of thousands of people struggling against the "web of insanity" that encompassed the entire country. In fact, thanks to their efforts the most terrible of

---

27 ПРО А-35

all possibilities did not materialize and peaceful heavens sit above the millions of inhabitants of our planet. Just as forty-five years ago this fragile peace is maintained at a very high cost.

Director of the Center for Army Research, Conversion, and Disarmament (Kiev), Valentin Badrak

OTHER BOOKS

BY

KSENIYA KIRILLOVA

In the Shadow of Mordor
(with Michael R. Davidson)

Successor
(with Michael R. Davidson)

Made in the USA
Columbia, SC
27 November 2020